WELCO

The cab driver drop[...] the elevator to the forty-second floor. 'I love to be high,' said Pauline. 'I mean high up, looking down over New York. How about you?' It was a tremendous view. 'Yes, I love it too,' I said.

I turned around. She was naked. 'You can look at that view any time. Right now, come and love me,' she said. She was truly beautiful. Her well-trimmed pubic thatch proved either that she was a genuine blonde, or that she had her pubes dyed too. Either way, it looked good to me. Her breasts were exquisite, seen totally revealed: firm, full, well-shaped, and tipped with erect nipples. She licked her lips, and smiled.

'Do I look good enough to eat?' she asked, holding out a hand. I grinned back at her. 'You most certainly do, ma'am,' I said. I took her hand, and she led me along a corridor and up a flight of stairs to the condominium's upper floor, and into her bedroom ...

Also in paperback from New English Library

The Pearl: volume 1
The Pearl: volume 2
The Pearl: volume 3
The Pearl Omnibus
The Oyster: volume 1
The Oyster: volume 2
The Oyster: volume 3
The Oyster: volume 4
The Oyster: volume 5
The Oyster Omnibus
Rosie – Her Intimate Diaries: volume 1
Rosie – Her Intimate Diaries: volume 2
Rosie – Her Intimate Diaries: volume 3
Rosie – Her Intimate Diaries: volume 4
Rosie – Her Intimate Diaries: Omnibus
The Black Pearl: volume 1
The Black Pearl: volume 2
The Black Pearl: volume 3
The Ruby: volume 1
The Ruby: volume 2
Arousal
House of Lust
The Uninhibited
In the Pink 1: Stripped for Action
Summer School 1: Warm Days, Hot Nights
Summer School 2: All-Night Girls
Summer School 3: Hot to Trot
Summer School 4: Up and Under

In the Pink: Sin City

Tony Andrews

NEW ENGLISH LIBRARY

Copyright © 1995 by Tony Andrews

The right of Tony Andrews to be identified as the Author of the Work has been asserted by him in accordance with the
Copyright, Designs and Patents Act 1988.

First published in Great Britain in 1995 by Hodder & Stoughton
A division of Hodder Headline PLC

A New English Library paperback

10 9 8 7 6 5 4 3 2 1

All rights reserved. No part of this publication may be reproduced, stored in a retrieval system, or transmitted, in any form or by any means without the prior written permission of the publisher, nor be otherwise circulated in any form of binding or cover other than that in which it is published and without a similar condition being imposed on the subsequent purchaser.

All characters in this publication are fictitious and any resemblance to real persons, living or dead, is purely coincidental.

British Library Cataloguing in Publication Data
Andrews, Tony
  Sin City. – (In the Pink Series; Vol. 2)
  I. Title II. Series
  823 [F]

ISBN 0 340 63492 8

Typeset by Avocet Typeset, Brill, Bucks
Printed and bound in Great Britain by
Cox & Wyman Ltd, Reading, Berkshire

Hodder and Stoughton
A division of Hodder Headline PLC
338 Euston Road
London NW1 3BH

CONTENTS

CHAPTER ONE
Daly's Dandelion — 1

CHAPTER TWO
Nice work if you can get it — 23

CHAPTER THREE
Getting down to it — 47

CHAPTER FOUR
On the Mat — 71

CHAPTER FIVE
On the Game — 111

CHAPTER SIX
Tit for Tat — 143

CHAPTER SEVEN
The Fourth of July — 181

CHAPTER ONE:
DALY'S DANDELION

When the Pan Am flight landed at Kennedy, I discovered, after clearing Customs and Immigration, that Fred wasn't there to meet me after all. He'd sent his secretary, Eileen. Well, it wasn't yet lunchtime in New York and, according to Eileen, he didn't surface much before late afternoon these days anyway. He'd sent her in a stretch limo, of course. The real VIP treatment. I wondered what he was trying to tell me. Knowing Fred, he'd probably done it just because he knew I'd be amused. It was my first stretch limo, and I was. Amused, I mean. But the news from Eileen wasn't good.

I'd been talking to her over the telephone for a matter of months now, but this was our first meeting. She was a pretty girl, with the sort of red hair that you see a lot of in South Wales, cut in a short, modern bob. And she had freckles to match. Fred had patently been attracted by her face and figure, but I was soon to discover that she was a first-class worker too. Basically, she ran the company when Fred wasn't there, which was most of the time, apparently. In our initial conversation, on the way into the city from the airport, she was obviously torn between loyalty to Fred, being genuinely worried about him, and the effect that his current behaviour was having on the rest of the staff.

I was torn between listening to her, and watching that fantastic view of Manhattan that you get coming in from

Kennedy, with those unmistakable skyscrapers rising up on the far side of the East River. In the end the view won, and I asked Eileen if she'd mind if I just looked at it for a while. She laughed, and apologized. 'Hey, I'm sorry, Tony,' she said. 'I guess when you live here you don't notice it.' We went in over the 54th Street Bridge, always my favourite approach, and then turned down Third Avenue until we came to the office, which was on Third, between 48th and 49th. I hadn't been to New York for over a year, but it looked pretty much the same as on my last visit, at least in the centre of town. The traffic didn't get any better. The cab drivers still believed that they owned the right of way. But then, they do in London too. It was June, and I was glad that I had worn a lightweight suit, despite the drizzle in London as I left. The cab was air-conditioned, and getting out onto the street was like being hit with a hammer. The temperature was 102 degrees, and it was humid. I scuttled across the sidewalk and into the cool interior of the building's atrium. The driver brought my bags in, and took them into the goods lift.

Eileen had explained that, since I was staying with Fred in his apartment, it would probably make sense to take both myself and my bags there rather later in the day. Hence bringing them to the office. She had instructions, she said, to introduce me to the rest of the staff, and then to take me to lunch. Was there anywhere special that I would like to go? No, thanks, I said, I'd be happy to leave it to her.

I met the staff in what seemed like a blur of pleasant faces, some male, some female, all smiling a welcome. I reckoned that I would get to know them soon enough, so I just let the names wash over me, not even trying to remember them. They all said they'd heard a lot about me from Fred, and I wondered what kind of bull he had been feeding them. I knew my job, and I wasn't frightened of anybody, but this was New York, and the magazine's circulation *was* over four million, by comparison with our UK total of less than a million. But hell, I guess that just meant more of everything. More ink. More paper. More photography. More girls. I positively perked up at the thought of more girls. A person cannot have too many girls. Not in my book. And then, finally, I'd met everyone, including the switchboard girl. 'Fantastic,' I said to Eileen. 'So where are you going to take me to lunch?' 'I thought you'd better start off as you mean to go on,' she said. 'So I've booked us a table at Le Cirque. Have you been there before?' I had to admit that I hadn't. The Four Seasons, yes. The Inn on the Park, yes. Windows on the World, yes. Le Cirque, no. But I'd heard of it, of course. We got a cab up to East 56th Street. We were lucky. It was a checker, and it was air-conditioned.

All the restaurants I've just mentioned are the kind of places you go to in New York if you're trying to impress someone, even if that someone is only yourself. Le Cirque is something else. It is almost certainly the most expensive restaurant in the city. It is low key, elegant, and full. If you or I were to try and make a reservation there, we almost certainly wouldn't succeed.

Fred had to be spending a fortune if he was eating there regularly enough for his secretary to be able to make a reservation in his name. New York City's movers and shakers were all around us. I recognized faces that I couldn't put names to; faces from Wall Street, Madison Avenue, Capitol Hill. I could see Joe Brooks, US *Penthouse*'s art director, with a couple of girls who had to be models. I'd known Joe back in England, when he had started out with Bob Guccione. He was English. He saw me looking at him, and waved a languid hand. At least Eileen was impressed, when she asked me who he was, and I told her. 'Wow,' she said. '*Penthouse* is one of our main competitors. That and *Playboy*. And, I guess, *Club*. Imagine you knowing *Penthouse*'s art director. Just wait till I get back to the office.'

Le Cirque's food is basically French inspired, but it has American overtones. You can get French food in London. I wanted something typically New York, so I started off with some linguini with clam sauce. Everyone who lives there knows that New York is one of the world's great fishing ports, but it's not an item of information that seems to travel very far. I don't know if you still can, but you used to be able to get over twenty different kinds of native oysters in the fish restaurant at Grand Central Station, down on East 42nd Street, probably the city's best fish restaurant. I followed the linguini with corned beef hash, to the approval of the waiter. 'You've been here before, sir,' he said. I didn't disabuse him. I just smiled.

Eileen obviously thought that I was mad, ordering corned beef hash. She tucked into vichyssoise, followed by lobster salad. She patently took the view that corned beef hash could be eaten in any neighbourhood restaurant (and in that, she was right). Le Cirque was for finer things. No matter. We both enjoyed our meal. Eileen was an excellent luncheon companion, and once she got over the fact that I didn't want to spend my entire lunch listening to her catalogue of Fred's problems, we got on famously. She told me that she was from out of state. Massachusetts, where her father (whose own father was a Polish immigrant) ran a garage. She was one of three sisters and also had a brother. She said that she had found the restrictions of living at home with her family in small-town America claustrophobic, and had left when she was twenty-one for the freedom of New York, which she now thought of as home. She kept in touch with her family, and always spent Christmas with them, but didn't feel the need to see them for the rest of the year. She lived over on the Upper West Side, she told me. New Yorkers are either East Siders or West Siders. The East Side is newer, and more expensive. The West Side is more traditional, with some really very beautiful old apartment buildings, but much of it is very run-down. It's rather like living north or south of the river, in London. You're either one or the other.

She'd had a number of lovers, she told me, since she had come to the Big City, but nothing that had really lasted. Most New York men, she opined, were 'either gay, married, or sexist pigs.' I wondered if the fact that she put her hand on mine as she said this was any kind of an indication that she was available, should I so desire. It was difficult to tell. 'I expect everyone here tells you,' she said, 'but I just love your accent. It's so cute. I could listen to it all day.' 'You'll soon get used to it,' I said. 'After a while, you won't even notice it.'

Whatever else I got up to in New York, I told myself, fucking the boss's secretary wasn't on the list. For God's sake, the place was rolling in pretty girls. I allowed Eileen to settle the bill, on the basis that it wasn't her money, and we left the restaurant. Until we got out onto the street, I was considering walking the seven blocks back to the office, but I had forgotten the intense heat. It was worse somehow, after the coolness of Le Cirque. Eileen saw off a large New York male for a cab that they were both waving down, and we made our way back through the early afternoon traffic. When we got back to the twenty-fourth floor offices, the receptionist said that Fred had telephoned a little while earlier to say that he was up and about, and ready for me to make my way to his apartment. Eileen wrote down his address for me—he was in an apartment block on Park and 64th—and showed me where my bags were stowed. One of the editorial people gave me a hand down with them, and hailed a cab for me.

When I got there, it was to find that Fred lived in a small (it was only twelve storeys high, and with but two apartments on each floor) but extremely elegant apartment block in one of the most expensive parts of town. Park Avenue, above the fifties, is a much sought-after address. The block had been built in the 1920s in Art Deco style, and had been beautifully preserved, with much gilt and polished mahogany, and with exquisite mirrors decorating the entrance hall. The lift looked primitive, but it seemed to function efficiently, and suddenly I was being welcomed by Fred, who was standing outside his twelfth-floor apartment, having been advised by the doorman that I was on my way up. Security in New York is all.

'Hey, Tony,' he said. 'Welcome. Did Eileen look after you? What did you think of the stretch limo? Where did she take you for lunch?' I laughed. 'Hi,' I said. 'Great to see you. Yes, Eileen looked after me very well. I thought the stretch limo was too much, and she took me to Le Cirque. But how are you?' 'Come in,' he said, 'and I'll tell you all about it. But first, let me show you your room.' I entered into a hallway that was furnished with magnificent antiques, and lined with leather-bound books for its entire length, which was the depth of the building. My room was at the back of the building, looking out in the direction of the East River, but there were too many taller buildings in the way to actually be able to see the river. But I did have a splendid view of the Con-Ed chimneys down around East 50th Street. (Con-Edison is the company which supplies electricity, gas, and steam—for heating—throughout New York). The bedroom was a large, well-furnished room, with its own bathroom *en suite* (obviously put in long after the block was built) and with enormous, walk-in closets for clothes, in the American fashion.

For those of you who haven't seen one, a closet is a small room, furnished with rails, on which to hang clothes, drawers for underclothes and socks and so on, and racks for shoes. It is usually about the size of a suburban house's spare bedroom. My bedroom had two of these closets leading off the wall opposite the large double bed. They are always much, *much* larger than the biggest wardrobe, and are the most sensible way to store clothes. Why the closet is somewhere that homosexuals supposedly come out of I have never known. 'Make yourself at home,' said Fred. 'I'll give you a set of keys in a minute. I expect you'd probably like to tidy up. I'll be in the sitting room when you're ready. Is it still Scotch and water, no ice?' 'As ever,' I said. 'Thank you. I shan't be a moment.'

I dumped my bags in one of the closets to unpack later, had a quick wash, combed my hair, and went through to the sitting room. Fred handed me a glass. 'Cheers,' he said. 'Welcome to New York.' We clinked glasses, and drank. Fred poured possibly the strongest drinks in the world. The room was enormous. The furniture, as everywhere, was antique. I noticed a beautiful inlaid backgammon table in a corner, that must have started life somewhere out East. 'Fancy a game?' asked Fred. 'I'd love one,' I said, 'but I think I'll wait until I've slept off my jet-lag, if you don't mind.' 'Oh, sure,' he said. 'I hadn't thought about that.' Fred was an excellent player, and we were fiercely competitive with each other at the game. We always played for money, and I think I had the slight edge over Fred, except that he had an irritating habit of losing, say, over a long evening, and then saying 'Double or quits?' and winning. But what the hell. But I certainly wouldn't sit down and play backgammon with him unless I was reasonably *compos mentis*.

I asked him about his alleged absence from the office, and told him of the rumours about the booze, birds, and cocaine. 'Oh, sure,' he said. 'They're all true. I shan't try to deny them. I've just got bored. The magazine's doing fantastically well, Wally's making a fucking fortune. And I'm not doing too badly. I just don't know what all the bloody fuss is about. I mean, I keep an eye on it, for God's sake. Those are competent people up there in the office. You'll see. I don't have to be there all the time. So I'm not. What the hell?'

It was a perfectly reasonable point of view, but not one that Wally was likely to agree with, and I said as much to Fred. 'Oh, I know,' he said. 'Wally's a pain. But so long as the money keeps rolling in, why the angst? We've caught up *Club*. I don't know if we'll ever overtake *Playboy* and *Penthouse*, but what if we don't? It isn't written in my contract that *Tiptop*'s American circulation has to exceed that of the other magazines. Think how long they've been at it out here. It's ridiculous.'

It's difficult, isn't it, when you can see both sides of an argument? Certainly, Fred had done a good job launching Wally's American magazine. Circulation, as Fred had said, was climbing rapidly, and had overtaken Paul Raymond's publication *Club*. Advertisement sales were excellent, and the whole operation was making huge amounts of money. But what Wally objected to was the fact that Fred seemed to have lost interest in the project, and to have abandoned any idea of work in favour of a pretty dissolute life of drugs, alcohol and sex. That he had installed competent people to carry on the day-to-day tasks of putting a monthly magazine together was neither here nor there, really, at least from Wally's point of view. Who was to say that if Fred was going to the office daily and doing his job, that the magazine's circulation wouldn't rise even more quickly? But Fred was my friend, and I simply didn't want to get involved in his differences with Wally, and I said so.

'Go back to London and have a rest, Fred,' I said. 'Relax, enjoy being in London, sort out your problems with Wally—you know you can. You're the number one son that he never had—and rest assured that I'll keep things going here. You've got to go. Wally insists on it. So why not go and enjoy it, instead of getting uptight about it? And try and slow down a bit. There's plenty of life out there to enjoy. You're not going to run out of fun tomorrow, you know. You don't have to do everything this week. It's not for me to moralize, but it's not unreasonable of Wally to expect you to spend some time in the office, now is it?' 'I suppose not, Tony,' he said. 'I suppose not. Now let's go and look for a little fun.' 'I think, if you'll forgive me, I'll join you for some supper, and then take myself off to bed,' I said. 'It's been a long day.' I looked at my watch. 'It might be seven in the evening to you, but it's after midnight for me, and I've been up since six British time. Do you mind?' 'No, of course I don't mind,' said Fred. 'I'm sorry, I always forget about time zones and jet-lag, and all that. We'll go off and have a nice relaxed supper somewhere, and then you can come back here and go to bed. Sleep as late as you like in the morning. It'll do you good.' 'Thanks,' I said. 'I will.'

We had a pleasant meal at the Waldorf-Astoria's Japanese restaurant, right down almost at the bottom end of Park Avenue. In those days, London's only Japanese restaurant, as far as I was aware, was the one in St. Christopher's Place, not far from Selfridges. This restaurant was much bigger, with a seemingly much more extensive menu. With my limited knowledge, I let Fred order, and we were plied with plate after plate of small, delicious dishes.

One of the earlier ones was sushi, raw fish wrapped around rice that's been soaked in vinegar. It was mouth-wateringly delightful, and was the beginning for me of a life-long love affair with sushi and sashimi. Fred drank numerous tumblers of saki, and I chose half a bottle of white Californian wine. After green tea and—for Fred—the inevitable brandies, we parted company. Me to go back to the apartment and a much-needed bed. Fred to take off for the delights of Manhattan at night. 'Don't wait up for me, Tony,' he said, as the doorman got us separate cabs on Park Avenue. 'I might be a little late.' Tell me about it, I thought.

I awoke the next morning refreshed by a good night's sleep. It was just after eight. There was no sight nor sound of or from Fred. The office, like the English one, opened at ten, so I got up, showered and shaved, made myself some coffee, and took a cab downtown. I was early, so I found a coffee shop and had some breakfast, by which time it was nearly ten. When I got to the office, everyone appeared to be in already, so it didn't seem that Fred's bad habits had affected anyone else. I spent most of the day with Eileen, who ran through pretty well everything with me, and by the end of the day I felt I knew basically what was happening.

'So where's the nearest singles bar?' I asked of Eileen at the end of the day. This was a phenomenon that had not, as yet, crossed the Atlantic, and I was curious to find out if they really were as described in the British newspapers. 'Oh, now let me think,' she said. 'I guess the nearest is Daly's Dandelion. It's two or three blocks up on Third Avenue. That's heading north.' She smiled at me. 'Don't worry. You'll soon get used to it. I imagine you'll probably find what you're looking for there. If by any chance you luck out, then there's Daly's Daffodil, about the same distance up on First Avenue. They're both good places. It's the same company, obviously. They get a nice class of customer. By and large. Or if you want to go up as far as Third and 64th, there Maxwell's Plum. That's probably the most famous of all the New York singles bars. It's also an excellent restaurant.' I thanked her, and she wished me luck. I had the same feeling then that I'd had in Le Cirque the day before; that I only had to raise my little finger, and she'd come running. Oh, well.

I walked slowly the three blocks up Third Avenue. It was warm, but I was dressed for it, and I took things gently. I just love walking the streets of New York. Daly's Dandelion turned out to be a largish bar with plenty of space, and with the late afternoon sun streaming through its windows. It was seriously crowded with what appeared to be well-dressed men and women of all ages, the women perhaps slightly outnumbering the men. I wondered what to drink for a moment, thinking that perhaps asking for whisky and water, no ice, might be a problem. I hadn't yet learned to say Scotch, straight up, which is the only way you'll get what you want in the States, if that's what you want. If you simply say whisky, you'll get rye or bourbon. But when in Rome ... I decided on a Bloody Mary. I'd just paid for it, and turned away from the bar to find a good place to stand, one that would allow me to observe the action, when a very pretty blonde girl came over to me. She was in her early thirties, was exquisitely made up, and was wearing a well-tailored navy blue lightweight suit and a colourful, flower-patterned, almost transparent silk blouse. I could see both the colour and the shape of her nipples. She stood about five ten in her medium-heeled court shoes, and I could smell the aroma of an expensive scent, which I didn't recognize.

'Hi,' she said. 'You're British, aren't you?' I admitted that I was, and told her my name. 'Terrific,' she said. 'Hello, Tony. I'm Pauline. Would you like to fuck?' I must admit that I was somewhat taken aback by her direct approach. I mean, you know, I've been around a bit, but did a beautiful woman whom you'd never seen before ever come up to you in a bar and say would you like to fuck? That was my introduction to New York singles bars. Of course, I said 'Yes.' I think I even said 'Thank you.'

'Great,' she said. 'There's no hurry, now that we're agreed about what we're going to do. Tell me about yourself. Are you on vacation?' 'No,' I replied. 'I'm over here to work. I'm editing *Tiptop* magazine while my editor-in-chief goes back to London for a spot of leave.' 'Wow,' she said. '*Tiptop*! That's wild. I guess I've picked myself a winner. You must have fucked more women than I've made trips to Tokyo.'

I must have looked a bit blank. 'Oh, I'm sorry,' she said. 'I should have explained that I'm a stewardess with Pan-Am.' 'Now it's my turn to say wow,' I said. 'I guess I'm going to join the Mile-High Club, even if only as a ground member.' 'Oh, I wouldn't take too much notice of that Mile-High Club nonsense,' she said. 'Can you really imagine anyone other than a total freak trying to fuck in an aircraft lavatory? There's just no room, for a start. Some girls say they've done it, but I haven't, and I've never met anyone who has. I know a few stewardesses who have fucked across a row of seats at the back of the aircraft at night, when most people are asleep, but that's it. But tell me about *Tiptop*. That's a great magazine. You treat your women with class, which is more than most of those men's magazines do. And you have some great-looking girls. Do you get to fuck anyone you want to?' 'Well, the answer to that has to be no,' I said. 'But I guess I do get the opportunity to meet more pretty girls than most men do. And, in a strange way, working on a magazine like *Tiptop* is a positive advantage. It didn't happen between you and me, because you came right out with your invitation. But in England, girls are rather less forward, and sometimes it can be a problem to work around to the question of sex without offending anyone. But working on the magazine, as I do, when you meet girls, they immediately start talking about sex. Which helps enormously, of course. And if they're in the girlie magazine business in any way, well, they lead pretty sexy lives themselves already. But tell me about yourself. Are you a New Yorker? Were you raised here?'

She finished her drink as I asked the question, and accepted the offer of another. She was drinking white wine spritzers, the woman-who-doesn't-really-drink's drink. I waved at the barman, and he brought us two more in moments. I've never met barmen anywhere in the world who have memories for what you're drinking like New York barmen, or who work so quickly and efficiently.

'Cheers,' she said. 'Isn't that what you Britishers say?' I raised my glass. 'I guess it is,' I said. 'Cheers.' 'To answer your question,' she said, 'no, I'm not a New Yorker. I was born and raised in California. In the Nappa Valley, where the wine comes from. But I moved up here in '64, and I've been here ever since. I like it. I enjoy my job, although it plays havoc with my body. And it gives me plenty of free time between trips. I've been on long-haul flights for some years now, and it gives you good breaks, both at home and around the world. And in my spare time, I like to fuck. I've no great ambitions to get married. I wouldn't mind a nice, close relationship with some decent guy, but you don't meet too many of those in New York. So I stay with the fucking. It keeps me happy.' She grinned over the top of her glass. 'And out of mischief, of course.'

I laughed. It was such an honest self-appraisal. This lady didn't seem to have too many illusions, either about herself, or about life. 'And speaking of fucking,' she said, 'as I was, shall we go and get on with it?' She moved very close to me, and looked into my eyes. I could smell her perfume again, and then, moments later, I felt her hand on my crotch. 'Are you feeling randy?' she asked. 'Do you think you'll enjoy fucking me?' Her hand sought, and found, my stiffening member. 'Oooh,' she said. 'That feels good. What a pity you can't feel me. I'm all wet. My pussy's dripping. If we don't get out of here soon, it'll start showing through my skirt.' She was standing up against me, so close that I could see down the front of her blouse. I could see her full, naked breasts, and her erect nipples. They were a dark, brownish red, and swollen with lust. They looked a bit like little brown thimbles. I wanted to suck them, and I licked my lips in anticipation.

She cleared her throat, and said huskily 'Do you like to suck pussy?' I nodded. 'Yes,' I said. 'I do. Very much.' 'Fantastic,' she said. 'Take me away and eat me. Now. Please. Suck my pussy for me. Then fuck me. Hard. Make me come. And I'll make you come. Any way you like.' She reached up and kissed me full on my mouth, her tongue inside, exploring. Then 'Will I be your first American fuck?' she asked. 'Yes,' I said. 'As a matter of fact, you will.' 'Then I'd better work at it, hadn't I?' she asked. 'I wouldn't want your first American fuck to be a disappointment.' She squeezed my now erect cock and, looking at me, she drained her glass. 'Come on, baby,' she said. 'Let's get a cab. It's party time.' She grabbed my hand, and we went outside into the still warm evening, and hailed a cab coming down Third Avenue. 'First and 86th,' she said to the driver. We got in, and he took the first left, and then made a left again, up Second Avenue.

'It's a fair way uptown,' said Pauline, 'but I like it. It's the part of the old East Side that used to be called German Town, back when the El was still running. The block's brand new, and I got in at the beginning, when they were still fairly cheap. It's a condo.' She let go of my hand, and patted my crotch. 'Good boy,' she said. 'Just making sure.' I assured her that I would like her apartment. The El was the old Elevated Railway that used to run right down the East Side, but which was eventually pulled down when the subways were built, leaving a speculator's dream in developable land area. Much of it now was second generation development, the old, smaller skyscrapers having been pulled down and replaced by bigger, taller, more expensive ones.

The cab driver dropped us off, and we took the elevator to the forty-second floor. 'I love to be high,' said Pauline. 'I mean high up, looking down over New York. How about you?' It was a tremendous view. You could see all the way down to

Battery Park, and the World Trade Center, and everything in between. The Rockefeller Center, the Chrysler Building, Central Park off over to the right. 'Yes, I love it too,' I said. I turned around. She was naked. 'You can look at that view any time. Right now, come and love me,' she said. She was truly beautiful. Her well-trimmed pubic thatch proved either that she was a genuine blonde, or that she had her pubes dyed too. Either way, her snatch looked good to me. I could just see a tiny, pink line at the centre, which had to be her cunt lips, and I could also see a trickle of clear, colourless liquid emanating from the bottom of them. Her breasts were exquisite, seen totally revealed; firm, full, well-shaped, and tipped with erect nipples. She licked her lips, and smiled.

'Do I look good enough to eat?' she asked, holding out a hand. I grinned back at her. 'You most certainly do, ma'am,' I said. I took her hand, and she led me along a corridor and up a flight of stairs to the condominium's upper floor, and into her bedroom. It was well furnished with contemporary, American-style, designer furniture, the most noticeable item being a large, modern, four poster bed, the 'posts' of chrome steel, and hung all about with pretty, white, lacy curtains. It was king-size. She let go of my hand, and I undressed, as quickly as I could manage. She lay on the bed on her back, her legs spread, one hand playing idly with her pussy as she watched me.

My cock was throbbingly erect as I dropped my trousers and underpants, and made my way over to the bed. I didn't feel that it was necessary to say anything. I just wanted to get at that lovely pussy. I knelt down in front of her, and she parted her legs even more widely, and took her hand away from her now very wet cunt. I leaned down and licked it, slowly, from top to bottom, savouring the taste and scent of freshly aroused, clean pussy. She tasted good. Like a sun-ripened, perhaps slightly over-ripe, still warm melon, with perhaps a touch of lime to bring out the flavour. My favourite fruit, I thought, as I began tonguing her, thrusting inside her welcoming, strongly scented love-hole. She squirmed and moved her hips up against my mouth, making deep-throated, little cat-like sounds in her throat as I sucked her. I used my hands to spread her puffy, lust-swollen lips even further apart, and felt for her clitoris with my tongue. It was easy to find, firmly at attention as it was, a small soldier standing guard against I don't know what. Certainly not her virginity. I concentrated on massaging it with my tongue, and soon felt her responding to its stimulation.

'Oh, yes baby,' she almost purred. 'That feels so good. I'm going to come now. You're making me come. I like it. Then you can fuck me. I'm coming ... I'm coming ... Yeeees ... Nooooow. Oh God, I'm coming. Oh, yes.' She thrust her hips up hard against my mouth, and put her hands behind my head and pressed it down onto herself, grinding her cunt against my mouth and tongue, writhing as she came, fucking my mouth with her pussy, until, slowly, her multiple orgasms began to dwindle. And then, finally, she was spent. She let go of my head, and patted it, then sat up and smiled down at me.

'Hey, baby,' she said. 'You really *do* like to suck pussy, don't you? That's the best cunnilingus I've ever had. After you, they ought to spell it cuntilingus. That was terrific. I thank you.' She bent down and kissed me. 'What a naughty boy,' she said. 'You taste of pussy. Where *have* you been?' 'Oh, nowhere special,' I said. 'Just paying lip service to a new friend.'

'Oh, wow,' she said. 'Lip service. I like it. You British are too much. Most of the stewardesses I work with at Pan-Am tell me that all male Brits are gay. You know. What you call queer. Homosexual. As in fucking each other. All I can say is they must have been moving in the wrong circles.' 'Oh, very good,' I said. 'Moving in the wrong circles. That's an improvement on "they were trying to increase the circle of their friends." It's as good as the one about the wife who was so worried when she discovered that her husband was gay, that she didn't know which way to turn.' Pauline exploded with laughter.

You're too much, sweetie,' she said. 'Come and fuck me. Or would you rather I sucked you off? Or both? You choose. After what you've just done for me, it's your treat. I just knew, when

I saw you come into Daly's Dandelion, that you were the one for me. That was before I heard you order your drink in that splendid British accent. So you choose. What'll it be?'

If I had been totally honest, I would have told her then and there that what I would have enjoyed more than anything else would have been to lie back and let her suck me off. Preferably very slowly. But it doesn't always pay to be selfish, sexually. I could see that she seriously wanted to be fucked. She had an urgent need for stiff cock up her fanny. She was wet, willing, and wanton, as the saying goes. And wanting. So I reckoned that if I provided the required fuck – which in itself wasn't going to cause me any pain, now was it? Then I would probably be storing up riches in heaven. Or something like that. I pretended to have difficulty in deciding what my preference would be, pantomiming my indecision. 'Hey, come on, baby,' she said. 'Don't give me all this shit. Do you want to fuck me, or don't you?' 'Of course I do, my darling,' I said. 'I want to fuck you. Now. From on top. Just like Mom and Pop. Please. Is that OK?' She lay back on the bed again, her legs spread wide. 'It's more than OK, baby,' she said. 'It's fantastic. I'm all yours. Come and get me.' I put a hand between her legs and felt how wet she still was. I slid a finger into her, and rubbed her clitoris, very gently. She moaned. 'Please fuck me,' she said. 'Please put your stiff prick in my cunt and fuck me. Fuck me silly. Fuck me hard. Please. Now?'

I climbed onto her, and she took my rampant prick and fed it into her open, waiting cunt, which closed around my cock as I thrust downwards. She was as tight as a mouse's earhole, as the saying goes. Lovely. Tight and wet and slippery. I felt her muscles embracing my cock as if they were massaging it, grabbing it and, as it were, masturbating it in long, hot, wet strokes. 'Mmmm,' she said, from far away. 'I like it. Do it to me, baby. Fuck me.'

I rode her hard, knowing that I couldn't last that long myself. From the moment she'd said 'Do you want to fuck?' in Daly's Dandelion, from the second that she had gripped hold of my cock through my trousers while we were still in the bar, for all the time that I had been sucking and licking her wet pussy, I had been building up a massive ejaculation, which needed very little action now to bring it into being. She reached down and gripped my cock around its base, masturbating me into herself as I fucked her. It was the final, delightful, erotic, all-consuming straw. I began to pump my ejaculate into her in prolonged spurts. 'Oh, my God,' she cried. 'You're coming. I can feel your spunk spurting up my cunt. It's making me come too. Ooooh, that's lovely.' And then it was over. For the moment. We were both satiated, one way or another. After that, I must admit that I dozed off there for a while, an arm around Pauline's shoulders, her arm around my neck, jet-lag bringing some still much-needed sleep. I can only hope I didn't snore.

She woke me up a while later. 'Hi, honey. It's after eight. I wondered if you'd like to go and eat? I haven't got much here other than juice and cereal and coffee. Being away so much, it isn't worth my keeping a lot of food in. It only goes stale, or off. But if you're hungry, there are any number of neighbourhood restaurants around. What do you say?' I got myself together as best I could. 'Yeah, that'd be great, sweetheart,' I said. 'You choose where. I'm easy. Anything you fancy is fine by me.'

She thought for a moment. 'I tell you what might be fun.' she said. 'There's a nice place down on Third Avenue at 73rd Street, which isn't too far from here, called Marty's, where they do a good selection of food, and there's a lovely guy there in the evenings who plays piano. His name is Patrick Cook. He's a songwriter, and a lyricist, and he writes musicals, but he plays piano in Marty's bar restaurant in the evenings to pay the rent. You know how it is.' 'Sounds good,' I said. 'Let me take a quick shower, and I'll be with you.' 'Let's shower together, honey,' she said. 'It'll be more fun.' So we did. And, of course, we had a knee-trembler in the shower, didn't we? Well, if you'd been me, so would you. I promise. I started off simply soaping her all over. I thought it would help. You know? And then she started doing the same for me, and before either of us really realized what we were doing, there we were, fucking. Well, why not? Afterwards, Pauline poured us a drink for while we dressed, and I felt that, in the circumstances, I could ask for a Scotch and water, no ice, which I did. She drank vodka and tonic, which I took as a good sign. Girls who drink white wine spritzers *all* the time can sometimes be a problem. Take it from me.

Marty's turned out to be one of those restaurants which they do so well in Manhattan. There was a big, crowded bar, with excellent service. Plenty of room to sit at a table, if that's what you wanted. A fairly extensive menu, of what I would describe as New York food. That's not a put-down. it's a compliment. Good stuff, most of which you won't find, at least all together, anywhere else but New York. Good, cocktail bar piano playing in the background. In Marty's case, it was a young, good-looking, red-haired, freckle-faced pianist, who waved at Pauline as she came in.

When he'd finished his number, Pauline took me over and introduced me. 'Patrick Cook, Tony Andrews,' she said. 'Tony's from London, England. He's over here editing *Tiptop* magazine for a while.' 'Gosh,' said Patrick. 'Do you know my father, Joe Cook?' 'I don't think so,' I said. 'Should I?' 'No, not really,' said Patrick. 'He's a writer. Television mostly. And books. But he writes the occasional piece for *Club* magazine. I thought perhaps you might have come across him.' I laughed. 'I've only been here a couple of days,' I said. 'But get Joe to give me a call. The number has to be in the 'phone book. I haven't got as far as a business card as yet.' 'Hey, thanks,' said Patrick. 'I'll tell him to do that.' He started to play again, and the restaurant manager found us a table. I ordered New England clam chowder (as opposed to Manhattan clam chowder) followed by a bowl of spaghetti Bolognese. Pauline ordered soft shelled crabs, and the same spaghetti, and I ordered a bottle of Californian red to go with it all.

I was fascinated, watching the ongoing scenario at the bar.

There were groups of both sexes, who obviously worked together, and who were having a few before they left to go home. There was a group of slowly changing people, who looked as if they were locals, using the place as we would a pub at home. And then there were the singles and the couples. As I watched, some of the singles paired up, and became a couple, and some of the couples broke up – usually with one of the pair leaving – and the remaining one becoming a single. It was quite enthralling.

The thing that I have always liked about New York restaurants is the fact that it doesn't matter where they are – they can be uptown, downtown, or midtown, they can be wildly expensive, or unbelievably reasonable, but they'll all have one thing in common: the waiters and waitresses appear to enjoy what they are doing. Waiting on table isn't seen as a down-market occupation. Nice people do it. Intelligent people do it. And aren't thought any the worse of for so doing. I don't know whether it's genuine or not, but it *appears* to be genuine, and as a customer, that's all that's necessary. 'Hi. I'm David. I'm your waiter for the evening. May I get you a drink?' Goes and gets drinks, and returns with them. Remembers who ordered what. 'Now let me tell you about today's specials. Oh, yes. I'm afraid we're out of the Boston Scrod. We've had such a run on it, you wouldn't believe. Now, I'll give you a little while to think about what you want to eat, and then I'll come and take your order. If you need me before that, shout.' Sounds familiar? I thought not.

We ate our food, chattering quietly to each other about life with a capital 'L.' Pauline, obviously, was well travelled. She seemed to enjoy her job with Pan-Am, although she was very aware of the long-term health problems associated with constant long-haul flying. 'The cabin pressurisation causes havoc with one's skin,' she said. 'And I haven't had a regular period for longer than I care to remember. But the money's good. And it beats the hell out of pounding a typewriter. But I shan't do it forever. The condo will soon be mine, and I sure as hell couldn't have afforded *that* on a stenographer's salary. And, of course, it's an investment, really. If I need the cash when I give up flying, I can always sell it and move out of town. It will have appreciated so much by then that it should keep me comfortably in my old age.' She asked me the usual questions about where I was born, and where did I go to school? How long had I been working as an editor on girlie magazines? Was I – had I ever been – married? Did I *want* to get married? All the things that girls ask men on their first evening out together.

I found myself very attracted to her. She was genuinely, down to-earth, attractively nice. When we'd finished our meal, I asked her if she would care to come back to the apartment for coffee and a liqueur, and she said yes, she'd love to. I was amused by her face when I gave the cab driver the address on Park and 64th Street. 'Wow, Tony,' she said. 'I've never been in an apartment on Park Avenue in all my years in New York.' 'There's always a first time,' I said, rather unimaginatively. I paid the cab off, and we were greeted by the apartment block's two doormen. Fred, they told me, had gone out not too long before. He hadn't left a message. I had explained to Pauline about my camping out in Fred's rented apartment, but she was still impressed when we got up to it. 'Have a look around,' I said, 'while I put some coffee on. But first, what will you have to drink? There's most usual things.' 'How about a glass of wine?' she asked. 'Red?' 'Sure,' I said. 'No problem.' There was a jug of Californian red open in the kitchen, and one of white, I knew, in the fridge. The glasses were in the living room. I poured Pauline her wine, and myself a Scotch and water. 'Cheers.' I raised my glass.

You Brits certainly do yourselves proud,' said Pauline. 'Do you live like this at home?' 'Frankly, no,' I said. 'But I live pretty well. It's not really possible to make realistic comparisons between London and New York. What we're talking about here is Manhattan, which is only one of what I always think of as five islands, although I know that's not true, strictly speaking' (The others are Queens, The Bronx, Staten Island, and Brooklyn). 'But most foreigners think Manhattan *is* New York. Or vice versa. Even so, its not a huge city in terms of area, even if you include Westchester and Nassau County. London is much more spread out, as you know. But living here on Park Avenue, in a block like this, is more like living in Mayfair than in Hampstead, which is where I live. I've not seen an area in Manhattan that truly compares with Hampstead. Maybe SoHo. I don't know. It's difficult. But as our boss's representative here in America, Fred – whom you'll meet, I'm sure – needs a certain amount of, status, for plain good business reasons. Paper manufacturers, for example, aren't going to be all that keen to sign millions of dollars' worth of annual paper contracts with a chap who rents a walk-up in Greenwich Village, for example. Not really.' I followed Pauline as she explored Fred's apartment. She loved my bedroom. 'Wow, she said. 'Some bed. That has to be fun.' When we had finished the guided tour, I suggested a game of backgammon, which she accepted with alacrity. Half-a dozen games later, and some thirty dollars the poorer, I could see why. 'I do play quite a lot,' she said, as I put the pieces away. 'But it was you who insisted on playing for money, now wasn't it?' I had to agree. It had been. 'I don't mind how much we play for,' I had said, 'as long as we play for something. How about ten cents a point?' 'Oh, come on, Tony,' she had replied. 'If we're going to play for money, let's at least make it interesting. How about a dollar a point?' To which I had happily agreed. My problem had been (and always is) that I find it difficult to refuse the doubling dice.

You really play quite a good game, you know,' said Pauline. 'But you need to learn when to refuse the doubling dice. I don't know if you were counting, but every time I offered it to you, you accepted it, and each time, you lost the game. If you'd said no, you wouldn't have lost as much money. It's as simple as that.' I grinned at her.

I know you're right, sweetheart,' I said. 'It's always been my problem. I think it has something to do with male chauvinism. I'm not a sexual chauvinist. At least, I don't think I am. But I'm a backgammon chauvinist. I can't ever believe that a woman is going to beat me. I've lost quite a lot of money over the years, for that single reason.' She laughed, and kissed me on the cheek. It was a pleasantly familiar gesture. 'Speaking of sex,' she said, 'much as I would like to try out that splendid bed, will you forgive me if I say thank you, and good night? I have to make an early flight tomorrow morning, and it's way past my working bedtime now. I've had a marvellous evening, and would very much like to think that we'll get together again when I get back from this trip. May I call you when I get back? I'm off to Tokyo, so that means a five-day rest break when I get there, so I should be back some time around the end of next week.' I agreed, naturally.

She was so beautiful, and she was absolutely delightful with it. Not to mention her healthily relaxed enthusiasm for sex. We exchanged telephone numbers, and I called down to the lobby to order her a cab. When they rang back to say the cab was waiting, I walked her to the elevator, and kissed her hungrily as we waited for it. She thrust her tongue down my throat, and then pulled away from me. 'I'm sorry, sweetheart,' she said. 'If I go on doing that, I'll miss my 'plane tomorrow.' Then the elevator arrived. I blew her a kiss as the doors closed.

I decided that I'd sit up for a while, and see if Fred came home within the next hour or so. I poured myself another Scotch, and switched on Fred's giant (by British standards) television. He was, like most New Yorkers, on cable television, the reason being that, with the multitude of skyscrapers, it is virtually impossible to get a picture any other way. I amused myself for a while, flicking through New York's fifty-nine TV stations, ranging from the national networks to one station where anyone can rent the studio for a hundred dollars an hour, and put on anything they like. Mostly, it's rubbish, but it's amusing if you've never seen it before. By midnight Fred hadn't appeared, so I went to bed.

CHAPTER TWO:
NICE WORK, IF YOU CAN GET IT

I got to the office by nine-thirty the following morning, but I was by no means the first in. Eileen was already there, as were most of the editorial and production people. There was a noticeable lack of ad sales staff, but they were probably starting their day out of the office, with existing or potential customers. Since my arrival, I had decided to start a monthly diary in the American issue of *Tiptop*, on the same basic principle as the one I had started in the UK edition, and I had asked the deputy editor, a pretty girl called Angie, to look out for any manuscripts that might have been submitted that could be suitable for such a feature. She had brought in quite a pile, and I began my day by sorting through some of them. The idea was simply to run a two-page, newsy feature, lavishly illustrated, telling readers about new developments in the world of sex.

New York was, I already knew, one of the three main gay cities in the world, the other two being San Francisco, and Sydney, Australia. London, it may surprise British gays to know, simply doesn't come into it. So when I found a piece describing the fact that New York gays announced their specific homosexual predilections by the colour and positioning of where they wore their handkerchiefs about their person, I decided to run a shortened version of it for *Tiptop*'s readers.

Not that I thought that *Tiptop* had too many gay readers. But it was a new, and amusing, look at an aspect of sex that would probably interest our heterosexual readers to hear about. At least it would teach them to be careful about where they wore their handkerchiefs. Down on Christopher Street, one of Greenwich Village's main thoroughfares, and site of a number of seriously gay bars, there's no longer any need to speak to any one to introduce your sexual preference, said the author of the manuscript. First of all, it's important to get the positioning of the pockets clearly stated. We are simply talking about the two rear hip pockets on any pair of self-respecting jeans. There is one on the left, and one on the right.

Right? Apparently, according to the author of the piece, a lacy number in the left-hand pocket means 'I want to fuck.' In the right-hand pocket, it means 'I want to get fucked.' Blue says that you like normal anal sex. Red says you like fist-fucking. Yellow indicates a penchant for water sports. 'Why piss in the street, when you can piss on a friend?' asks the writer. A difficult question to answer, that one. Put your yellow hanky in the left pocket, you're a sadist. Wear it on the right, and you're a masochist. Different strokes for different folks, as they say. I quite liked the idea, and called through to Angie, who arrived in my office almost immediately. I slid the manuscript across the desk towards her.

'I quite like this, Angie,' I said. 'Have you read it?' She picked it up and looked at it. 'Sure,' she said. 'I've read all those manuscripts on your desk. They wouldn't be there otherwise.' 'Sorry, love,' I said. 'Forgive me. Second question. Do you think it's right for this diary type feature we discussed yesterday? Do you think its OK for *Tiptop*'s readership? 'Yeah, Tone,' she said. Nobody had ever called me Tone in my life before. I'm simply not a Tone. I considered asking her not to call me that, and then I thought, what the hell? If she wants to call me Tone, she may. 'Sure. I think it's a good piece,' she went on, oblivious to my reaction. 'Provided that we ham it up a little. You know, don't take it too seriously. We could have some real terrific shots taken of male asses wearing the various different coloured handkerchiefs in their jeans, with backgrounds indicating their preferences. You know, we could show a guy with a red hanky in his pocket in the act of bending over and dropping his jeans, with a huge forearm and fist in the foreground, waiting ready to oblige him. Lots of butch tattoos on the arm, of course. Yeah. I like it. You want me to edit the piece, and set up the photography?'

Please,' I said. 'But get someone to check it out first. For all I know, it might be a send-up. We need to make certain that it's accurate.' 'Oh, sure,' she said. 'That won't take any time at all.' 'It won't?' I asked. 'Nah,' she said. 'I'll check it out with the art department.' She looked at me, completely straight-faced. 'Whatever you say, sweetie,' I said. 'On your head be it.' What was she? Some kind of fag hag?

Just as Angie left, Eileen rang through. 'There's a young girl here to see you, Tony,' she said. 'She hasn't got an appointment, but she's very pretty. Unusual, too. She can't hear me, so you can say anything from 'Sure,' to 'You must be joking.' What's it to be?' I thought for a moment. A very pretty girl would make for a very pleasant interlude. 'Sure, Eileen,' I said. 'Send her in.' A few moments later there was a knock on the door, and Eileen opened it, ushering in the lady in question. 'This is Lucy, Tony,' she said. 'Lucy, this is Tony Andrews. Have fun.' She shut the door. I stood up. For just a tiny moment I was speechless, and then I remembered my manners. I stepped forward, and held out my hand. 'Hi, Lucy,' I said. 'I'm Tony. Come and sit down.' She took my hand, but she didn't shake it. She pulled me towards her, and gave me a big, very wet kiss. 'Hi, honey.' she said.

She looked down at me, and I'm six foot. She was wearing three inch stiletto heels. She was completely bald. Shaven. Her scalp shone, as if polished. She was black. And she was very, very beautiful. Just then the telephone rang, and I waved Lucy to a chair, and went to answer it. It was *Tiptop*'s American printer, with a production problem. He'd been passed on to me by our production editor, with whom he seemed to have a problem. I talked to him for about five minutes, totally preoccupied, and at the end of the conversation, I put the 'phone down, and looked for Lucy.

She'd gone. Disappeared. Where to, I couldn't imagine. Until I felt a hand on my fly. The hand unzipped me, and a warm, soft, very feminine hand took out my prick, which, taken by surprise, took a few moments to rise to the occasion. Then I felt a warm, wet mouth encompass my now rigid cock, and I knew for certain where Lucy had got to. I saw no good reason to complain about this rather unusual (bearing in mind the brevity of our friendship) approach, and decided to lean back and enjoy it. I just hoped no one would come into the office while this was happening. I picked up the 'phone, and asked Eileen to hold all my calls. 'Hold everything, please,' I said. 'Lucy and I don't want to be interrupted for half an hour or so.' 'Hmmm,' said Eileen. 'I see.' Lucy's tongue and lips, not to mention fingers, were all in motion, producing the most exquisite, erotic sensations in my tool. I started, involuntarily, to move my hips, beginning a fucking motion, fucking those soft, warm wet lips, feeling her tongue massaging my cockhead, feeling her fingers masturbating the base of my cock lightly, sensuously. My ejaculation began to gather, deep down. It was going to be a big one.

It was the strangest sensation, feeling an orgasm coming on as a result of an expert, very practised mouth job, but not being able to see the person who was the cause of what was, very shortly, going to be an excellent effect. In my mind, I gripped that bald, shining black head, and I began to fuck Lucy's mouth with determination. I was going to come in her mouth. If she didn't like it, she had only herself to blame. I felt the spunk rising, rising, and then, suddenly, I was jetting it into her mouth. She didn't hesitate, she didn't withdraw. She kept on sucking, and she swallowed my spunk as I spurted it into her willing mouth. I kept my hips moving as I ejaculated into her, and she kept sucking and milking me, until there was nothing left to milk. I withdrew, gently. In a moment, Lucy appeared from below the desk, smiling a huge smile. 'Great, eh, man?' she asked. I nodded, not sure that I was quite ready to speak. And then I found my voice.

'Terrific,' I said. 'Really fantastic. Thank you. That was good. Really good.' 'It was good for me too,' she said. 'Your come tastes good. Really good. Creamy.' She licked her lips. 'Did you enjoy fucking my mouth?' She made a big 'O' of her lips, and mimed what could only be described as a cock-sucking mouth, making gobbling sounds as she did so. 'I did,' I said. 'Very much.' 'Then you'll love my pussy,' she said. 'It's smaller. Tighter. It'll grip your cock better. Look,' she said. She lifted up her short skirt, pulled aside some very sexy, gauzy, transparent black panties, and revealed that her pussy, like her head, was quite bald. In the centre of her pudenda, her almost black cunt lips stood exposed, puffy with desire, oozing a clear liquid. I felt my cock begin to stiffen again. 'What do you think?' she asked. 'Do you want to fuck it, baby? It's quite wet. You'll slide in beautifully. No problem at all. What do you say?'

'I say that yes, I'd love to fuck your pretty, bald, tight, wet little snatch,' I said. 'But not right now, sweetheart. For two reasons. One is that, after that beautiful blow-job, I'm not going to be at my peak for a while, and I'd hate not to be at my best for you. The other is that, sadly, I *do* have some work to do. So, if I may, I'll take a rain check, darling.' She rearranged her skimpy panties, pouting her full lips in sham disappointment. 'Well,' she said. 'It's your choice, man. Don't say I didn't offer. Now, what I came here for originally is for some modelling work. How about it, honey?' I looked at her. She was some model, that was for sure, but she didn't seem right for the usual kind of *Tiptop* pictures. She was almost *too* striking.

'Hang on, honey,' I said. 'I'll get my art director in here.' I rang through to Eileen. 'Do me a favour, Eileen love,' I said. Ask David if he'll pop in here for a moment, will you? I want him to have a look at this model Lucy who's with me.' 'Sure,

Tony,' she said. 'He'll be with you momentarily.' He arrived moments later, and I introduced him to Lucy. She gave him a big wet kiss too, which didn't do a lot for him, since he was gay. 'Lucy here wonders if she could model for us,' I explained to David. 'I thought that should be your decision.' 'Oh, fine,' he said. 'Thanks. OK, baby, strip off, will you?' Lucy looked a little surprised, but she did as she was told, taking off her summer dress to reveal the black panties that she had flashed at me earlier, and which I could now see were accompanied by a matching, gauzy, minuscule black garter belt, and black stockings. She wasn't wearing a bra.

'That'll do fine,' said David. 'You needn't go any further. Walk up and down a bit, will you, and turn around a few times, please?' 'Don't you want to see my pussy?' Lucy asked. 'I shaved it specially this morning.' 'Not particularly,' said David, winking at me. 'I'm more of an ass man myself, and I can see that quite clearly.' Lucy grinned a wide grin at him, and started to walk elegantly up and down my office. Her breasts were small but prettily shaped, with pointed, almost black nipples that — of course — matched her pussy lips perfectly. That enticing part of her anatomy showed quite clearly through the gauze of her panties, and there was a damp patch just beneath it, where she was dribbling her love juice, the flow presumably started by her arousal while sucking my cock. I felt my cock jerk beneath my trousers, and tried to look at some part of Lucy that wasn't going to give me a hard-on. There wasn't anything. I looked at David instead. That worked.

'OK, Lucy, baby. Thank you. You can get dressed again now,' he said. 'So what do you think?' asked Lucy. 'Will you give me some work?' 'We'll let you know, baby,' he replied. 'Just leave your name and number with the girl in reception, will you?' Watching Lucy dressing was just as sexually exciting as watching her undress. First she bent down and straightened her stocking seams, her naked breasts swaying slightly as she bent down. Then she pulled her panties up tightly around her waist, with the result that part of the crotch was pulled into her cunt, a sight I have always found sexually stimulating. My cock was having a problem again. I put a hand into my pocket and rearranged things more comfortably. Lucy saw what I was doing, and grinned.

She then lifted up her dress and dropped it over her head, lifting her arms as she did so and, pulling the dress down, she then adjusted each breast individually until she was comfortable. She looked around for her bag, found it where she'd left it down on the floor beside my desk and, picking it up and opening it, she took out a small wallet containing visiting cards, and gave one to each of us. 'Thank you, gentlemen,' she said. 'I'll give one in at reception on the way out. Thank you for your time.' She looked directly at me. 'If there's anything I can do for either of you,' she said, 'just call me. OK?' She blew a kiss, and she was on her way.

When the door had shut behind her, David said 'Quite a gal. I'm sure we could find her something, although I'm not sure exactly what right now. She'd be too much, I think, for a normal girl set. It's a great body, but it's not going to photograph like a great body. We either need some sort of gimmick ...' He stopped short for a moment. Then 'Why don't I have some test shots done, Tony?' he asked. 'Then we'll have a better idea of how best to use her. I think it would be a pity just to let her go.' 'Fine,' I said. 'I'm happy with that. Thank you.' He moved towards the door, and then turned back and grinned at me. 'Just in case you missed it,' he said, 'I think she was trying to tell you something. Or sell you something. Like her pussy ... Anyway, you've got her number. See you.' He left, closing the door quietly behind him.

Moments later, Eileen knocked and came in. 'Hey,' she said. 'So what did Miss Darkest Africa want? Patently not a haircut.' She cocked an eyebrow at me. 'You didn't, did you?' she asked. 'Didn't what?' I said, trying to look all innocent. 'Fuck her,' said Eileen. 'What, you mean here in the office?' I asked. 'Yes,' said Eileen. 'Here in the office. Did you, or didn't you?' 'Eileen,' I said. 'Trust me. I can stand here with my hand on my heart, and tell you that I didn't, and haven't, fucked her. Here, in the office. Or anywhere else. But that's not to say that I might not fuck her somewhere in the future.'

'You can say that again,' said Eileen. 'I can think of three places, for a start.' 'What do you mean?' I asked. 'Three places?' 'Well, you said it,' said Eileen. 'Fuck her somewhere in the future. Somewhere. I can think of three places. Her pussy, her ass, and her mouth. And I'll bet she's an expert at jacking off, too. You choose.' 'Eileen, darling,' I said. 'Don't be so bitchy. It doesn't become you. While the boss is away, I'm the boss, right? Let's have a little respect where it's due. Hmmmm?' Eileen looked at me, I must admit, slightly acidly. 'First of all,' she said, 'the boss isn't away yet. He might not be here in the office, but away he ain't. Secondly, I'm supposed to look after you. Right? That includes, in my book, protecting you from six-foot-tall, bald, black hookers. Model my foot. The only thing she models is about an inch and a half across, ten inches deep, is about two inches away from her asshole, and is permanently wet. In a word, her cunt. If you're that short, ask Aunty Eileen. I can do better than that Harlem tart. Any time.' She turned on her heel and left. I didn't stop her. I believe that what she had just done is called telling it like it is. She'd rather taken the pleasure out of my morning to date. I need a change, I thought. I know what I'll do, I said to myself. I'll go and have a look at the *Tiptop* photographic studio, downtown. I rang through to Eileen, and when she picked up the 'phone, I simply said, 'I'm off out. I may be back, or not. I'll call you later,' and put the 'phone down.

I took a cab down to the studio, which was on Canal Street. Not the most salubrious area in New York. I rang the bell, which was answered after a while by a very pretty girl, a black-haired, diminutive little lady whose name, I discovered later, was Betsy. She managed the studio, and did a bit of everything. Helping with make-up, with hair-styling, with lighting, with photography, with obtaining props. You name it, Betsy could do it. 'Yeah,' she said, patently unimpressed with my appearance. 'Hi,' I said. 'I'm Tony Andrews. I work with Fred.' Her attitude changed immediately. She nearly choked on her gum. 'Oh,' she said, remembering to smile, 'Tony. Hi. I'm Betsy. Come in. Please.' She held the door open. 'George is just shooting a girl set. Can I get you anything? Coffee? Tea? A beer?' I went in. 'Beer would be good. Thank you.' The studio was enormous. It had been a warehouse originally. Betsy introduced me to George. George Barter. He was photographing a stunning blonde called Lisa. Lisa was lying on a mattress on a set in a corner of the studio, surrounded by lights, made to look as if she was sunbathing in her back yard (American for garden). She was naked but for a very short pair of cut-down denim shorts, and she had her right hand down inside them, between her legs, obviously with the intention of persuading *Tiptop*'s readers that she was playing with her pussy. She had the most fantastic pair of tits that I could remember seeing for a very long time. Really full, as if with milk. Bursting. Round, globular, with pale pink aureolae and nipples, the nipples themselves much larger than usual, long, erectly hard, standing up like great teats.

George took a number of further shots from those that he had patently taken before I arrived. 'I think we'll have the shorts off now, baby,' he said. 'OK?' 'Sure, honey,' said Lisa. She stood up and took off her shorts. She had obviously divested herself of any underwear much earlier on, for there were no elastic marks on her waist or thighs. 'Will you kneel on the mattress, please, honey?' said George. Lisa knelt on the mattress. This spread her buttocks widely, and I found myself staring up her pink, puckered, tight little anus, which was sited just above her lushly blonde, hairy cunt. She was slim-hipped, but her buttocks were full and round, and the view of her rear from where I was standing was something else. At that point, Betsy brought me the beer she had offered a while ago, and George called a halt while we all took a breather. Lisa didn't bother to put on anything to cover up her nakedness, but stood up, bollock-naked, a can of Schlitz in her hand. 'So you're from British *Tiptop*?' she asked, standing in front of me. 'That's me,' I said. I kept my eyes on her face, to avoid staring at those fabulous tits. The nipples were still hard. Lisa stroked first one, then the other, with the ice-cold beer can. 'It helps keep them hard,' she explained. 'I know,' I said, rather unnecessarily. She grinned broadly at me.

'You can look at them if you like, Tony,' she said. 'You don't have to keep staring at my face. They're just tits. But they *are* real. They're all mine. No implants. Feel.' She took my right hand, and placed it on her left breast. I squeezed it, gently. It was real, all right. The flesh was firm and warm, but soft. There was no implant, that was obvious. I could feel the hard, cold nipple against my palm, and my cock started to stiffen. I took my hand away. 'Beautiful,' I said. 'Really nice. Thank you.' 'Any time,' she said, smiling up at me. I wondered if she meant it. George looked at his watch. 'Time to get back to work, children,' he said. Lisa put down her beer can after a last anointing of her nipples with its cold exterior, and went back to her mattress.

Let's have some more of that pretty ass, Lisa,' George said. 'Could you lie on your stomach, and put your hands behind you, palms down. One on each buttock?' Lisa did as she was asked, placing her hands behind her on her buttocks. The very positioning of her hands involuntarily pulled the cheeks of her bottom apart, and that little pink cornflower winked at me again. 'Terrific,' said George, kneeling down, the better to centre on her rectum. 'Now just spread your cheeks the tiniest bit. Let's give the boys a thrill.' Lisa looked over her shoulder at the camera, her mouth half-open in a sexy pout, her hands spreading her plump, firm buttocks even farther apart. 'How's that?' she asked George, who was clicking away non-stop. 'That's terrific, darling, just terrific,' he said. He carried on for a while, instructing Lisa to raise a leg here, place an arm there, until he was satisfied. 'Fine, sweetheart,' he said. 'Now let's start with the panties. Betsy?' Betsy came over to him with an armful of exotic, assorted knickers. George ruffled through them slowly, looking and discarding, until he found what he was looking for.

It was a pair of tiny, plain white, lacy-fronted knickers that would reveal far more than they could ever possibly cover. 'These will be fine, thanks,' he said to Betsy. 'Show Lisa how to do the 'no one's watching me and I've pulled my panties down and I'm playing with my pussy' bit, will you, please?' Betsy took the knickers over to Lisa, and they chatted away for a couple of minutes. Then Lisa put the knickers on, and lay down on the mattress, and then Betsy pulled the knickers down, just below the top of the blonde model's thighs, revealing her hairy pussy. Betsy said 'Excuse me,' and bent forward and pulled Lisa's outer labia apart, then showed Lisa how George wanted her to spread her vulva with her fingers, revealing the pink wetness deep inside.

Lisa seemed totally unembarrassed, as did George. He got her to move her hands and fingers around into different positions, but always with a variation of the open pussy shots, taking many different pictures of Lisa apparently in the throes of masturbation, but to hear him, he might have been instructing his model in the way to arrange a bunch of flowers. It was as unemotional as that. I could, nevertheless, detect the fact that Lisa's pussy was getting wetter and wetter, and I watched as the love juice started to run down her thighs. Neither George nor Betsy seemed to notice it, and Lisa herself said nothing. And then George had come to the end of the open pussy shots, and without saying anything, Betsy took a warm, damp flannel over to Lisa and handed it to her. Lisa took it, and wiped herself clean. I nearly came in my trousers.

Over a period of time, George photographed Lisa as she slowly put on more clothes. He got her from the knickers-down state to the 'I'm wearing my knickers and feeling myself through them' sequence. This was followed by the 'I've taken my bra off, and now I'm in my knickers and my white hold-up stockings' mode. The white stockings had lacy tops, and looked intensely erotic against Lisa's deep tan. The next shot was the 'If I pull the crotch of my knicks aside, I can show you my pussy' picture. This was followed by the 'I've got all my clothes on (in this instance the shorts and a tight, white T-shirt) but if I sit like this and raise my right leg, you can look right up my shorts and see my pussy showing through my transparent knickers.' At which point they stopped for lunch.

Lunch had been ordered by Betsy and sent in from a local deli. There was a good selection of cold meats, with a variety of pickles and things to go with it, and lots of excellent salad, followed by cheeses, and accompanied by a liberal supply of Californian red jug wine. Betsy looked after everyone, handing round plates and napkins and glasses, and making certain we all had everything before she started looking after herself. She kept up a constantly amusing chatter as she did so, mostly gossip about personalities on the New York fashion and photographic scene. Lisa had put a robe on while we ate, but she didn't seem too bothered about tying it up, and I had plenty of opportunity to continue to admire her amazing tits at close quarters. She told me that she came from Philadelphia, where her parents were quite wealthy. She didn't need to work, she said, but she found both Philadelphia and not working boring after a while, and had come to New York looking for a little excitement. She found posing nude satisfying, and she liked the people that she met in the girlie magazine business.

She had no wish, she said, to go into pornographic movies, not being motivated, as most of the girls who were in it were, she said, by the comparatively large amounts of money on offer for any girl who was pretty, with a good body, and who would fuck in front of a camera. 'I prefer to do my fucking in private,' she said, smiling at me. 'How about you?'

I agreed with her, whilst thinking to myself that it was a strange statement, coming, as it did, from a nude model, and we got onto the subject of the recently opened Plato's Retreat, a sex club up on West 74th Street, over on the West Side, which apparently was a sexual free-for-all, where anything went. No, she hadn't been there, said Lisa, for the reason already stated – she liked to do her fucking in private. But she'd heard about it from girlfriends who had been there. Apart from the usual kind of things like plunge pools, steam rooms, bars, and a restaurant, apparently there were rooms and open areas for any and every kind of heterosexual sex, plus lesbianism, and so on. In these areas, you could either participate, or simply watch, while there were smaller, private rooms for hire, if that was what you wanted. Apparently it was a pretty wild scene. It sounded absolutely right for an item in my proposed monthly sexual diary for *Tiptop*, and I made a mental note to ask Pauline if she'd be amused to come with me. Men, I gathered, were not permitted entrance on their own.

At that point, George announced that it was time to get back to work, and I began to take my leave. They were going to do exactly what they had been doing all morning, but with a different collection of clothes (underclothes!) and a different set. It had already been built in one of the other corners of the warehouse, and from the school desk, books, blackboard and easel, and various educational impediments, I could guess that the clothes were almost certain to be a very short gymslip, with a tight white shirt, and navy blue knickers. I wondered if they were going to use the cane that was hanging up alongside the easel. I thought of Lisa's plump buttocks, and almost offered to stay. But work is work, and I decided to press on.

I had decided, during lunch, to look up a guy whom Fred had told me about: Doug Johns, a man described as a genital sculptor. I had his address and telephone number scribbled down in my diary somewhere. I looked it up, and before I left the *Tiptop* studio, I rang Doug to see if it was convenient to go visit him. He wasn't too far away, down around the bottom end of Park Avenue. He answered the telephone, and when I explained who I was, and why I wanted to see him, he said great, come right away. I found a cab, and was there within ten minutes. He was a pretty laid back kind of guy, with shoulder-length hair, a full beard and glasses. He had, he said, been sculpting genitals for some years now. He began by making hash pipes in the shape of cocks. 'At first, I felt that I was doing something rather sleazy,' he told me. But he quickly discovered that all his friends wanted one, and he was soon producing them by the dozen. The real surprise, he says, was that as he progressed he found he was losing the sexual repression that he'd had since childhood. 'For the first time in my life, I found that I was able to talk freely about sex,' he said. 'I had always been interested in sex, but had always been afraid to do anything about it. Now, suddenly, I had found the key with which to unlock sexual knowledge.'

Doug continued with his carvings and produced many hundreds of pieces, until he slowly reached a point where his work began to pose a serious question that had to be answered: could he actually produce truly creative, erotic art? And if he could, would he be able to make a living by it? Would it develop into an artistic career? 'I wanted to be a creative artist,' he said. 'I hadn't been in a sexual relationship for over a year, and I was frustrated on both fronts. And then I just picked up a piece of wood, and started carving.' That was the beginning of the successful emergence of Doug Johns, artist.

Carving, as he did male and female genitalia, you might be forgiven for believing that he had difficulty in finding models. In fact, he said, the reverse was true. Since he had begun his career in earnest, over two hundred people – one third men, two thirds women – had come to his loft to pose. 'I have no difficulty in finding models at all,' he said. 'Many of them stand out in my memory. Most of them have been recommended by friends who have themselves already posed for me.' Among those he remembered from the worlds of film and publishing were Marc Stevens and Tina Russell, of porno movie fame, and Fiona Richmond, Paul Raymond's *Club* magazine woman around the world. Doug showed me a ceramic, fire glazed, exact replica of Marc Stevens's fully erect ten-and-a-half inches. It was a humbling moment. It was in the form of a hash pipe, and yes, you sucked the cock head to get your smoke. Any other questions?

Nowadays, curiously enough, when Doug sculpts cocks, he only does the tip. I asked him why. 'Simply because every man who ever came to me asked me to add a couple of inches to the length, in the days when I used to do the whole organ. Apart from what you could call artistic integrity, there's the everyday, male ego to cope with. I'm not in the business of putting people down. So these days I just do tips. Everyone's got a tip. It's so much simpler.

'A woman's cunt, on the other hand,' he said, 'is just like an orchid.' He opened a long, deep drawer. It was filled with wax cunts. 'But you can never tell what shape her cunt is going to be from looking at her, like you often can with ass or tits. Tall, skinny women can have full, fat cunt lips, and vice versa. And the two cunt lips, like the halves of people's faces, are never exactly the same. Look at this one,' he said, tracing the outline of a labia with a loving finger. 'She looks symmetrical, but actually, she isn't. Look here.' He was right. And looking at the drawer of sculpted pussies, I could suddenly see from whence all the flower symbolism in erotic art comes. In his genital sculpting, Doug has long sought a genuine genital hermaphrodite, to pose for him for an afternoon's sitting. Despite assurances that the sculpture would be undertaken in the strictest confidence, he has not yet, to my knowledge, found any volunteers. I arranged a convenient day and time for some photography of Doug's unusual creative work, and left, wondering whether or not to bother to go back to the office. It was just six, and the chances were there would be no one there, but since I more or less had to pass it anyway on my way uptown, I decided that I would stop off on the way home. In fact, Eileen was still there. She smiled when she saw me. 'Hey, I've got some messages for you, Tony. May I bring them into your office in a moment?' 'Of course, sweetheart,' I said, smiling back, and glad that she seemed to have regained her good humour.

She came into my office moments later, and put a pile of

messages on my desk. 'There's nothing there that can't wait until tomorrow,' she said. 'But there's one thing that can't wait.' 'What's that?' I asked. She got up and shut my office door, and turned the key in the lock. Then she came over to me, and sat on my knee as I sat in my chair. 'This,' she said. And she put her arms around my neck, and kissed me wetly on the mouth, her tongue thrusting down my throat. She explored my mouth and tongue with hers for a long few minutes, and then disengaged, taking a deep breath. 'I've been wanting to do that from the first moment that I saw you at the airport,' she said. 'I just adore that British accent, and I want to fuck you. And I want you to fuck me. And I want to suck your cock, while you suck my pussy. I just want to do dirty, sexy, lovely things with you. Shall we start now?' She kissed me again, preventing me from answering her last question. When I could withdraw from her mouth, I did, and said 'Sweetheart, I'm greatly flattered. And I adore you too. But you're my boss's secretary, and I'm not supposed to fuck you. It's bad for business. And Fred is my mate, and he'll be furious when he finds out.' 'What do you mean, finds out?' she said. 'He's gone.'

'Gone where?' I asked. 'Home,' she said. 'You know. That's why you came out here. So that he could go home. Now he's gone. One of those messages is from him. He says have a good time. So, shall we start now? Huh?' It was a bit of a surprise, I must say. Not the lovely Eileen's approach. That didn't surprise me, to be fair. But Fred's sudden departure. I thought at least he might have wanted to go through the next two or three issues with me before he left. Or ask if I had any questions. Something. Anything. But that was Fred. I should have been used to him by now. It was, in a way, a sort of compliment, I suppose. 'I tell you what, sweetheart,' I said to Eileen. 'Let's stop talking about fucking, and go out and have a bite to eat. What do you say?'

Eileen was nothing if not predictable. 'I'd rather eat *you*, honey,' she said. 'But if that's what you want to do, sure. Where would you like to go?' 'You choose, baby,' I said.

'Anywhere you fancy is fine with me.' She settled for Giraf, on East 58th Street, not too far away. And yes, the restaurant *does* spell its name with one F. It turned out to be a chic, romantic, classy sort of place. The food was mainly Northern Italian, with a few French dishes here and there. Eileen was obviously a regular customer, and she introduced me to the owner, Tom White, a former ad man turned restaurateur. I chose Mussels Marechiaro with Fettucine Verdi, and Eileen plumped for the Fettucine alla Carbonara. We chattered about nothing in particular whilst we ate our meal, and then we got down to the business in hand with our coffees. I ordered a Strega, and Eileen a Galliano. 'Cheers, love,' I said. 'Cheers, Tony,' she said. 'That was really good. Now then. What's the problem? You seemed taken aback by Fred's departure, but you must have been expecting it, surely? It was hardly a surprise.'

'Well, yes and no,' I said. 'I mean, there are a million things I don't know about his apartment, for example. I don't know who his landlord is, or whether I'm staying there legally, with the landlord's knowledge and permission. I mean, it's a sub-let, isn't it? From the lease-holder, to Fred, with the landlord's permission. But where do I stand?' She leaned across the table towards me and patted my arm. 'Don't worry about a thing, sweetie,' she said. 'Aunty Eileen has taken care of all those problems, before you came out. You're a legal sub-tenant, approved by the landlord, with his full knowledge. The only thing the landlord doesn't know, as far as I'm aware, is that *his* sub-tenant is screwing Tiptop Publications over here for twice what the apartment costs him. But that's life, I guess. What next? Let's get this Lucy tart out of the way. I mean, really, Tony! What on earth are you thinking of?'

'I don't think I understand,' I said, trying to look innocent. 'Don't give me that shit, please,' said Eileen. 'You're going to fuck that black so-called model, aren't you? Come on, now. Tell me the truth.' 'Well,' I said, a little sheepishly, 'it *had* crossed my mind. You know ... Research for the magazine. An item for my sex diary. Don't you think?' 'Bullshit,' she said.

'You just want to fuck her because she's black, six feet tall, and bald. Isn't that so?' 'And she's got a bald pussy,' I said, meanly. 'And she gives terrific head. But I stand by my point of view. How many people do you know who've fucked a six-foot-tall, bald negress, with a shaved pussy, and lived to tell the tale?'

Eileen slapped my wrist. 'I knew it,' she said. 'I just knew it. Hold my calls for a while, you said. I knew it was bullshit. The only difference was that I thought you were fucking her. Now you tell me she was giving you head. Why can't I give you head? I may not be bald, God forbid, but I give great head.' I reached over and squeezed her arm. 'Because we'll do an awful lot better if we stay as friends, my love,' I said. Any relationship you and I might have would be doomed to disaster before it started. I mean, just think about it. Just suppose that you and I were fucking each other' (she smiled at me) 'and that the fucking had got to the stage where we thought we loved each other' (she sighed.) 'Then imagine what you would have done if – purely in the interests of *Tiptop*'s readers – I had rung through and said hold my calls. Just like I did. You'd be beating my door down before Lucy had her panties off. Now, wouldn't you?' She grinned at me. 'I guess so,' she said. 'But it would have been fun, wouldn't it? But you don't need that kind of thing, Tony. Really you don't.'

'So what am I going to fill my sex diary with every month then?' I asked. 'It's not that difficult,' she said. 'I brought you this current copy of *Club Quest*. It's a spin-off from Paul Raymond's *Club* magazine. It seems to be aimed specifically at New Yorkers. They've got a sort of up-front diary, called Trickz and Tradez. Look.' She handed me a small, digest-size publication, and I flicked through it. It seemed to be trying to appeal to everyone: straight, gay, lesbian, enema freaks. You name it. They even had fashion, book reviews, restaurant recommendations, and the latest porno movies discussed at some length. But the basis was, of course, pretty girls with no knickers on. Pink was everywhere. There was one very pretty girl with the largest vaginal lips I have ever seen, before or since. I looked at the magazine's up-front section, but to my mind it wasn't particularly exciting. It basically read like a swap shop, with people offering erotic material for sale or trade. I reckoned that I'd have to find my own diary items, and young Lucy looked like a starter to me. I said as much to Eileen. This time she didn't quibble, but just shrugged her shoulders. 'You'll be sorry,' she said. 'But Aunty Eileen will always be around waiting for you. Just let me know when you need me. ' 'I really appreciate that, sweetheart, ' I said. 'I really do. And now, if you'll forgive me, I shall call you a cab and say goodnight.'

Ten minutes later I was in a cab myself, on my way downtown to Lucy, having telephoned her after I'd left Eileen. 'Hey, baby,' she chortled. 'So you're coming to play. What a gas.' She repeated the address. 'I'll see you when you get here. Ciao.' 'Here' was an elegant townhouse in the low forties. It was expensively furnished, and there was decent art hanging and standing around. 'What do you think?' she asked. 'Do you like it?' She reached out a hand and grabbed my cock. 'Wow,' she said. 'Am I going to have fun with that. But what would you like to drink, baby? Champagne? Wine?' I asked for a Scotch and water, no ice. 'That sure is a hell of a way to drink Scotch, baby,' she said. 'But if that's what you want, that's what you shall have. She moved over to a large drinks cabinet, and mixed my drink. 'Here, baby,' she said. 'Salut.' She was drinking white wine. 'So, baby,' she said. 'What have you been up to?' 'Not a lot,' I said. 'Work. You know. The usual stuff. Nothing exciting.' 'Don't worry, baby,' she said, taking me by the hand. 'You come upstairs with Lucy, and we'll get up to some pretty exciting stuff. You'll enjoy it. I promise. Have you been thinking about my shaved pussy? Did you get a hard-on when you thought about it? Did you think about that blow-job I gave you?'

She let go of my hand, and walked up the stairs ahead of me. She was wearing a short, black wool skirt, and a black jumper.

I looked at her ass as she swayed up in front of me, and I really did begin to get a hard-on. She led the way up to the first floor, and into a large bedroom, dominated by a king-size bed. There were mirrors everywhere. The bed linen was all-white and lacy. The bed itself was gilt, about late nineteenth century, I would say, and it had a deep, firm but soft mattress. I sat on the edge of it, and began to undress.

Lucy took off her jumper, revealing her beautiful breasts, with their almost black nipples and aureolae. Then she bent and pulled her skirt down, stepping out of it and discarding it onto the white carpet. That left her in white silk knickers, which had a lace inset at the front, a white, lacy suspender belt, and black, seamed stockings. The knickers looked as if they were sprayed on. She twirled around for me. 'What do you think, baby?' she asked. 'Do you like it?' 'I love it,' I said. 'Keep it on. For a while, anyway.' 'Do you like kinky sex, baby?' she asked. 'Just tell me what you want. Lucy likes kinky sex. You want me to beat you? Tie you up? You want to spank me?' She looked at me, quizzically. 'Not specially, honey, thank you,' I said. 'I'm just an old-fashioned knicker fetishist at heart. Nothing too advanced.' 'Great,' she said. 'Come over here.' She sat on the edge of the bed and spread her legs.

'You can kiss my bald pussy through my tight little white panties,' she said. 'Would you like that?' I think I mumbled something that she took as a yes. 'That will make my pussy all wet, and my panties all wet, and then you can take them home with you when you go, and sniff them while you masturbate. They'll be scented with pussy. Strong pussy. My pussy.' She laughed. 'That's what pantie – sorry, knicker – fetishists, like, isn't it, baby?' 'That's certainly part of it,' I said. I was naked now, my prick throbbing stiffly in front of me. I went over and knelt down before her, and just looked at her. I could see the black lips of her cunt through the lacy panel in her white silk knickers. Her garter belt was minimal, the suspenders long, stretching down over her thighs to the darker bands at the top of her stockings. The contrast between the soft, silky whiteness of her lingerie, and the soft black satin of her skin, was highly erotic. I could smell the scent of her arousal. Talking dirty obviously turned her on too.

Her black skin through the black stockings was another erotic contrast, and I ran my hands down her thighs and over the stockings, pulled tight over her firm skin. The feel of all those contrasting surfaces was fantastic. I touched her between her legs, gently. The silk felt wet. I rubbed the material, slowly, and she gasped, drawing in her breath sharply. 'Oh, baby,' she said. Nothing else. I traced the outline of her cunt lips, and then I grasped her around her plump buttocks and pulled her towards my mouth, pressing my lips against her pussy, revelling in her shaven, baldness through the soft silk. She was wet between her legs, and I made her even wetter. I could taste the love juice dribbling out of her, copiously now.

'Oh, baby,' she said again. I pushed her down backwards onto the bed, and got myself into a better position to really suck her through the soaking wet crotch of her knickers. I could feel her pussy lips through the thin material, and I needed, suddenly, to pull her knickers down and suck her properly. I raised my mouth up from her for the moment that it took to pull her panties down, leaving just the white garter belt and the black stockings. I dropped the knickers on the floor, and forced my tongue between her willing pussy lips, thrusting it deeply into her. She tasted strongly, slightly musky. Gamey. I had to fuck her now. I got astride her, and she grasped my rigid cock and guided it into her. She was hot, tight, and wet. All the things she had said she would be. She was starting to sweat now, and perspiration trickled down her pert breasts in tiny streams.

'Oh, baby,' she said, for the third time. 'I like it. Oh, yes. That's good. Please don't stop.' I hadn't the slightest intention of stopping. As I looked down at her, her eyes shut now, her mouth slightly open, I could see sweat on her bald head, running down onto her neck. She opened her eyes. 'Hey,' she said. 'You're good. Why didn't you tell me?' I kept on fucking her with long, slow strokes. She had a pussy like a young nun's in terms of tightness. It's being shaved added to the fantasy. 'You didn't ask,' I said, grinning down at her. 'But thank you.' 'I'm ready now,' she said. 'Does it bother you if I finish it off for myself?' 'Not in the least bit,' I said. 'Feel free.' She slid a finger down into her cunt, between my cock and her vaginal wall, and I could feel her searching for, and finding, her clitoris. She shut her eyes again, and started rubbing her clitoris, slowly but strongly. The feel of her finger, rubbing down there, was akin to having her masturbate me whilst I fucked her, and I too began the ride to orgasm. Soon she was panting, and she started to writhe under me. I began to fuck her as hard as I could, encouraging my ejaculation as I helped her orgasm to peak. She suddenly started screaming out loud, saying 'Oh, my God. Oh, Jesus. Oh, yes,' and her finger moved even more quickly as she climaxed. Just as she reached her apex, I came with her, and began to shoot my sperm into her in what felt like great jets. 'Oh, yes, baby,' she shouted. 'Now you're coming too. I can feel your hot spunk inside me. Oh, God. Oh, Jesus. Yes. Oh. Oh. Oh.'

She slowly relaxed, and began to quieten down. 'I'm sorry, baby,' she said. 'I'm a bit of a shouter. I should have said.' 'No problem, honey,' I said. 'They're your neighbours, not mine.' She laughed. 'You'd probably like a shower now, baby,' she said. 'But first let me suck your cock clean for you. My mamma always told me that every self-respecting girl should suck her man's cock clean after sex.' She looked up at me and grinned. 'I'm naughty, aren't I?' she said. 'But I like the taste of pussy too. Did I tell you that? Mine, or someone else's. I love to suck girl's little pussies. You must come and watch me some time. But right now, just lean back and enjoy this.' I did as I was instructed, and she did exactly what she had offered to do. You might suppose that I was brought to another ejaculation by her oral ministrations, but in fact it was much more a gentle exercise in hygiene than any kind of a sexual work out. After which we showered together, and I took my leave.

'You come back soon now, baby, y'hear,' she commanded. 'Lucy be waiting for you. Any time. Ciao now.' I caught a cab and went home. It was only when I was in the cab that I realised I'd forgotten Lucy's present of her knickers. Fred's apartment didn't look any different from when I had left it that morning. Fred had a cleaning woman who came in every day. I hadn't met her yet, but she was very efficient. She also did laundry. One simply left anything one wanted washed and ironed in one's room, and it was back there that evening, beautifully done. There was a laundry room in the basement of the apartment block, complete with washing and drying machines, irons and ironing boards. Fred had told me that this was standard practice in New York, at least in the more up-market blocks. I poured myself a drink and switched the box on for a while, but I didn't find anything to catch my imagination, so I went to bed. I had an early morning meeting at the offices of *Tiptop*'s American distribution company, so an earlyish night wouldn't be a bad thing. I slept the sleep of the innocent.

CHAPTER THREE
GETTING DOWN TO IT

The following morning was another punitively hot day, with the streets of Manhattan like iron canyons, the sun beating down like a hammer on an anvil. I got the doorman to go out and find me a cab, and was relieved to discover that the distribution company's offices, up and across town, on Broadway and 111th Street, were modern and fully air-conditioned. One of the many things that Europeans discover about New York to their surprise is that Broadway is an avenue. It's not just the place by Times Square where most of the theatres are. It runs almost the whole length of Manhattan, from north to south, as do all the island's avenues. Up on the thirty-fourth floor of the building, I asked at reception for Bill Carlson, and was greeted moments later by a girl whom I took to be his secretary. She was dark haired, tall, and very well put together. Her short skirt exposed great legs. 'Tony?' she asked. 'Hi,' I said. 'Hi. I'm Linda, Bill's assistant. If you'll come with me, Bill will be with us momentarily,' She had a fabulous Bronx or Brooklyn accent. I couldn't tell which. I followed her through a pair of glass doors and down a corridor to a large, well furnished office, with a terrific view looking west out towards New Jersey.

Distribution is one of the vital elements of successful magazine publishing. First, you have to get the product right. Your readers have to like the magazine that you are producing enough to relate to it, and to want to buy it. The second most vital thing is to make sure that it is available wherever they want to pick it up. If they should go to a bookstall and ask for it, and find – for whatever reason – that it isn't there, they may never ask for it again. Truly. Some readers are as fickle as that. In a nation as large as America, that can be a problem. The day your new issue is printed, you want it to be on sale everywhere throughout the country.

Being realistic, of course, that just doesn't happen. But with effort, by being nice, by cajoling, by bullying, by bribing, by doing whatever is necessary, you can at least be sure that your magazine will be on sale, in sufficient quantities, in all the major outlets in all the major cities in the country. But at the end of the day, you are almost entirely in the hands of your distributor.

However, there is one vital difference between Britain and America when it comes to magazine distribution. In Britain, your distributor's sales team takes orders. That means that they visit all the outlets regularly, and while of course they try to get the retailers to increase their orders, when push comes to shove, taking orders is what it is all about. In the States, a publisher decides – obviously with advice from his distributor – on how many copies of his magazine he thinks he can sell, and that is the quantity he will print. The distributor's sales team simply distribute the copies, and encourage the retailers to sell them. It is a finely balanced decision, but sales records show that it is a more efficient way of increasing sales than the English way.

In neither country can the retailer lose out, for the copies of the magazine are on a sale-or-return basis. If there are any copies of last month's (or week's) left over when this month's copies are delivered, the previous month's returns are taken away, and the retailer is credited with their value. There is a very small number of magazines which are on firm sale. That means that whatever the retailer orders, they become his property. He pays the publisher for them whether he sells them or not. These are usually specialist magazines with very small circulations, whose sales have been stagnant for years.

Just then Bill arrived and introduced himself. 'Tony, Hi,' he said, taking my hand in his, within which it almost disappeared. 'Fred's gone off for a spot of leave, I gather.' 'That's right,' I said, withdrawing my hand from his vice-like grip. 'He'll be away for about a month, I guess.' Bill got Linda to bring us in some coffee, and then we settled down to go through the computer print-outs of the last three months' sales, state by state. They showed, on analysis, a steady overall increase of about fifteen per cent a month, which was tremendous.

Sales were concentrated on the east and west coasts, with virtually no sales at all in that enormous space in the centre of the continent known as Middle America. This pattern is reflected in practically everything that is sold in America, from shoe polish to newspapers, but it is particularly so with girlie magazines. Another synonym for Middle America is the Bible Belt, which is, I think, self-explanatory. Whatever you want to call it, that part of America is known, sadly, for its unemployment, its low educational standards, and its low per-capita income. The only thing that does outstandingly well there is the distribution of food stamps. 'I guess we're doing pretty well, all things considered,' said Bill. 'Sales are going up where they should be going up. Returns are down, and are continuing to fall. We're in every major chain in America. The future looks good. So long as you people can keep up the quality of the magazine – by which I mean the quality of the editorial, as well as the quality the print – I don't foresee any problems. We've got our professional finger right on the pulse. If any problems should arise, we'll be the first to know.' 'Thank you very much, Bill,' I said. 'That's all extremely encouraging.' 'My pleasure, sir,' he said. 'Now then, how about a bit of lunch?' 'That would be nice, Bill,' I said, looking at my watch. It was after twelve. I had no idea that we had been talking for so long. Suddenly I needed a drink. 'What do you fancy?' he asked. 'Anything, Bill, anything,' I said. 'I love it all.' 'Has anyone taken you to Palm Restaurant yet?' he asked. 'No,' I said. 'But I've heard of it. It serves steak and lobster, doesn't it? Supposedly the best steak in New York?' 'Well, I guess there's a lot of restaurants in the city that would lay claim to that title,' said Bill. 'But they're certainly in there up at the top. It's a bit of a journey downtown – it's on Second Avenue, in the forties – but I think you'll agree that it's worth it.' He picked up the 'phone. 'Linda. Yes, honey. Is our cab ready? Good. Thank you.' He looked over at me. 'The cab's waiting, Tony,' he said. 'Let's go.'

We were lucky, the ride downtown didn't take too long. It was New York that invented gridlock, but today the traffic was flowing fairly smoothly. It was the beginning of the summer, and all those families who could afford it had moved out of town for the duration. To the Hamptons, to Long Island, to Fire Island. To anywhere by the sea, where a breeze made the long, hot days more bearable. This left the husband back in the heat of New York city, commuting to the rented summer house at the weekends.

This, of course, gave rise to much hilarity and celebration amongst the married, male population of New York, for suddenly, once a year, there was no one home to complain about late nights, too much drinking, or, in some cases, lipstick on one's collar, real or imagined. Some men looked forward to it as much as their kids looked forward to the summer holidays, and ladies having affairs with married men celebrated with their loved ones in the traditional manner. They fucked them stupid. I asked Bill if he was married, and when he said yes, I asked him, quite bluntly, if this improved his sex life during the long vacation. He laughed. 'I understand the question, Tony,' he said. 'But believe it or not, after over twenty years of marriage, and three kids – whom I love – I'm still in love with my wife, Barbara, and she with me. Our sex life is good, in that it's frequent, and we both enjoy it. It may not be as passionate as it was at first, but I haven't strayed through all those years, and I have no intention of starting now. What the summer does mean for me is that I can sit around and play poker with my friends all night, and not get nagged for staying up too late, and making the games room stink of stale cigarette smoke.'

We arrived at Palm, which was throbbing. It's a smallish, delightfully old-fashioned restaurant, with dark oak panelling, waiters in black trousers and white aprons, and fabulous steaks. The customers were almost all – but not completely – male, and it was obviously a place where men liked to lunch with men, eat some real food, and drink some real drink. Bill was welcomed as an obviously regular customer, and I guessed he used it a good bit for entertaining his customers. There was nothing in the contract between his company and *Tiptop* that said he had to entertain anyone, but it did occur to me that, from the profits he was making from us, he could well afford the occasional lunch. Even at Palm. Cheap it isn't. But to be fair, both he and his company earned their profit, and it would be just as accurate to say that I could afford – on *Tiptop*'s behalf – to take him to lunch. Bill ordered me a Scotch, 'straight up, water on the side, hold the ice.' While waiting for our drinks, Bill pointed out the old prints on the walls and, the living proof of the restaurant's popularity, the restaurant across the road, almost directly opposite, called Palm Too. Nice. 'But if you ever want to book a table here,' said Bill, 'just let me know. The one across the road isn't for the likes of you and me. It's for out-of-towners.' It was a kindness, and typical of the man, as I was slowly becoming aware.

Reading the menu, I saw something called Surf 'n Turf; described as a whole Maine lobster, broiled in butter, followed by a sixteen-ounce fillet steak, grilled to order, the two together with vegetables of your choice. As the most expensive item on the menu, I wasn't surprised when Bill suggested it. I think he was a mite surprised when I said thank you, but no, thank you. I settled for a smaller fillet steak, rare, with hash browns, and a salad, preceded by clam chowder. Bill had to explain to them that I wanted the salad *with* the steak, not before it, as is the American custom. Bill joined me with the steak, and, to go with our food, he ordered an excellent French burgundy from a very extensive wine list. It came before the food, and after tasting it, Bill filled our glasses, and raised his to mine. 'To overtaking *Playboy* and *Penthouse*,' he said. 'I really think we can do it. And to you and me. Cheers.'

The steak, when it came, was perfectly cooked, and mouth-wateringly delicious. We ate slowly, Bill regaling me with stories from his years in the magazine distribution business, and asking me about publishing in Britain. Unlike the vast majority of successful American businessmen, he had never been to Europe. He had been too young for the war, he said, and had always found places to go on holiday that he preferred to Europe. Listening to him, I could understand why, for he had been to Mexico a number of times, to various Caribbean islands, to Hawaii, to Canada, and pretty well all over his own country. Who needed Europe, I had to ask myself?

He explained that he came from a small family, the son of a carpenter, working in White Plains. He'd done well at school, and had gained a scholarship to New York University, where he'd studied business management. He'd got a good degree, and had applied for a job at the distribution company where he was now vice-president, sales. He'd started at the bottom, as part of a trainee management scheme, working with the sales force, so he knew the job inside and out. He'd been lucky – he said – and the company's turnover and profits had improved regularly over the years, leading to his present position. It struck me that what he called luck, I would probably call hard work, but it was nice to meet an American who, for a change, didn't attribute his company's success entirely to his own solo efforts.

'But enough of that, Tony,' he said, as we got to the coffee stage. 'First of all, what will you have with your coffee? How about a little cognac? No? What, then?' I decided on a glass of port, and was pleased to see that didn't cause a problem at

Palm. Not too many New York restaurants serve port. Or, at least, not decent port. Palm does. 'And now that's settled,' said Bill, 'tell me about your business. I mean, do you really all spend all your time getting laid, like Fred tells me?' I had to laugh. 'Maybe when you're as successful as Fred is, you do,' I replied. 'I'm still at the stage where I have to work as well. So "no" is the honest answer to your question. But there are certainly advantages to working on a girlie magazine.' I spelled out the usual, but still truthful, bits, about there being rather more attractive women about the office than in most businesses, and that there was seldom any reason to try and work around to the subject of sex, since that was the nature of the business that we were all in, and it was foremost in everyone's minds for that reason anyway.

And in addition, there were those girls who believed, rightly or wrongly, that being featured in one of *Tiptop*'s girl sets – preferably the centrefold – was the beginning of the road to fame and fortune, and (to my never-ending pleasure) many of them thought that attempting to force their sexual favours upon one of the editors was a good place to begin. That, plus the fact that the women were, by the very fact of being there, young and pretty. And if you know any young and pretty girls who live in a sophisticated city who aren't enthusiastic about sex, well, you've got a serious problem. Bill laughed.

'But I've spent quite a lot of time with Fred. You know, lunch, dinner, that sort of thing. And I've spent many a night away from home playing poker with Fred in his apartment – to my wife's intense irritation. But I say to her, business is business sweetheart, whether it's sitting in the office, or playing poker in Park Avenue. If that's what the client wants, and if I am able to provide it, then that's what the client gets.' He winked at me. 'Mind you, Tony,' he continued, 'I do love to play poker with a good school, and Fred knows some really smart players.' 'Tell me about it, ' I said. 'It took playing poker with Fred for me to realize that I was never going to be a poker player. There was a time when I thought that I was a fairly competent player, but I gave it up after my first few games with him. I simply couldn't afford it.' Bill laughed again.

And then, 'Say, Tony, how well do you know Fred?' he asked, looking serious for a moment. I thought for a minute. I wondered why he wanted to know. 'Oh, I've known him for about five years altogether,' I said, eventually. 'For about four years working for the London magazine as a freelance, and then almost a year working inside the company as an editor. I count him amongst my few real friends,' I ended, wanting to make my position clear.

'Oh, great,' said Bill. 'Then I can speak to you in confidence, as one friend of Fred's to another. I'm fond of Fred too, and I don't think it's any secret to anyone that *Tiptop*'s business is our single largest, most profitable client. So I not only like him, and enjoy his company, but we all of us enjoy the business. You'll understand that, of course.' I nodded my agreement. 'And I would never mention this to anyone officially. Wally, for instance. I met Wally with Fred when they both came out here originally, looking for a distributor. But I think I've got to know you well enough over lunch to tell you my problem, which is this. In all the time that *Tiptop* has been out here now, I've seen Fred dozens and dozens of times. You'd expect that, of course. But I've never met him in his office, and he's never visited mine. The only meetings we have are social ones. I simply can't get any kind of business sense out of him. If I raise business matters with him at the beginning or the end of a social meeting, be it a meal, or a poker game, he'll say, 'Oh, come, on Bill. Not now. This is for fun.' If I telephone him with a problem, he's not available. So all right, one way or another, a decision is taken, and the business carries on, and, thank God, it's getting better and better. But sometimes, lacking any other option, I take those decisions myself. Now that's not right. Well, is it?'

I didn't reply immediately, and he carried on. 'What worries me is that, to all intents and purposes, there isn't really anyone in charge of *Tiptop*'s business out here. I mean, Wally's the company president, but he's in London, and he doesn't seem to want to know anything, other than that the company is profitable, and getting more profitable. I feel that I'm being forced to take decisions that are not really mine to take. They're Fred's. Fred is the only vice-president, and he doesn't want to know either. Now, what do you think, Tony? You've been out here long enough to see what the set-up is in the office. What's your opinion? I've seriously been losing sleep over this.'

I thought for a moment. Bill was absolutely right of course. It probably seemed like madness to him. I tried to steer a line between reassuring him, and telling him the truth. 'Bill, first of all let me say thank you for confiding in me. I appreciate your trust,' I began. 'I respect your confidence, of course. But I don't think things are quite as bad as they may seem to you. First of all, the company out here – corporation, as it is, in fact – is soundly set up. It is a wholly-owned subsidiary of the London operation, and that in itself is as rich as Croesus. So there aren't likely to be any sudden, unexpected money problems. There might be only Fred out here as a VP, but there are two of New York's finest legal and accountancy firms appointed to look after our business out here.' I mentioned two world-famous companies, the attorneys on Madison Avenue, and the accountants on Third Avenue. Bill whistled. 'I had no idea,' he said.

'And they are in daily touch with our office administrators, whom you are possibly not aware of,' I continued. 'They are accountants themselves, and a couple of them have legal training. And then although all those people – the in-house staff and the consultants – are technically answerable to Fred, they also have access to Wally any time they think they need it. So, you see, one way or another, Wally is pretty much in control, whatever the situation may look like from the outside.

'Secondly, Fred is Fred. He has a very short attention span. And he loathes what he regards as the boring detail. He hates to quibble about paper costs, or giving rises to staff, or agreeing that so-and-so can go on holiday. His gift is seeing a market, understanding his readers – even before the magazine has appeared – and searching out the right contributors in terms of journalists and writers to provide the material that is required. After that, as far as he's concerned, it is simply a matter of fine tuning. As he sees it, the company employs other people to actually undertake the dreary day-to-day business of getting issues together, getting them printed and distributed, and worrying about things like taxes, staff salaries, and holidays. After the first three issues, if I know my Fred, all he will expect to do is look at each issue as it is made up – before it goes to press – make any last-minutes alterations that he may think necessary, and attend the occasional editorial meeting to comment on the most recent issue as it comes off the presses. And that, he considers, doesn't warrant spending too much time in the office. He'd rather screw girls, snort cocaine, drink, eat, sleep all day, and play all night. But it doesn't mean that he doesn't know what is going on.'

I was almost finished now. 'But I appreciate your concern, Bill. What I've said doesn't actually help you, in that, if you feel the need to talk business with Fred, leave aside the fact that he's not here at the moment, it isn't going to resolve that problem. But at least it might make you feel that there are actually a few people keeping an eye on what is going on. And if it's any help, whilst I'm out here, feel free to call me any time. In fact, why don't you call me every week, to make base, and tell me if you have any problems that I can help with, and I'll do the same with you? OK?'

'Hey, that's terrific, Tony,' said Bill. 'I can't tell you how much better that makes me feel. And my colleagues, when I pass on the good news . . .' He hesitated for a moment. 'I may tell them everything that you've told me, mayn't I?' he asked. 'There's nothing that's secret there, is there?' 'Absolutely nothing, Bill,' I said. 'But while I don't imagine it's a secret from anyone, I 'd appreciate it if you'd leave out the bit about the cocaine.' Bill laughed. 'Yes, of course,' he said. 'No problem. Now, lets have a final coffee, another liqueur, and then let's go look for a little fun. Do you have to go back to the office?' I looked at my watch. It was nearly four o'clock. There didn't seem much point. 'Actually, no,' I said. 'What did you have in mind?' 'Did you ever see a real New York burlesque strip show?' he asked. I had to admit that I hadn't. Bill summoned the waiter, settled his bill, and we were on our way. We took a cab to a bar down off Broadway at 42nd Street, and we sat there, sipping our drinks in the soft warmth, while Bill gave me a run down on what was available around town.

'Burlesque is a dying art in America, sadly,' he said. 'There was a time, oh, forty or fifty years ago, when, if you knew where to go, there was real, top-notch burlesque in every major city. Great girls, great routines. But that's pretty much gone now, with just a few exceptions. These days, the punters just want to see pussy, so pussy is what they get. There is, for example, the Fun City Theatre, on 42nd Street, between 6th and 7th Avenues. It's a real theatre – small, but real – and it features ethnic girls – blacks and Spanish – doing fifteen, twenty minute numbers, which are really quite classy. There are also, on the same premises, but separately, hard core movies, peep shows, and a porno book shop.'

'The Bottomless Pit, on 53rd Street, between Third and Lexington, is what I would call a pussy bar. There's no show as such, but there's a big, round bar, on which the strippers circulate, and strip, and where all, but all, of the girls flash beaver. It's not expensive, either, you simply buy drinks at $2.50 a throw. There's no cover charge. If you want to stuff dollar bills into the girls' garters, you won't find anyone objecting. The higher the denomination of the bill, the longer you get a real close look at the pussy of your choice. Perhaps the nearest to real burlesque is Melody Burlesque on 48th Street and Broadway. It's real raunchy. There are usually at least five different strippers on every evening, and this show proves that burlesque ain't quite dead yet. It's still wriggling at the Melody!

'There's also traditional bumping and grinding, combined with contemporary flashing, at a number of the other strip shows around 42nd Street, including Follies Burlesk, on Broadway at 46th Street; at Roxy Burlesk, at 244 West 42nd Street, which, people tell me, sometimes features live male/female sex. And then there's Psychedelic Burlesk, on Eighth Avenue, at 42nd Street, which has a troop of strippers performing daily.' 'Fascinating, Bill,' I said. 'Tell me, can customers have it away with the girls at any of these places?' 'I don't honestly know,' he replied. 'I've never asked. But people tell me that at some places you can, and some places you can't. I believe it comes down to agreement between you, the girls, the management, and the money. It's certainly worth asking, if there's someone you especially fancy. Most of the guys I know that go there go there to get a hard on. They then get a cab home, and give their wives a little excitement. You know what I mean?' 'I do, Bill,' I said. 'Sadly, I do.'

'If it's live sex shows you're after, the Show World Center on Eighth Avenue at 42nd Street is probably the place for you. It's supposed to be the best in town. It has three separate live sex theatres. One is a peepshow in the basement, featuring two girl exhibitions. In the other two theatres, they feature live sex in between hard core films. One features live 'girls only' exhibitions, with always two, sometimes three girls getting into the action, whilst the third theatre features both two girls and one-girl-and-a-guy shows. I've been to all three. They're great shows, actually. With good story lines, both funny and imaginative, and there are good bodies on the participants, plus they all seem to really enjoy what they are doing. The theatres are all clean, and the audiences seem just ordinary folk, like you and me. Upstairs there's another peepshow, and a sex shop. It's all good news.

'Just along the street from there, on Eighth Avenue at 47th Street, is the Hollywood Twin Theatre, which does much the same sort of thing, but not quite so well. The girls are pretty though. It's certainly worth a visit. I could go on and on, but I think I've mentioned anywhere really worth mentioning. There's The Doll, on Seventh Avenue at 48th Street; the Avon 7, also on Seventh at 48th. Then there's the Love Theatre, on 42nd Street, between Sixth and Seventh. Oh, and a million more. What do you fancy?' In the end, I decided to leave it up to Bill.

He was, after all, the obvious expert, and eventually we went, more for the fun of it than anything else, he emphasized, to the Bottomless Pit. Topless and Bottomless Pit would have been a more accurate description. At $2.50 a drink (in the days when a drink at a decent hotel would cost you $1.50) it was cheap. And no one hustled us for drinks. The girls were all young, had great bodies, were all skin shades from deepest black to palest white, and most shades in between, and wore very little other than garter belts and stockings. They strolled, minced, or walked around the circular bar, basically in time to the music, although none of them was going to win a Tony for their dancing. But they smiled, and were both cheeky and provocative, blowing little pouting kisses when they caught your eye. I followed Bill's example in seeing how to play the game. If you waved a dollar bill at them, they knelt, or squatted in front of you, whilst you tucked the note into their garter, which action had the benefit of splitting their beaver, giving you an eyeful almost literally, since they were on the top of the bar – of moist pussy, in shades from palest pink to black. The higher the denomination of the note, the longer they stayed. A dollar got you a smile, and a thank-you. Twenty dollars got you five minutes conversation, with the fingers slipping down to open the pussy to its fullest extent, showing you a delightfully moist, shining interior, from which emanated the cock-hardening scent of hot, wet, aroused sex.

It's a great way to spend a late afternoon/early evening. It sure beat the hell out of staying on at the office. After sampling, as it were, a number of the girls, I decided that the one that I liked the most was the one who, to my mind, represented that unique, all-American sports emblem, the cheer leader. A Dallas Cowgirl she wasn't, but she was young, pretty, had terrific legs, and I could just imagine her in the tight tunic and short, short, pleated skirt of her college team.

Even better here, she was naked, apart from the garter that was stuffed with notes, proving that I wasn't alone in my appreciation of her. Her rosy cheeks were flushed with her efforts as she capered seemingly happily around the arena. She was attractively made-up, and her hair was cut short and shone with cleanliness. She it was I tried with my first twenty dollar bill, having previously spread around a few fives and tens. I held it up as she came around my way the next time. 'Hey, mister,' she said, squatting in front of me and looking right at me as I slid the note beneath her garter, 'I surely do appreciate that.' Her accent was pure cornball, from somewhere out there in the wide open spaces of America's West. 'It's my pleasure, sweetheart,' I said. 'Hey, you're a limey,' she came out with. 'And you like pussy. I can tell.' She slid her right hand down between her legs and, in the squatting position that she had assumed to allow me to slide my twenty under the elastic of her garter, she spread her vaginal lips. Wide. The original tunnel of love.

If you like pussy, how do you like mine, baby?' she asked. 'I like it a lot, sweetheart,' I said. 'So what brings you to the Big Apple?' she interrupted with, before I could proceed any further down that particular road. 'Are you on vacation?' 'No,' I said. 'I work here. 'What at?' she asked. 'I'm one of the editors from *Tiptop* magazine,' I said. 'Do you know it?' She looked amazed, I'm not too sure why. '*Tiptop*?' she said. 'Wow. Hey this is where *I* make a pass at *you*. What're you doing after this, honey?' 'Are you serious?' I asked. 'I sure as hell am,' she said. 'But hang in there. I can see that the boss is getting fidgety. Let me do a couple of circuits, and I'll be back. You don't have to make it a twenty next time, baby. A single will do. Don't worry. No one else can see what it's worth.'

She pranced, and strolled, and semi-bumped and ground her way around the circular bar twice more, stopping to spend strictly regulated time with other punters holding up their greenback offerings to her. She was quite right. You couldn't see what particular denomination anyone was holding up, since all American dollar notes are the same size and colour. Only the figure in the top left- and right-hand corners tells you what they're worth (and of course the amount is spelt out in words as well) and you can't see that from more than a couple of feet away. After the two circuits she came and squatted in front of me again.

'Hey, baby,' she said, almost breathlessly. 'I finish at seven. That's in about fifteen minutes. What do you say I meet you in P.J. Clarke's at seven fifteen? Do you know P.J. Clarke's?'
'Sure, sweetheart,' I said. 'I'll be there. Thank you. Terrific.'
She blew me a kiss, and got up and continued with her stop and start progress around the bar. Everyone in New York knows P.J. Clarke's. It is the oldest Irish bar (of many) in the city. It is not, as a matter of interest, on its original site. It used to be much farther uptown. But it has been at 915 Third Avenue for longer than most people can remember.

It is a delightful place, although at peak times it does get a bit full. It is another of those dark oak-panelled, mahogany furnished bars, with pictures of early customers in the black, high-collared suits, white shirts, and enormous Derbys (American for bowler hats) of those early Victorian days. There is the bar itself, which serves decent Guinness, and any other drink you care to think of. It also serves bowls of probably the best Chili around. It may not be the hottest, but it is certainly the most delicious. It comes with beans and crackers. If you want anything other than chili, then you need to go to the restaurant, proper, which is through the back of the bar. There they serve good, wholesome American food, from burgers and ribs to steaks and broils. You need to book. If you've never been to P.J. Clarke's, put it up at the top of your list of places to visit. Ahead of the Empire State Building. Ahead of the Statue of Liberty. Ahead of the Bronx Zoo. Ahead of Bloomingdales. Ahead of the Guggenheim Museum. Ahead of Central Park. Ahead of everything. And then I also have to advise you, if you are male, to make certain that you pay a visit to the men's room off the front bar before you leave. It is a unique monument to early Victorian plumbing.

But back to The Bottomless Pit. I leaned over and told Bill what was happening. 'Hey, how about that?' he said. 'Let's walk around the corner to P.J.'s. I'll buy us a quick drink, and then I'll leave you to your own devices. You're obviously in luck tonight.' We left the strip show. I waved goodbye to the blonde cheerleader (as I thought of her) and she shook her tits, and winked at me. P.J.'s was about ten minutes walk away, through the early evening crowd. The bar itself, when we got there, was heaving with the last of the after-work drinkers, but it was starting to thin slowly, as commuters began looking at their watches, and taking off to catch trains from Grand Central Station to White Plains, Westchester, Floral Park, New Jersey, and points north, south, and west.

Bill ordered me a Scotch and water, no ice, and himself a cognac. 'Well, cheers, Tony,' he said. 'It looks like you've got yourself set up for the evening. Good luck.' He raised his glass, and swallowed thirstily. I raised mine back. 'Cheers, Bill. And thank you for a delightful lunch. Day. Evening. Whatever.' I laughed. It had been a long day. 'I've enjoyed myself immensely. Thanks a lot.' 'My pleasure, Tony,' he said. 'It's been good to meet you. I've enjoyed your company. And you've very much put my mind at rest. My thanks to you too.' We drank our drinks slowly, Bill entertaining me with stories of what he described as the old New York. We all do it, about the places that we know and love. He was talking about the Fifties. And then he looked at his watch, and announced that his wife would be expecting him home for supper shortly. We parted good friends, and I felt that it had been a day well spent, apart from the excellent food at Palm, and the fun and frolics at The Bottomless Pit.

Such is the service at P.J. Clarke's, that all I had to do was to raise my empty glass to the barman and a replacement was in front of me within seconds. I made movements that indicated that I was looking for money, and the barman said 'You stayin' on a while, sir?' 'Er, yes,' I said. 'Then I'll run a tab for you,' he said. 'You can settle it when you leave.' What a civilized way to run a country. If only we could learn to do the same in England. Why are we such a backward country in these matters?

Right then the cheerleader came in through the door, and came up to me and gave me a great big kiss. I enjoyed the envious looks from the other men in the bar. 'Hi, baby,' she said. 'I'm sorry to keep you waiting.' 'No problem,' I said. 'What'll you have to drink?' 'Thank you,' she said. 'I'll have a Beefeater martini, straight up. A slice.' The barman mixed it, and brought it, within moments. 'So cheers,' I said. 'What's your name?' 'Oh, I'm sorry,' she said Dee Dee. From Deirdre, which I don't like. What's yours?' 'Tony,' I said. 'Hi, Tony,' she said. 'Here's to us.' 'Hi, Dee Dee,' I said. 'To us. Cheers.' She drank her martini as if she hadn't had a drink all day. Perhaps she hadn't. 'You must think I'm very forward,' she said. 'No, not really,' I said, comparing her now – dressed in a pretty, pale beige cotton suit, with her high heels and stockings, her hair well combed, her make-up well put together – with the earlier vision of her naked but for her garter.

'No. Not at all. Tell me, how would you like to see if we can get a table at the back?' I asked. 'Then we can sit in comfort and tell each other our life stories. Or whatever.' She looked at me a little askance. Maybe that 'or whatever' was a little over the top. 'Forgive me,' I said. 'It's been a long day. I've probably had just a tiny bit too much to drink. What I actually mean is that I'd really like it if you felt you would care to join me for supper in the restaurant at the back. OK?' 'Put that way, baby,' she said, 'how could I refuse? Yeah, I'd like that. Thank you.' I excused myself and walked through to the restaurant. It was early for them, as yet, and yes, sure they had a table for two. I told them I'd be back in ten minutes. I looked for the barman. He was right in front of me. 'Going through to the restaurant, sir?' he enquired. When I told him yes, he said he'd pass my bar check through to them. I tipped him, and thanked him. What a fantastic system. (British operators of massive hotel chains, please note. It would make a change from turning every place that they take over into a characterless, money-making machine. God forbid that any of them should ever get control of the Savoy Group). We went through to the back, and were shown to our table in a pleasant, quiet corner. 'Will you have some wine with your meal, Dee Dee?' I asked, 'or would you rather stay on martinis?' 'Wine would be good,' she said. 'Red, please. If that's OK?' 'It's OK,' I said, and ordered some. We both settled for the bacon cheeseburger, with Thousand Island dressing and fries, and we agreed to share a tomato and onion salad. We gave the restaurant's fried onion rings – for which they are famous – a miss.

'So, Dee Dee,' I said. 'Tell me about yourself.' 'There's not a lot to tell, really,' she said, beginning as all people do when you ask them to tell you about themselves. 'I was born in Bismarck, in North Dakota. It's about a thousand miles from anywhere. I guess Minneapolis, in Minnesota, is the nearest city. I went to grade school, and my childhood was quite normal, until I was fourteen, when my father left my mother and went off with another woman. After a while my mother shacked up with this guy Paul. I didn't like him, but what I couldn't put up with was when he started abusing me.

'When my mother was out, he'd come into my room, and he'd press me up against the wall, and then he'd feel my breasts, and put his hand up my skirt and into my panties, and force his fingers into me. And the next thing, he'd get his cock out, and try and make me masturbate him. And he'd ask me to suck him off. Or he'd say "Why don't you lie down and let me fuck you, sweetie? You don't know what you're missing." He was disgusting. I didn't want to tell my mother. However awful I thought he was, she loved him, and she hadn't had that much happiness. I didn't want to spoil that. So one day, not long after my eighteenth birthday, I just upped and left. I took the

Greyhound bus down here to New York, thinking, like everyone does, that I'd soon get a job. But it just didn't happen. I could get jobs waitressing, and things like that, but I couldn't earn enough to afford somewhere to live. So, very quickly, it became obvious that there were only two ways to earn enough to keep myself. One was to become a hooker. The other, a stripper in a topless, bottomless bar. You may not see a whole world of difference between the two, but, believe me, if you're a girl, and you're broke, there is. I might be showing all I've got to anyone with the price of a drink at the Bottomless Pit, but at least it's still mine. I walk out of there at the end of the day, and haven't sold it. It's a battle, sometimes, and I get pawed a lot, but there are heavyweight bouncers there – I don't know if you noticed them?'

I had, and I said so. 'So if there's a real problem, I've only got to nod, and the punters are out on their ear. Literally. The good news is that, with the tips, I earn really good money. It's not pleasant work.' She laughed. 'Although it does, sometimes, have its amusing moments. But I make as much in a good day as I'd make all week as a waitress. That allows me to afford a little studio of my own, over on the West Side. And live my own life. Which pretty well brings me up to date. But the reason that I threw myself at you, when you said you were from *Tiptop*, is that what I really want to do is nude modelling. I don't know whether they're right or not, but the other girls at the club say I've got a terrific body. What do you think? Do you think I might make a model for your magazine?'

Dee Dee looked at me anxiously, biting her lower lip. I looked back at her. At that moment the waitress brought our burgers. I waited until she had dealt with everything, and then I looked at Dee Dee, and smiled. 'I'm not making any promises,' I said, 'only because it isn't my sole decision. But it is my opinion that, yes, you'd make a splendid model for *Tiptop*. And I'll be happy to do everything that I can to arrange for that to happen for you. I'm reasonably certain that I can get a test shoot set up for you. Just leave it with me. OK?'

She jumped up from her chair and came around the table and gave me a big hug and a kiss, to the amusement of the other diners in the restaurant, and to my intense embarrassment. One or two of them cheered, and someone shouted 'Go for it, bud. Go for it.' 'Oh, you are *my* man,' she said. 'You are really *my* man. Thank you. Thank you. Thank you.' She kissed me again. I disentangled myself, and said 'Hey, honey. That's nice. But there's no need. Really.' She went back to her chair. We tucked into our burgers, and talked of life. Like you do. Close to, and without the Bottomless Pit makeup, she was even prettier. I couldn't help thinking of what lay beneath the summer suit. It seemed strange, sitting here in a civilized restaurant, talking normally to a girl who, less than an hour ago, had been squatting naked in front of me, spreading wide the lips of her cunt. But that aside, she was both intelligent and street wise. She was no blue stocking, but she could hold her own, conversationally, more than comfortably.

She wasn't at all the kind of girl that I had expected. She hadn't yet become hardened by what she was doing. She still had ambition, and patently saw her occupation as a means to an end, and not a way of life in itself. Unlike the average stripper, whose main interest, in my limited experience, is in money and worldly goods, she was interested in what was going on about her. And she still believed, she said, in love. 'I'm not a virgin,' she said, looking at me from beneath thick eyelashes with her piercingly dark blue eyes, 'I enjoy sex, although I don't exactly put it about. But I would like to settle down one day into a permanent relationship. Perhaps not just yet awhile, but one day. You know, marriage, kids, a little place called home. All that sort of shit. It appeals to me. Right now,' she continued, 'I'm sowing some extremely selective wild oats.'

She grinned impishly at me. 'Now listen here, Tony. I don't want you to misunderstand what I'm going to say. You've said that you'll do your best to help me to get some nude modelling work with *Tiptop*. I think you know that I'm tremendously

GETTING DOWN TO IT

excited about that. And frankly, if you'd said to me that part of the deal was to drop my panties for you, then I'd drop my panties for you.' I could feel my prick responding to her implied invitation. Down, sir, I said to myself, not very emphatically. 'Because that is an opportunity to give up the revolting way that I'm having to make a living by right now, and anything that can get me out of that has to be worth a fuck or two, however bad you may think that paints my morals. That is why I want to spell out to you that, since you've been a decent enough person specifically not to make that part of the deal, I don't want you to think that I'm saying what I'm going to say just because I'm grateful. Understand?'

Frankly, that was all a bit too convoluted for me, and I said so. Did she want to fuck, or didn't she? I do like to be clear about people's intentions, when it comes to sex. 'I'm sort of a little confused,' I said. 'Spell it out for me in simple words, will you, please?' 'Sure,' she said. 'I want you to take me out of here and to somewhere where you can fuck the living daylights out of me. I'm not offering my body to say thank you. I'm offering it simply because I fancy you. I want your cock inside me. Is that simple enough?' I almost blushed. When I'd got myself together, I found my Amex, and paid the bill (it's a bit of a *non sequitor*, but in New York, if you pay with cash, they think you haven't got any money). 'It's not far,' I said. 'Ten minutes at most.' We found a cab, and she slipped an arm through mine as we got into it. Her fragrance smelt sexy. I wondered if her knickers were damp. I made a mental note to look and see.

The doormen at the apartment block were beginning to give each other knowing looks, each time I arrived back there with a different girl. It didn't do my ego any harm at all. I wondered what in God's name they must have thought about Fred. Dee Dee loved the apartment, and made a whirlwind tour before disappearing into the bathroom for a while. She then came looking for me. I was in the bedroom. In bed. Naturally. I watched her undress, and yes, her knickers *were* damp.

Actually, they were *wet*. The pale green satin fabric was *dark* green between her legs. She saw where I was looking, and looked down at herself. She laughed. 'Think of it as a compliment,' she said. 'Pussy wants you. Pussy has been wanting you since you tucked a twenty under my garter. Girls feel sexy too, you know.'

All she had been wearing under her suit were knickers and tights. She threw them down where she stood, and came over and climbed into bed beside me. She put her arms around me and pressed me down onto the pillow, and then she started kissing me hungrily, while her right hand searched for, and found, my rampant cock. 'Hmmmm,' she said. 'How lovely. That's a whopper.' I felt for her cunt, and found it where I already knew it was. It was very wet indeed. Dee Dee patently either wasn't into foreplay, or she seriously wanted to fuck.

Either way, she climbed on top of me, and, spreading her cunt lips with her right hand, she fed my cock into her with the other. She was tight and wet, and she knelt forward and pressed down on my cock, which had the effect of sucking me deeply inside her. I could feel her cunt muscles working as she started to ride me, and I put my hands around her firm buttocks and pulled her down as hard as I could. She groaned, and spread her legs even wider, riding me hard now, urgently beginning the ascent up towards orgasm. She bent forward, still fucking me hard, and thrust a hard nipple into my mouth. I sucked it, and felt it swell even more. I worked at it with my mouth and teeth, and after a while she pulled back and then, leaning forward again, placed the other nipple into my mouth, patently asking for the same treatment.

I began kneading her buttocks, and my fingers found the cleavage between them. I ran a finger down it, arriving at her anus. I gently massaged the puckered flesh, and felt it slowly become lubricated. Then I eased a finger inside her, and began finger fucking her arsehole. She groaned again, and began working even harder, and then, suddenly, she was screaming her pleasure as she came, bucking and riding as if on horseback. I began to fuck her as hard as I could, and brought myself to orgasm, feeling my semen spurting up inside her. 'Oh yes, baby,' she said. 'That's good. That's real good. Fuck me now. Now. Oh, yes. Oh God. I can feel your hot spunk inside me. I'm coming now. Yes. Yes. Ahhhh.' She shuddered through her climax, and rolled off me, leaving me gasping. I lay there, breathing long, slow breaths, until my heartbeat slowed down, and my breath came more easily. 'Wow,' said Dee Dee. 'That was great, man. Really good.' 'My pleasure, sweetheart,' I said. 'All I did was lie there and think of England.' She laughed. 'I've read that expression somewhere,' she said. 'It's what married women in Britain in Victorian times were supposed to do when their husbands fucked then, wasn't it? Lie back and think of England. Terrific.'

I didn't particularly want Dee Dee to stay the night. Not because I didn't fancy continuing to get to know her, sexually and in every other way, but because it had been a long day, first with Bill, then with Dee Dee. It was getting late, and, frankly, I was tired. Tomorrow was another day. It wasn't a problem, she said. She quite understood. I gave her my office and apartment telephone numbers, and took down hers, and promised that I'd get back in touch, once I'd spoken to my art director, David, about her auditioning for him. 'Don't worry, David won't jump you,' I said. 'He's gay. And he's awfully nice with it. *And* he's got an excellent eye for a pretty girl. So he'll just love you. Come and see me when you've seen him. But I'll be in touch anyway. I called down for a cab for her, and went down with her when it arrived. I gave the driver five bucks. Dee Dee looked almost tearful. Whether with happiness, or something else, who knows? She kissed me goodbye, and I gave her a big squeeze before she got into the cab. She waved out of the rear window until the cab was lost in the traffic.

CHAPTER FOUR
ON THE MAT

There was a stack of messages at the office the following morning, due to my lack of attendance the previous day. Before I did anything else, I walked through to the art department, and gave David Dee Dee's telephone number, asking him if he would be good enough to have a look at her, and if he thought she was worth a test shoot. I suggested that perhaps, if he had not already set up the test shoot for Lucy, that he might arrange for them both to be done by the same photographer on the same day. He said no, he hadn't yet set anything up, and he agreed to arrange the two together, if he agreed that Dee Dee qualified. I called her when I got back to my office, and she was ecstatic. 'Shall I call him now, right away, Tony?' she asked, anxiously. 'No, honey,' I said. 'Let him call you. He'll get around to it soon enough, believe you me.'

There were three messages from Pauline, all of which added up to 'Where are you? I'm home. Please call me. Pauline.' Eileen had added a scrawled 'Shall I tell her you're downtown with Lucy?' at the bottom of one of them, followed by an exclamation mark. I grinned to myself, and picked up the telephone. She answered on the first ring. 'Darling,' she said. 'How lovely. There you are. I rang your office all day yesterday, and your secretary said something about a distribution meeting. And there was no reply from the apartment in the early evening. What were you distributing? Money?' I laughed. 'Hey, Pauline, sweetheart. How are you? How was Tokyo? When am I going to see you?' 'Tokyo was good. How about now?' she suggested. 'I can't, darling,' I said. 'But I can meet you for a quick lunch, and then, if you're free, we'll have a nice long, leisurely dinner, and then we'll have to see what we can think of to do after that. How does that sound?' 'Sounds good,' she said. 'Shall I come and pick you up at the office?' 'Please do,' I said. 'That would be nice. About twelve thirty?' 'Great,' she said. 'I'll be there.'

She was on time, something that I was to discover was important to her – unusual, in my experience, in a woman and we agreed (since we were also going to eat out that evening) that we'd eat something fairly light for lunch. 'There's a great little sushi bar not far from here,' she suggested. 'It's on 51st, between Third and Lexington. Do you like sushi?' 'I'm learning to love it,' I said. 'That would suit me fine. Let's go.'

When we got there it was busy, but they found us two seats up at the bar, and we spent enjoyable minutes making our selection. We both ordered Nigiri. 'That'll do me for starters,' I said, having ordered tuna, salmon, shrimp, octopus, and cucumber. 'How about you?' Pauline ordered everything that I had, bar the octopus, for which she substituted eel. We watched as one of the two sushi barmen dexterously prepared our food, turning small portions of compressed cold, seasoned rice into finger-shaped and roll-shaped pieces around the fillings that we had chosen, and covering the outsides with thin sheets of seaweed. We added miso soup and Japanese pickles to our order, and accompanied our food with warm saki. Delicious! As we ate, Pauline told me that in her opinion, the Japanese food one got in New York was, by and large, every bit as good as that in Tokyo, provided one chose where one ate it reasonably carefully. Looking about me, I could see that almost all our fellow customers were Japanese. Over our food, once we had got past the 'what have you been doing?' and 'what's happened since I last saw you?' and the 'do you still love me?' bits, I brought up the question of Plato's Retreat, and told Pauline that I fancied visiting it, to see whether or not it would make a suitable story for my proposed *Tiptop* sex diary.

She told me that she had heard about it, but that she hadn't been there, and I asked her if she fancied trying it out after dinner that evening. She was silent for a moment. 'Do you know, Tony,' she said, 'that if anyone had asked me that a few weeks back, I would have said, yeah, terrific. Sure. Let's go. Right now, since I've met you, I feel rather differently. I mean, when we met at Daly's Dandelion, I was just looking for sexual exercise. Sexual excitement. Now, I don't want to share you with anyone. I want you all to myself. Does that sound strange?'

I wasn't sure what to say. It didn't sound particularly strange, but it did imply a certain amount of commitment. Eventually, I said 'No. It doesn't sound strange. In fact, I very much appreciate what you're saying. But to put your mind at rest, I wasn't thinking of taking part in any kind of multi-person orgy, but simply of going to Plato's Retreat to see what goes on there, and of reporting my findings, if they're at all interesting, to my readers. And of course, I've no intention of announcing that I'm representing *Tiptop* when I get there. We would be totally incognito.' 'In that case, honey,' she said, 'I'm with you. I'm yours. Always.' She smiled at me, and leaned over and kissed me. Somehow, it made me feel really mean. Life's a shit, isn't it?

Plato's Retreat was up on West 74th street. When it originally opened, it called itself a sex club, and it kept its address at 270 West 74th a secret, offering only its telephone number – 212 646 1169 – to those interested enough to track it down. Couples were admitted for $20, and single women for $8. No single men were allowed entry. The club is solely heterosexual. We paid our money, and were told that the entrance fee included drinks and the use of all facilities. It was in an enormous basement which had previously been a rather seedy, run-down health club. Now it boasted a disco, with the dance floor surrounded by sheeted mats. There was a full-size heated pool, a steam bath, and a sauna. It was still seedy, but there was an air of sexual excitement, almost frenzy, about the place, as Pauline and I checked in. It quickly became obvious that the club flourished on a basic principle of 'change partners.' As often as possible.

Couples on the dance floor as we arrived were mostly totally naked. We stripped off, and left our clothes in lockers, to which we were given a key each, and a piece of string with which to attach it to some part of our bodies. I chose my wrist, Pauline her neck. We got ourselves a drink, and sat down on a rather tatty sofa, to watch what was going on around us. Apart from the frenetic dancing, and a certain amount of action on the mats around the dance floor, which were really in an area too dark for us to discern with much certainty exactly what was going on there (although we could obviously make an informed guess), we could see very little. So we took our drinks in our hands, and started a slow perambulation around the premises. There were couples in the steam bath indulging in oral sex. Through the haze of steam we glimpsed naked, sweating bodies, indulging each other. Rampant penises were thrusting between lipsticked lips, and down hungry throats, while masculine tongues and mouths serviced spread *labia minora* and *majora*. No-one seemed to care that they were being observed. Indeed, I think that for many, the audience was a major part of the attraction. All the world's a stage, as Shakespeare put it. One guy was fucking one of the women up her ass, to her intense pleasure. What their relationship was – if any – I do not know.

The same kind of scene was being played out in the sauna and in fact we recognized a couple of the bodies that we'd first seen in the steam room, now indulging orally with different partners in the sauna. With all this live sex going on around me, it surprised me that I didn't have even the beginnings of an erection. In fact, to be honest, the whole thing was a bit of a turn-off. After the sauna, we visited the pool. The over chlorinated waters fairly resounded with the sound of fucking. The water itself, and the wet, naked backs of women slapping against the pool walls as they copulated, mixing with the sounds emanating from the disco, fairly had the surface of the pool whipped into a frenzy. The whole thing was quite extraordinary, and – to me – completely asexual.

I asked Pauline what she thought, and she said that she would be happy to leave as soon as I felt that I had gathered enough material. I felt obliged to talk to some of the participants, and was surprised to discover that most of them were in fact married, and were there with their marriage partners. I watched a particular couple for a while, and saw them first have sex together, then split, looking for – and finding – new partners. I saw the husband watching with what? Interest? Excitement? Jealousy? as his attractive wife was fucked successively by three different men. Two black, one white. All three were, putting it bluntly, better endowed than he. Every time she came, she screamed. By the time she was apparently finished, she was complaining of a raw cunt. The last I saw, she was jerking off some guy whilst her husband watched yet again.

He'd fucked just one other woman whilst his wife indulged herself. I wondered which of them was the motivating factor behind their visits. As we left the area in which they were performing, she was scolding him for allowing her to behave in the way she had. He should have stopped her long ago, she announced. He knew, she said, that she couldn't stop herself.

Talking to individual women, who for the moments that I spoke to them were without their partners, or who had arrived singly, they mostly simply said that they came there to fuck. One woman had an interesting theory. 'I come in here alone,' she said. 'And I leave alone. A lot of the couples here pretend that they are married, or into some kind of ongoing relationship. But you'll find that most of them don't even know each other that well. They just pair up for the purpose of getting in here. Once they're in, they find the sex that they're looking for in a reasonably controlled, safety-in-numbers atmosphere. On top of that,' she said, 'it's every woman's fantasy. I just come in here, and guys grab me, and they fuck me. It's what I come for, and I love it. Do you wanna fuck?' I made my excuses, as they say in the *News of the World*, and left. I'd been keeping Pauline as close to me as possible, once I discovered that she didn't want to take part in what was going on around her. It surprised me that she didn't, remembering where we had met, but I had to agree with her that the whole set-up was pretty unattractive. She kept a whole caravan of would-be partners at a distance, without getting them too upset.

As journalist Jared Brady wrote recently in a personal view of Plato's Retreat: 'The primal thump of Quaaluded, boozed, amyl nitrated, and otherwise wild bodies could strike a responsive chord, even between the legs of a eunuch. The heavy breathing rumbles, like the thunder of Sodom and Gomorrah. The moans are like the sirens of hell. The patrons are not in a health club, but in a Temple of Sex: a fornicating crowd pushing its way through the Kingdom of Come. They are holy rollers, a congregation of panters, intent on gaining the heights (or is it the depths?) of ecstasy. At five in the morning, they slowly exit out from their heaven, both raw and revived, both exhausted and nearly ecclesiastical, with their faith renewed by some hard on deity of nymphomania. Pleasure is the only cross they bear.'

Pauline and I left long before five. Just after midnight, we went back to Fred's apartment, faintly depressed by the whole affair. Could sex be so desperate? Could sexual fulfilment be so dejected? Could sexual freedom be so petty? Could fun be so unamusing? We took a long, luxurious shower, and then we fucked each other slowly, lovingly, enjoying each other's bodies, warming to our task as slowly we banished Plato's Retreat from our minds. We gradually became able to laugh at ourselves again, and to giggle as we explored each other's orifices and prominent parts. I think it's called love. It beats an orgy any day, for my money. She stayed the night, and we made gentle, sensual love, brought on, I believe, by the desperate, urgent awfulness of what we had witnessed at Plato's Retreat. For a couple who both, probably, are more usually into the baser kinds of sex for pleasure, we managed what can only be described, in retrospect, as kindly sensuality. Caring. Loving. We fell asleep around dawn, and I crawled out of bed at a quarter to ten, leaving Pauline a note asking her to ring me at the office when she awoke. Eileen took one look at me when I arrived at the office, and scurried away, returning moments later with heavily sugared black coffee, and a lot of (I thought) undeserved accusations.

'You've been up all night fucking that black tart,' she accused. 'Have you got a doctor? Shall I make you an appointment with mine? Have you washed it? Sterilized it? You didn't suck her pussy, did you? God. You won't need a mouthwash, more of an injection of antibiotics. Show me your gums.' I gave her a sort of mechanical grin, exposing my upper and lower gum. 'Hmmmm,' she said. 'It doesn't look diseased. But the infection probably hasn't taken hold fully yet.' She was going to go on, but I raised up a weak hand, and she stopped, her mouth open to continue the flow as soon as I had finished.

'Hold it right there, darling,' I said. 'Enough. Enough. Now, let's get something straight. One. I haven't been anywhere near the lovely Lucy. I assume that's to whom you refer in this evil diatribe?' I paused, waiting for some kind of an answer. 'I don't know what tribe she comes from,' said Eileen. 'All those Africans look the same to me. But yes, that is to whom I refer.' 'Well, I just want you to know that the lady with whom I have been trysting the night away is none other than the lovely Pauline.' (I had told Eileen of being picked up by Pauline in Daly's Dandelion. It was she, after all, who had recommended the place to me). 'Be that as it may, I do not see why you have to slander the lovely Lucy. What makes you think so lowly of her? She's never done you any harm. What's all this rubbish about diseases? Come on, now. What's it all about?'

Eileen looked at her feet, and then at me, and sat down in one of the chairs opposite my desk. 'Look, Tony,' she said. 'Whatever you do with your life here in New York is your business, OK? But just remember one thing. You're a stranger here. A foreigner. Before you arrived, and again, just before he left, Fred asked me to watch out for you. To help you. Guide you. Look out for your interests. On top of which, I don't mind admitting, I've fallen for you. So I personally want to look after you, as well as simply doing what Fred asked OK? And I just have this bad feeling about that black tart.' I frowned at her repetition of the word, and she apologized.

'I'm sorry, love. I'm not usually prejudiced. Some of my best friends, as they say. Lucy may be pretty, I'll give you that.' I smiled at her. 'Oh, all right then. Beautiful.' I nodded. 'She may be beautiful,' she continued, 'but I don't think she's very clean. I suspect that she is extremely promiscuous, and I think you ought to be careful. OK?' I sighed. 'All right, Eileen, sweetheart,' I said. 'I accept your explanation. And thank you for your concern. I do, really. But on this particular occasion, I'm not guilty. Enough of that. What else?' 'I think the only thing of any interest is that a girl from London keeps calling you.' Eileen looked down at her notebook. 'Don't tell me,' I said. 'Annabel. Right?'

Eileen looked surprised. 'How could you possibly know that?' she asked. 'Don't ask,' I said. 'Call it intuition. Anything else?' 'Just one thing,' she replied. 'John Boyce, the ad director, wonders if you can spare him some time today? He just wants to run over things generally. He says it's not urgent, but he'd like to get together with you when you have the time.' 'Ask him to come along now,' I said. 'If it's convenient. If it's not, you fit him in. I'm easy.'

My God, I thought. Annabel. Darling Annabel. I hadn't called her once since I'd been in New York. I hadn't given her Fred's apartment number, she only had the office one. I hadn't even sent her a postcard. I looked at my watch. It was nearly eleven. That meant it was nearly four in the afternoon in London. Chances were that she'd still be at home. I picked up the 'phone, and dialled her penthouse number. The 'phone picked up on the first ring. I hoped she hadn't been sitting by it. Waiting. 'Hello,' she said. The soft tone of her familiar voice sent shivers down my neck. 'Hi, baby,' I said. 'It's me.' 'Darling,' she said, her voice suddenly vibrant, exuding warmth. 'It really is you. I thought you'd disappeared. How are you? How's New York? Are you having fun? I miss you. Are you fucking lots of lovely New York ladies?' I laughed. What else could I do? 'I'm. fine, darling, just fine, thank you. And New York is good. A lot of hard work. A lot to learn. Some fun. No New York ladies. Not yet, anyway. But how are you? Are you OK? Is everything all right?' Better a barefaced lie than the wounding truth, I thought. There was a slight pause before she replied. Then, 'I'm all right, darling,' she said. 'Missing you, of course. Playing with myself rather a lot. But life goes on. All's well at the club. It's quietish, being the summer. Lots of people are away. I thought I might accept your suggestion before you left, and come over and stay with you for a while. What do you think?' I thought that would be terrific, and I said so. I was getting a hard-on at the idea of her playing with herself. Naughty fingers. Damp knickers. Wet pussy.

'That would be fantastic, darling. Wonderful. When do you want to come? Any time suits me. You can stay with me in Fred's apartment. There's plenty of room, and it's amazingly central. You can walk most places if you want to, although I wouldn't advise it. It's very hot.' 'Oh, gosh,' she said. 'That's lovely. I thought you might say you were too busy. Let me have words with the club this evening, and I'll call you tomorrow. Do you really mean any time? I mean, like next week? That sort of thing?' 'The sooner the better, darling,' I said. 'Just let me know when. And let me know the flight times, and I'll come and pick you up.' 'Oh, darling,' she said. 'I think I'm going to cry. I'll hang up now. Speak to you as soon as I've got firm dates and flight times. Be good. I love you, darling. Goodbye now.' 'I love you too, sweetheart,' I said, and we hung up. I was genuinely pleased. There might be a lot of available pussy about in New York, but Annabel was something else. I began to realize how much I'd been missing her. The 'phone rang. It was Eileen. 'John can come through now, if it's convenient,' she said. 'Sure,' I said. 'Send him through. Some coffee would be nice, if that's not too much to ask. Please.' 'No problem,' she said. 'Give me five minutes.' Just then John Boyce came into the office. I'd met him before, of course, when I'd arrived. He was a pleasant, extrovert guy of around forty. He was shortish and plumpish, outgoing in the way that sales people are. Eileen followed him in with the coffee, which she poured and handed round. John stood back by the door until she had finished.

He then held out his hand. 'Hi, Tony,' he said. 'Good of you to see me. I appreciate it. 'Good to see you, John,' I said. 'And it's no problem. It's what I'm here for. Another time, you don't need to ask Eileen. Just come in. If I'm busy, I'll say so.' 'Oh, terrific,' he said. 'Thank you. Now then, I just wanted to touch base on a couple of things, if I may. Fred is always enthusiastic, but he's not much of a detail man, if you know what I mean.' I grinned at him. 'I know what you mean, John,' I said. 'But he's a bloody good editor.' 'Oh, that for sure,' said John. 'That for sure. Now, first of all, are you the right person for me to discuss editorial matters with?' I thought for a moment. 'If you mean, am I able to take decisions in Fred's absence, yes, I am,' I said. 'Good,' said John. 'I've been trying to get Fred to tone down the girl sets ever since I first joined *Tiptop*. You know what I mean. Less pink. What I'd call a slightly less gynaecological approach to some of the sets. I don't mind them, but serious advertisers don't like them.'

'Why would you want him to do that, John?' I asked. 'Well, as I've said to Fred, we're missing out on some really big advertisers in a number of fields, simply because our girl sets are too strong. If we could only tone them down a bit, there are companies in the motor manufacturing business, the cigarette business and the drinks business who I'm pretty sure I could persuade to spend at least part of their budget with us.' He looked at me eagerly, as if trying to read my mind. I'd heard it all before, of course, from Wally's and Fred's advertisement sales people in London. In the girlie magazine business it's an ongoing difference of opinion between editors and publishers on the one hand, whose point of view is that it is the girl sets that basically sell the magazine to the readers, and distributors and advertisement sales people on the other, who always claim that it is the – in their opinion – unnecessary strength of the girl sets which is preventing them from getting maximum distribution/obtaining the really big advertising clients.

Certainly, in London, W.H. Smith's and Menzies, the two largest chains of retail bookstalls, didn't take *Tiptop*. Nor did they take *Penthouse* or *Men Only*, although they take all three these days. Strange that, looking back, for even in the UK, all men's magazines are about a hundred per cent 'stronger,' visually, than they were all those years ago. Back in the late Seventies in the States, as I've already mentioned in *Stripped for Action*,* photographic reproduction of the male and female genitalia – the latter gaping open or not – were not legally considered pornographic. This meant fewer distribution problems, although some large advertisers took a rather disapproving view of publications such as ours. Happily, plenty of others took a quite different view.

What it really comes down to is that readers buy magazines because they like the editorial content. They don't buy magazines because they like the advertisements. If you can appeal to a large audience of readers, then certain advertisers, who sell products that they believe will appeal to your readers, will buy advertising space from you, provided that the cost is acceptable on a financially sound basis, known as cost-per thousand, or CPT.

Put simply, if a newspaper or a magazine has a readership of

---

*Published in paperback by New English Library.

one thousand people, and it sells its advertising pages at five pounds a page, you can see that the CPT is five pounds. If a competitive publication has only five hundred readers but it sells its pages at the same cost of five pounds, then its CPT is ten pounds. You can see which is the better buy for the advertiser, assuming both readerships are in his market.

So, in my opinion, and in that of most other editors and publishers, one simply does not alter the editorial tone of a magazine to satisfy either ad sales people or advertisers. One hopes to find a happy medium between the two. These facts I related to John. As a more than competent salesman, I wasn't telling him anything that he didn't know already. He simply thought that his approach was worth a try. Had he been able to sucker me in and persuade me to tone down the girl sets in an attempt to sell more advertising pages, his commission – and that of his sales team – would have soared.

He grinned at me, but he didn't argue, and he moved on to his next point, which was to ask if I would change Fred's ruling against *Tiptop* accepting what are called inserts – those nasty sheets of paper that fall out of many a magazine as soon as you pick it up off the bookstall. These inserts appeal to certain advertisers, since they are considerably cheaper to buy than conventional advertisements in a publication. Other than in times of recession, when advertising money is as hard to come by as any other kind of money, most publishers refuse them on the grounds that they lower the tone of the publication. The time that it takes to insert them, although done by machine in most cases, can also slow down delivery from the printer, something that every publisher wants to avoid. Going on sale on time each day, week, or month, is absolutely vital.

John's last point was that, since – despite his criticisms – he was managing to sell more and more advertising as our sales increased monthly, he thought it was time that we upgraded our original advertisement sales material. I hadn't seen it, and he showed it to me. It was perfectly acceptable for the purpose for which it had been designed, which was for *Tiptop*'s launch in America, but it certainly was out of date and, now that we were immensely profitable, I felt that we could, and should, come up with something rather more lavish. Something with which John could impress his clients.

I told him that I agreed with his wish, and said that I'd approve a budget for him, and asked him to get Eileen to set up a meeting with him, his team, and David, the art director, to discuss the requirements, and arrange to get some roughs out. He went off, happy that I had approved at least one of his requests. I still believe that the first two were simply try-ons. I rang through to Eileen, and asked her if she fancied joining me for lunch. She was pleased to say yes, and it pleased me too. She was always good, relaxed, amusing company. I took her to the sushi bar that Pauline had introduced me to, and we gossiped over sushi for her, sashimi for me, with the same miso soup, rice and Japanese pickles. We accompanied it with an excellent bottle of dry Californian wine from the Napa Valley. There are worse ways of spending a lunch hour. Eileen asked me who Annabel was so, realizing that I would probably need her help during Annabel's visit, I told her what there was to tell about my relationship with Annabel. When I'd finished, she said 'But you haven't said whether you really love her or not. Is this it? Is this the big one? You know. Wedding bells, all that?'

I looked across the table at her. 'I haven't said that, because I don't know,' I told her. 'When I'm with her, I don't want anyone else. When I'm not with her, I'll fuck anything that moves, given half an opportunity.' 'Except me,' said Eileen, rather acidly, I thought. 'But let's not go on about that right now.' No, I thought to myself. Please let us not go on about that right now. Not ever.

Aloud I said 'How do you tell? Surely, if this relationship with Annabel was real love – whatever that might be – surely I wouldn't be interested in other women? Would I?' 'You'd only give up tomcatting around if someone cut your dick off,' she answered. 'Or your balls. I've been tempted myself, once or twice.' 'Oh, come on, Eileen love,' I said. 'Do me a favour. I've never been anything other than totally up front with you. About you, anyway. What I get up to with other women, strictly speaking, isn't any of your goddamn business.' 'Oh, thanks a lot,' she said. 'Here,' she went on, mercifully changing the subject, 'You eat this. I don't like squid.' I took the squid, resting on its bed of vinegared rice, and ate it with relish. 'Thank you,' I said. 'But you haven't answered my question.' 'That's probably because you haven't asked one,' she replied. 'Unless you're going all the way back to "How do you tell?" To which the answer is, I actually haven't the faintest idea. I always thought I'd know when it happened, and it hasn't happened yet. Not really. You know, no sudden increase in my heart rate. No feeling of flying through the air. No rush of blood to the brain. No heavenly choirs. None of those things. But let me ask *you* a question. Or two. OK?'

'Sure,' I said, refilling our glasses with the end of the chardonnay. 'Fire away. Do you think we ought to have the other half?' 'Why not?' she said. 'It is Thursday.' I waved at the waiter, and then raised the empty bottle, pointing at it. He nodded, and went away. Eileen took a long pull at her wine, and then set the glass down, rather purposefully, and fidgeted about in her chair, until she found a more comfortable position. She looked directly into my eyes. 'You do like me, don't you?' she asked. 'I'm not wrong about that, am I?' 'Of course I do,' I told her. 'And no, of course you're not.' She looked slightly reassured. 'So where do I go wrong then?' she asked. I waited for more, but that was apparently it.

'What do you mean, where do you go wrong?' I asked her back, my heart sinking. 'I don't understand. Wrong about what? I suddenly knew only too well about what, but I wasn't going to admit it. 'Oh, for God's sake, Tony,' she said. 'You know perfectly well what I mean. Why don't you fancy me? Don't you find me attractive. I'm young – I'm only twenty-five – and I'm fit. I'm in quite good shape. I've been trying to show you for weeks now just how good a shape I'm in, and you don't want to know. I haven't got any antisocial diseases. What in God's name is the problem? Have I got BO or something? Please tell me. It's driving me mad.' I took a deep breath. Just then the waiter brought the new bottle of wine, and I took a welcome breather as we waited for him to open it. All of a sudden I'd had enough of Eileen and her whinging on about wanting to be fucked. If that was what she wanted, then that was what she'd get. When the waiter had gone, I leaned forward across the narrow table, and I took Eileen's wrist and held it.

'Now listen to me, young lady,' I said. 'When we've finished our lunch, I'm gong to take you back to Fred's apartment, and I'm going to fuck the living daylights out of you.' Her eyes widened into great rounds of surprise. I took no notice. 'I'm going to tear your knickers off, and fuck you until your cunt's so sore, you'll wish you'd never heard of me. At that stage, I'm going to make you suck me off. Probably more than once. Until it becomes really hard work. Then I might bugger you. Do you like it up your ass? If you don't know, you'll find out, this afternoon.' She was smiling now. 'There's just one proviso,' I said. 'No. Two.' 'Anything,' she said. 'Anything. But what are they?' 'I don't want any talk about love,' I said. 'This is sex. Just sex. Sex that you've asked for. OK?' 'Of course, darling,' she said. 'Of course. What's the other?' 'That's easy,' I told her. 'You don't tell Annabel. Not about you and me. Not about anyone. Is that a deal?' She was smiling all over her pretty face now. 'It's a deal, my darling,' she said. 'Can we go now?' I had to laugh. She was completely irrepressible. I waved at the waiter, and asked him for the bill. Ten minutes later we were in a cab on our way uptown. Eileen had her hand on my swelling cock as we rode up Fifth Avenue. I wondered if the driver was watching in his mirror, and then I thought, what the hell. He should be so lucky. I leaned sideways and whispered into Eileen's ear. 'From the moment you pass through Fred's apartment door,' I said, 'you are my sexual slave.' She turned half sideways and looked at me, smiling. 'After that,' I continued, 'you will do what I tell you to do, when I tell you to do it. If I say masturbate me, you will masturbate me. If I say drop your knickers, you will drop your knickers. If this is unacceptable, say so now, and I'll stop the cab, and you can get out. Do you understand?' She leaned across and kissed me. 'Yes, master,' she said. 'I can't wait.'

I got the usual knowing looks from the doormen at the apartment, but I ignored them as I normally did. One has to keep servants in their place. Eileen had been to the apartment before, of course, collecting and delivering papers for Fred, that sort of thing. She walked straight into the bedroom, and turned to face me, waiting. 'What's the matter?' I asked. 'Nothing's the matter,' she said. 'Then what are you waiting for?' I asked. 'You said you were going to tear my panties off,' she said. I went over to her, and knelt on the carpet in front of her, and raised her skirt. 'Here,' I said. 'Hold this.' She held the skirt up around her waist, revealing pale lemon panties, trimmed with white. They were lacy, and ever so slightly frilly. I could smell the scent of hot, pulsating pussy. I put my hand between her legs. 'Open your legs,' I demanded. She did as she was told. I felt her knicker crotch. It was encouragingly damp, and I could feel her swollen pussy lips through the thin material. I stroked them for a moment, and she closed her legs around my hand. 'Mmmmm,' she said. 'That's nice.' I reached up and, taking the waist of her knickers, I pulled. Hard. It split, with a satisfyingly tearing sound, and I ripped the knickers apart, pulling the remains of them down her legs. She stepped out of them. Her curly, gingery red pubic bush matched her short, gingery red hair. 'Strip off,' I said, 'and lie on your back on the bed.'

I watched her as she undressed. She was smiling happily to herself. I almost expected her to start humming, but she didn't. I took off my own clothes as I watched, allowing my stiff prick the freedom it was crying out for. She looked over towards me, and her face creased into a welcoming smile when she saw my cock. 'Here, baby,' she said. 'Eileen's ready for you, honey. Come to mummy, darling.' I walked over to the bed and stood in front of her, my prick inches in front of her face as she sat up. I didn't have to say anything, she reached out and drew me to her, her mouth open, and she licked her lips before she took its length into her mouth. She drew it in deeply, then took it out again, and looked at it.

She then started to lick it, slurping her saliva its full length, and then blowing softly on it, cooling it. She teased its head pulling the foreskin carefully down and licking the purple glans, taking it into her mouth and sucking strongly, as if on a lollipop. My prick hardened even more, and as she drew it out of her mouth the next time I could see the colourless pre-ejaculate liquid oozing from its eye. 'What about a little soixante-neuf, sweetheart?' I asked. She drew himself out of her mouth and smiled up at me. 'Sure, baby,' she said. 'I'd like that.' She lay back on the bed, her legs spread wide, and I knelt over her head as she guided my cock back into her mouth again, her tongue wet and warm on its stiff length. I buried my head in her red-haired crotch, relishing the slightly gamey flavour of her pussy that I find unique amongst redheads. She tasted strongly of my favourite female odour, that of aroused cunt. Her pussy lips were strangely dark for a white girl, a sort of purply brown in colour, and they were thick and fleshy, glistening wet with her juices.

They were long, almost like hairless spaniel's ears, and I sucked their length into my mouth and held them there, tonguing them and sucking, revelling in their succulence. Eileen began to move slowly under me, her pubis thrusting upwards against my mouth, her knees closing about my head, and she began making little mewing noises deep in her throat.

I let her labia out of my mouth and, spreading them wide with my fingers, appreciating their inner pinkness as I did so – such a contrast to the outer, deep purple – and searched with my tongue for her clitoris. It wasn't difficult to find, standing to attention as it was, guardian-like of her inner privacy, sentinel to her womb. I could feel the first contractions of an orgasm in her vaginal muscles, and I tongued her all the harder, bringing her to a shuddering climax as she shouted out her pleasure as she came. 'Oh, yes, baby, that's good. I'm coming. I'm coming. Oh, yes. Oh, fuck. Oh God.' I felt my own ejaculation building, and I pumped at her, fucking her mouth now as she sucked me in between her shouts, and then I was spurting my come down her throat. She gulped and swallowed, and sucked and swallowed again, until I was sucked dry. We rolled apart, and we both lay there for a while, our hearts beating wildly, our breaths coming in gasps, and then finally slowing down. After a while I got up off the bed. I was thirsty. 'Do you fancy a drink, sweetheart?' I asked. She thought for a moment.

'Sure,' she said. 'Thank you. I'd like a glass of white wine, if I may.' 'You may, of course,' I said, and went through to the kitchen and the fridge, and poured her a glass of white, and then got together a scotch and water for myself. When I got back to the bedroom, Eileen was sitting up, still naked, with her handbag open beside her, and the makings of a joint in front of her. 'Do you smoke grass?' she asked. 'No, not really,' I said. 'Not any more. I used to. I'm not seriously into anything these days, other than booze. But if it's around, I'd rather 'ludes, or coke, than grass. But you go ahead. It doesn't bother me in the least. Do you smoke it much?' 'I guess I do,' she replied. 'It relaxes me. I'm a much better fuck when I'm high than when I'm straight. We *are* going to fuck, aren't we?' She smiled as she raised the over-size joint and licked along the length of the paper, rolling it professionally, and then nipping off the ends.

I gave her the glass of wine, and raised my glass in salute to her. 'Of course we are,' I said. 'You don't think I'd get this far and let you get away without fucking you, do you? And in any case, if I did, I'd never hear the end of it. It would be nag, nag, nag, in the office. All day, every day. I can hear it now. Do you know, I think you've probably set a new record, at least as far as I'm concerned.' I grinned at her. 'Oh, yeah,' she said. 'What's that?' 'I'm reasonably certain,' I said, 'that you're the only woman in my life ever to nag me into bed.' 'Oh, fuck off, Tony,' she said, laughing. 'All I can say is, when we actually get around to it, that I hope you enjoy it. Have you got any complaints, so far?' 'No complaints at all,' I said. Nor had I. Her fellatio had been of the finest. Top drawer. And I said so. 'Well, thanks, honey,' she said. 'My cunnilingus was of a pretty high order too, if you really want to know.'

'Tell me, Eileen,' I said. 'Do you like girls? You know, sex with girls? Have you ever had any kind of a sexual relationship with another woman?' She looked at me, but she didn't say anything for a moment. And then, 'Whatever makes you ask that? Do I look like a fucking dyke, or something?' she asked. She looked angry. 'Oh, come on, Eileen,' I said. 'Don't go all po-faced on me. Most girls have a little lezzie experience at some stage in their lives, even if it's only to discover that they don't like it. It's not the end of the world.'

She lit her joint, and inhaled deeply, holding the smoke down in her lungs, then releasing it, slowly. The scent of grass suddenly permeated the bedroom. 'I don't know why I'm getting so fucking uptight,' she said, through another stream of smoke. 'To answer your question, yes, I did once have a lesbian relationship.' She inhaled again. She was really taking the stuff down. 'A long one. I lived with another woman for two years. I thought at the time, since you ask, that I had discovered what sex was really all about. Fran, her name was. Short for Francine. She was a commercial artist, working in the art department of an advertising agency. She used to suck pussy like an angel.' She looked over at me with a wry smile. 'She was almost as good at it as you are.' She took another long toke. 'I guess it was the gentleness of it that got me hung up on it. I was a secretary at the agency where she worked. This would be what, four years ago now? I was four years younger, and if I say it myself, I was prettier then. The men used to chase me quite seriously in those days, and I don't mind admitting, I used to put it about a bit. But that was all that they wanted. They didn't want a relationship. They didn't even want a conversation. They just wanted a fuck. After which, mostly, they'd catch a train home to suburbia, and their wife and family.

'I was having a drink after work with Fran and some of the other girls one evening, and we were sitting around, you know, shooting the shit about men. And then, after a while, there was just Fran and me. I was feeling pretty low that evening, I remember, and she suggested that she take me home and cook for me, which sounded caring. I'd had quite a lot of wine to drink by then, and I drank more when I got to her apartment. She had a neat little studio over on the West Side. And before I knew what was happening, really, she had my panties down, and she was doing things to me that I'd never had done to me before. Not so gently, nor so lovingly, nor so caringly, anyway.

'I guess she just plain seduced me. And I loved every minute of it. A few weeks later I moved in there with her, and I stayed for two years. It was crowded, but we liked to be close. You asked me if I'd ever had any kind of lesbian sex. Honey, I've had *every* kind of lesbian sex. You name it . . . I've probably had more dildoes up my pussy than you've had hot dinners, as you British like to say. Fran used to play my cooze with her fingers like musicians play the harp. I used to come just looking at her. Because she *cared*, you see. She *loved* me. She'd suck me until I came and came, and then I'd lie there, and she'd just play with me, with her fingers, and I'd come and come again. And then she'd sometimes strap on a big dildo, and fuck me with it. And of course, after a while, she got me doing all these things to her. I enjoyed that too. She was such a pretty, feminine looking little thing, and actually she was the biggest dyke in creation. She loved seducing young girls. And, just like me, they all loved it.'

'What happened, then?' I asked. 'Did you change your mind, or what?' 'She simply found another girl, eventually,' said Eileen, genuinely rather sadly, I thought. 'A girl younger than me. And she asked me to leave. And I just went back to men. I thought about other girls, and I went to one or two of the better lesbian clubs, to see what I thought of the women there. But it was only Fran that appealed to me. I've met women since that I like, but no one that I've wanted to have a sexual relationship with. I think that was a one-off. If she hadn't thrown me out, I think I'd still be there. But there's no going back.' She stubbed out what had become the end of her joint, and smiled at me again. Rather more happily this time.

'So come and fuck me, lover,' she said. 'I'm ready for you now.' She lay back on the bed and opened her legs, fingering herself lasciviously, spreading her fleshy labia wide and thrusting two fingers down into her wetly recipient pussy. 'Ooooh,' she said. 'That feels good to me. Come and see how it feels to you, baby.' Her references to her lesbian interlude had my cock rigid again, and I put down my now empty scotch glass and walked across to the bed. She held her arms out, open for me, and I climbed across her, kneeling down, my knees outside her thighs, as I eased into her. She was gloriously wet, and gloriously tight. 'Wow, baby,' she said. 'At last. Here you are. I just love your cock fucking me.' 'Talk dirty to me, Eileen, sweetheart,' I said. 'Tell me all about you and Fran doing unspeakable things to each other. Tell me naughty things about you both.'

'Does that turn you on, baby?' she asked. 'Sure I will. I remember that first long, hot summer. Fran's little studio wasn't air-conditioned, and we'd both sleep naked on the sheets of her double bed at night, our windows open, hoping for a little breeze, and she'd play with my pussy all night. She'd frig me until I was sore, and then she'd say, "Suck me, Eileen. Lick my pussy with your soft, wet tongue." And she'd spread her legs, and hold her pussy lips apart, and I'd get my head down between her legs, and at first I'd just kiss her.

'I loved the taste of her, the smell of her, the feel of her soft lips under my mouth. And down below her pussy I could see her tiny, puckered little asshole, and I'd kiss that, and she'd wriggle, and she'd say, "No, darling. Not there. That's so naughty." And I'd kiss her down there harder, and I'd force my tongue inside her, and she'd reach down and press my head hard up against herself, and all the time she'd be saying "No, baby. No, darling. Not there." And she'd be wriggling, and then she'd stop saying no, and I'd start to finger-fuck her there, and she'd reach down and start to masturbate herself while I finger-fucked her asshole. She loved it really. She just didn't like to admit it. And then, after a while, she'd ask me to go and get a dildo, and fuck her asshole with that, and when she came she'd scream out with pleasure.' Eileen stopped for a moment, pressing her hips up against me, beginning to feel the start of her orgasm.

'Don't stop,' I said. 'Please don't stop. I'm going to come soon, thinking about you two lying on a bed together, playing with each other's pussies.' 'Sometimes,' said Eileen, 'she had to go away with a team from the agency, to make a presentation to some client, or to some prospective client, and occasionally she'd stay away for the night. And I'd be so lonely. I'd go to the laundry basket, and I'd find a pair of her worn panties, and I'd take them to bed with me, and I'd press the crotch of them into my nose whilst I masturbated, smelling the scent of her pussy on her pantie crotch, and I'd go to sleep with them pressed like that to my face. I never told her about that.

'Another time, I persuaded her to let me shave her. You know, shave off all the hair around her pussy. I found that fantastically sexy. Not so much the actual shaving, but the end result. I loved to kiss and suck all that lovely soft, smooth skin, leading up to those lovely pussy lips. And I'd rub all sorts of oils and unguents into her pudenda. I'd spend hours just stroking her and licking her down there. And, of course, I shaved the hair off from around her tight little asshole too, and I'd rub oil in there, and then my finger would slip, and my oily finger would finger-fuck her until she was pleading with me to go and get a dildo, and do the job properly. And I'd make her say, "please, Eileen. Please, my darling." I'd do anything for her if she said "Please," nicely.' I could feel my ejaculation gathering, threatening to burst my balls, as I fed my sexual fantasies on Eileen's descriptions of her lesbian affair. I began to move faster, fuck harder, feeling her tight pussy squeezing my rod, and as she felt me gathering for my approaching release, she started to move and thrust up against me, fuelling her own impending culmination. 'Oh, yes, baby,' she said. 'That's real fucking. That's no dildo. That's good, hard cock fucking my cunt.'

I rode her as hard as I could, and then, all at once, I came, jetting my sperm into her, hot spurts of come pulsing into her cunt. And then she was coming with me, shouting and writhing, celebrating her orgasm both physically and vocally, until we both were spent. She reached out as I slid off her, and put an arm about my shoulders. She looked at me and smiled. Tears were running down her cheeks. 'Thank you, baby,' she said. 'Thank you so much.' I put my arm around her, and gave her a big squeeze, and a big kiss. 'Thank *you*, darling,' I said. 'That was very beautiful.' We both fell asleep almost immediately. Not surprisingly, I suppose. When I awoke the next morning it was seven, and the summer sun was streaming through the bedroom windows. Eileen was still fast asleep.

I looked at her naked body at rest. She was in excellent condition, more due, at her age I suspect, to a great deal of dedicated hard work at some gymnasium, than to nature itself. I put on a robe, and found one for her amongst Fred's things, leaving it on a chair beside the bed for when she woke, and I went through to the kitchen, where I squeezed orange juice with Fred's electric juicer, and put on some coffee. I heard the *New York Times* hit the floor outside the apartment door with a thud just after eight, and opened the door to collect it. I was discovering what was happening in the rest of the world, when Eileen came through into the kitchen. She was wearing Fred's gown, which looked much better on her than it did on him, size apart, and she had obviously done things to her hair and face.

She looked years younger than I remembered her.

'Hi, honey,' I said. 'Juice? Cereal? Toast? Eggs any style? Coffee? Tea? What would you like? There's most things, apart from decent sausages. Even Zabar's don't seem to be able to manage those.' Zabar's, at 2245 Broadway, is, in the opinion of most New Yorkers that I know – and most certainly in mine – the best delicatessen in New York. Or anywhere else in the world, for that matter.

Since they're American, it seems perfectly reasonable to me that they cater for American tastes which, again perfectly reasonably, are different from British tastes in various areas. It is a fact that Americans do not like the kind of sausages that we British like. Nor do they like British-style bacon, preferring what most of us would regard as rather poor quality streaky bacon, cooked to a crisp. For the same understandable reasons, it is not possible to buy kippers in New York. Nor potted shrimps. And there again, of course, in the matter of language, there are similar differences. The plural of 'shrimp' in America is 'shrimp'. But then it is not easy to find in London properly made bagels, lox, and good quality cream cheese, a staple New York diet at Sunday brunch, eaten accompanied by Bloody Marys, or Mimosas (vodka, champagne and orange juice) by the jugful. It's possible, but it's not easy, and even more rare to find all three together. But wouldn't life be dull if we were all the same?

Eileen settled for juice, coffee, toast and jelly. You will know that in the States, 'jelly' means jam. In this instance, cherry jelly. I poured juice and coffee, put sliced bread in the toaster, found butter and jelly, and passed her the milk and sugar, neither of which she took. 'So what news of Fred?' she asked. 'Absolutely none it all, as far as I'm concerned,' I said. 'I haven't heard a word, either from him or from Wally. I thought *you* might have heard something.' 'No,' she said. 'Like you. Nothing. It's a bit of a worry, really.' She spread butter, then jelly, on her toast. 'I wondered if perhaps you'd telephoned him at home in England? I mean, you've got his home number, haven't you?' 'Yes, sure,' I replied. 'But I tend only to use it in real emergencies, and there haven't been any yet, touch wood. I always take the view, with Fred, that no news is good news. I reckon that if there were any serious problems, we'd have heard by now. Don't you think?'

She crunched toast, and was silent for a moment. 'Well, up to recently, I'd agree with you. But do you know just how far Fred is into cocaine these days?' she asked. I shook my head. 'He was taking a couple of grams a night. That's a hell of a lot, even if you're spreading it about amongst your friends. And at two hundred dollars a gram, it's a lot of money to sniff up your nose every evening. We all like a snort. At least I do. Provided that someone else is paying for it' She looked at me, quizzically. 'Oh, sure. Me, too,' I said. 'Count me in.' 'But Fred was addicted,' she went on. 'He was also getting very paranoid. They say cocaine is not addictive, but it is. It may not be physically addictive, but it's psychologically addictive. You get to the state, eventually, where you can't do without a snort to recapture that lovely warm feeling of confidence. To bolster your ego. Make you feel that every word you utter is meaningful. Fred's been in that state for a long time now. And he just doesn't need the coke, he needs the booze as well. In my opinion, he's not far off a basket case. I don't believe he's capable, any longer, of doing what he's paid to do. And someone – I don't know who – but someone in the office is telling Wally exactly what is going on.'

'I think you're right,' I said, remembering my conversations with Wally before I came out. 'Have you any idea who it might be?' She shook her head. 'Not really,' she said. 'Except to say that I'm sure it isn't anyone in either the editorial or the art departments. They all love him. There isn't anyone there who would do such a thing.' She looked at me, carefully. 'I can trust you, Tone,' she said. 'Can't I? Forgive me for asking, and you know I love you. But in a quite different way, I love Fred too.' I patted her arm. 'Of course you can, sweetheart,' I said. 'I count myself amongst Fred's few real friends. I wouldn't cause him any harm for any reason in the world. I love him too, in my own way. You know I do. Think how long I've fended you off, simply out of loyalty to Fred.' She had the grace to grin back at me. 'Yes, of course. I wasn't thinking. Forgive me. But to get back to the point, while I can't prove it, I think it's one of the consultant companies. You know, either the legal advisers, or the tax consultants. I don't think it's anyone actually inside our offices. And it certainly isn't anyone from the distributors. But it's someone with a fairly high degree of access to confidential information. Which points to the lawyers, or the accountants, really.' I hadn't met anyone from either company. They tended to deal with Wally directly, either over the telephone, or else they'd fly over to London, if they needed to. Or if Wally wanted them there.

'You must have *some* idea, Eileen,' I said. 'For example, we haven't got any seriously legally qualified people in the office, but we've got accountants. They're technically answerable to Fred, but I doubt they get much change out of him, knowing what he thinks of accountants. And if they've had questions to which they couldn't get answers, then they'd go to Wally's accountancy firm here, and if they didn't know the answer, or didn't want to take the decision, they'd go directly to Wally. It makes sense really, doesn't it?'

'Tell me about it,' she said. 'Of course it makes sense. And I've been trying to warn Fred for months. But he simply won't listen. "So let them go to Wally," he'd say. "I'm doing my job. I've got this fucking magazine off the ground, and I've made it profitable. Sales and profits are going up monthly. What more does anyone want?" He's just plain and simple opted out. He prefers drinking, and fucking, and snorting. And who doesn't? I'm not criticizing him for his choice of pastimes. I'm simply saying that he should spend at least some time in the office. Talk to the staff. Talk to the suppliers. Talk to the advertisers. And, most important of all, talk to Wally. Don't you agree?' 'Well, yes, of course I do,' I answered. 'But if he won't listen to you, why should he listen to me? I tried to talk to him a couple of times, when I first arrived, but he simply didn't want to know. He reckoned that since the magazine was making a healthy profit, he didn't need to do anything else. He took the view that he'd started it up, got it off the ground, found the people to keep on running the various component parts of it, on a daily basis, and that was that. He thought that for Wally to expect him to be in the office every day was ridiculous.' Eileen sighed, deeply. 'May I have some more coffee, please?' she asked, passing me her cup.

I looked at the pot. It was a pretty dismal sight. And cold, too. 'Let me make some more,' I said. 'It won't take a moment.' I got up and went through the necessary motions. When I sat down again, Eileen said, 'I suppose one of the problems is that he's making too much money.' 'I suppose that could be the case,' I replied. 'But I've no idea, actually, what his salary is.' 'It's not his salary that is the problem,' she said. It's the ten per cent that he gets, worldwide, from all *Tiptop* publications, anywhere and everywhere in the world.' I whistled. I hadn't the slightest notion of what that figure might amount to, other than that it had to be a great deal of money.

'Put it this way,' said Eileen. 'I've never seen him pay less than thirty thousand dollars a month into his bank account here. Whether that's gross or net I've no idea. Either way, it ain't a pittance.' She was damn' right. This was back in 1976 remember. $360,000 a year is a lot of money now. Think of how much it was twenty years ago. 'Phew,' I said. 'I think maybe I'll commit suicide.' 'That, of course, is just for starters,' said Eileen. 'I'm not saying he's not worth it. I'm just trying to put his income into perspective, in relation to his booze and drug problems. After earning as much a month – even if it *is* gross – as most people earn in a year, then he lives in this splendid apartment at the company's expense.

'They pay his rent, and all his outgoings – down to that newspaper you're reading. Gas. Electricity. Service charge. Christmas gratuities to the apartment block staff. His cleaner. You name it, *Tiptop* pays for it. On top of which, he can spend a thousand dollars a week on entertaining without having to supply any details. Over that, he has to ask Wally to approve it before he spends it. So, terrific. He's worth every cent of it. *When* he's working. All of which adds up to the fact that he actually lives for free. I'm sure he doesn't, but if he really wanted to, he could put his salary into his savings account every month. I don't believe, in fact, that he's got a savings account. He snorts it all. Or most of it.'

What a horrifying story, I thought. It was actually worse than I had envisaged. Accepting that we can always live other people's lives for them better than they can themselves, I mean, really! He was earning a prince's ransom, by anybody's standards. But then, Fred was Fred. He always had been, and he always would be. He had certain unique abilities, which I've detailed before, earlier on. And he had certain disadvantages. You couldn't have one, it would seem, without the other. But it did seem, from what Eileen was saying, that suddenly – or not so suddenly, actually, thinking about it – things had gone a bit too far. Even for Fred. He'd had trouble with booze in the past. He was one of the world's over-indulgers. He simply couldn't ever say no. But cocaine was a rather more serious problem, I suspected, without knowing too much about it. I'd heard all the same stories that you have, I expect. People having the cartilage in their noses rebuilt surgically, having destroyed the original with cocaine, that sort of thing.

But far more serious, really (assuming you could afford the nose surgery, which patently Fred could) was the paranoia. Even in my short time with him before he took off, unannounced (as far as I was concerned) for London, he was under the illusion that Wally was persecuting him. What was to be done? As far as I could see, there wasn't anything that I *could* do. At least, certainly not until he returned to the United States. At which time I would be due to return to England.

'I don't know, Eileen love,' I said. 'It's difficult to know what to do for the best. As far as I can see, it's simply a matter of waiting until Fred asks for help. Or of waiting until he comes back here. Or both. I don't want to speak to Wally, and ask him what's going on. I don't believe that's my business, for a start. And even if I did ask him, there's no guarantee that he'd tell me. Wally's quite a private person about his relationship with Fred. Did you know that they had a sort of father/son relationship?' Eileen looked genuinely surprised. 'Good grief, no I didn't,' she said. 'It's quite easily explained,' I said. 'Wally's never been married. No, no, he's not gay,' I said, seeing her expression. 'Lots of women. He just hasn't married any of them. So he's never had any children. And it's always been my theory that he sees Fred as the son he's never had. It's much more than a business relationship. He really worships Fred. Which is why I don't want to ask him what's going on. So, in the circumstances, I guess it's simply wait and see.' Eileen pondered, for a while, then, albeit rather slowly, said 'I guess so. Poor Fred.'

She looked at her watch. 'Jesus,' she said. 'Look at the time. I'd best get myself together and shower and take a cab down to the office. Are you coming in first thing today? If so, it would probably be prudent to take different cabs. You never know who's watching.' She bent down and kissed the top of my head. 'Last night was something else. I loved every minute of it. I do hope you haven't got any regrets.' She looked at me, suddenly all nervous about my reply. 'Not for a single moment, my darling,' I said. 'Not a one.' I got up and gave her a big, passionate kiss. I was tempted, just for a moment, to say the hell with the office, and take her back to bed again, but common sense triumphed. Sadly. When we had both run out of breath, I stopped kissing her, and held her at arms length. 'I tell you what we'll do, sweetie,' I said. 'We've got two bathrooms here, so we can both be ready at about the same time. Like in fifteen minutes. OK?' 'OK,' she agreed. 'And then we can take the same cab downtown, but I'll get him to drop me off a couple of blocks away from the office, and I'll walk the last bit. That way, you'll be installed by the time I get there. How about that?' 'Terrific,' she said, and took herself off.

Half an hour later I gave Eileen the cab fare, and got the driver to drop me off on Park and 50th Street, and I started to walk slowly East along 50th to Third. It was hot as hell, even at a quarter to ten in the morning, and New York's traffic was at its noisiest. I took my time, window shopping, and looking at the people. New York is one of the best cities in the world for both those occupations, and I was looking half over my shoulder, admiring the rear view of an attractive, leggy girl in an extremely short skirt, when I bumped into someone – literally – coming the other way. I began to apologize, as did the pretty girl whom I saw was my protagonist.

My mouth literally dropped open as she smiled at me and said 'Tony! What on earth are you doing here?' I grinned back at her. 'I might just as well ask you the same question, June,' I said. She looked at her watch. 'How are you off for time?' she asked. 'I'm not in a hurry. Have you time for a coffee?' 'Of course I have,' I said. 'What a lovely surprise.' We walked down Third Avenue until we came to a coffee shop, where we made ourselves comfortable, and brought ourselves up to date with each other over numerous cups of excellent, frothy cappuccino.

I'd known June for some years. She had been a secretary in an agency that I used to use to type up manuscripts before I had a PC and did them myself as I went along. The last I'd heard, she'd gone off to America on holiday, and I hadn't heard of her since. That must have been about five years ago. She put me right. It was actually seven. She had, as I thought, come over to New York for two weeks' holiday. She'd come with a girlfriend, and they'd had a ball doing all the things that tourists do in the Big Apple. They'd done the Empire State Building, the Guggenheim Museum, the Statue of Liberty, Wall Street, the Bronx Zoo. They'd even been out to Shea Stadium for a baseball match. And they'd loved every minute of it. They had obviously been approached by a variety of men on their holiday, and June had fallen heavily for an attractive young attorney that she'd met in Maxwell's Plum.

To cut a long story short, the attorney had followed her back to London shortly after her holiday, and they had ended up getting married. She had apparently lived the life of Riley in Manhattan. In those days, girls marrying American citizens automatically got residency and work permits known as Green Cards and that was at the time when it was thought to be prestigious in New York, if you were American, to have an English secretary. She quickly found herself a job with a large advertising agency, working for the creative director, while her attorney husband earned good money with one of Manhattan's top law firms. They lived in considerable luxury in a brand new co-op on the Upper East Side.

Things had gone well for four years, but then her husband had left her for a younger, American girl. Being essentially an Englishwoman in a foreign country, and with a husband who was an attorney, she apparently got the rough end of the divorce settlement, financially, and she soon reached a situation where she was no longer able to maintain the lifestyle to which she had become so happily accustomed. Even a good secretary's salary couldn't support the way she was used to living. She then faced a difficult decision. She either had to find herself a much better job – for which she was the first to admit she had very little in the way of qualifications – or quit, sell up, and go back to England. 'So what did you do?' I asked, curiously. Obviously whatever she had done had worked out, since she was still here. She looked at me long and hard. 'Let me come back to that in a minute,' she said. 'You haven't told me yet what you are doing over here.' I told her about joining *Tiptop* in London, and then coming out here to enable Fred to take a well earned rest. I didn't go into any details about his booze and drug problems. I didn't know June that well.

'So you're still writing about sex, she said, smiling. 'I remember all those steaming manuscripts in London. I used to get soggy knickers typing them. They really were very sexy,' she finished. 'Well, thank you,' I said. 'I shall take that as a compliment.' 'Oh, it most certainly is,' she said. 'I used to have to make photocopies for all the other girls. They used to take them home with them, and I expect they did exactly the same when they got home as I did.' 'And what might that have been?' I asked, knowing perfectly well what the answer was.

'You know exactly what I'm talking about,' she said, grinning at me. 'We used to read them and play with ourselves. We girls didn't have good sex lives, back in those days.' 'And now?' I asked. 'Is your sex life busier here in New York.' 'You have no idea,' she said. 'So let me tell you. But this is between you and me. OK? You and me and about three hundred other people.' She laughed. 'But it's not for general discussion. Right?' 'Of course,' I said. 'Your secret is still a secret with me.' 'I work in a brothel,' she said, and stopped, looking at me to see what my reaction might be. I was, I admit, somewhat surprised, but I tried not to show it. 'Terrific,' I said. 'It's got to be better than working in a secretarial agency. 'In fact,' she went on, 'I don't just work there. I own it.' I laughed out loud. 'Absolutely *fantastic*,' I said, and I meant it. 'Oh,' she said, 'I'm so pleased that you're amused. I thought that you might be shocked.' 'Good God,' I said, 'why should I be shocked?' 'Well, it *is* breaking the law,' she said. I honestly hadn't thought of that. It was, of course. 'Well, it's a bloody silly law, is all I can say,' I said. 'Do you have problems? I mean, you know, the police, things like that?'

'No not really,' she said. 'It's a very small, very exclusive brothel. I run it from my apartment in a very large apartment block down on Roosevelt Driveway, on 34th Street. I only have six girls working for me, so that my customers, spread out over the day, or the evening, don't stand out. If anyone noticed anything like my neighbours, for example – they probably think I give a lot of parties. I make sure that I *do* give parties, to which I invite them. So they don't worry about the ones they think they don't get invited to. I just pay off the doormen every week. It's as simple as that, really. You must come and see it.

I'd like that. You don't have to use the services, of course. But come and have a drink, and meet the girls.' She grinned at me, and reached over and squeezed my arm. 'They'd probably fight over you to give you a freebie,' she said, laughing. 'But you don't have to give me an answer now.' She dug around in her handbag. 'Here's my card,' she said. 'There's no need to call, or make an appointment, or anything like that. Just arrive, if that's what you'd like to do. Any time after eleven in the morning, and up to three, four the next morning. Drinks are on the house. And may I have your telephone number? Where are you staying while you're here?'

I gave her Fred's number, and the address of his apartment. 'Oh,' she said. 'How the other half live, eh? Hey, you can invite me up there sometime. I'd love to see it. I've got some friends who live on Sutton Place. That's pretty swanky. But I've never been in an apartment on Park Avenue.' 'Come any time you like, June,' I said. 'Just call to make sure I'm there. Or call me at the office and arrange a time with me. You'd be surprised how many people have said to me that they've never been in an apartment on Park Avenue.' 'No, I wouldn't,' she said. 'I guess about ninety-five per cent of the inhabitants of New York have never been in an apartment on Park Avenue. Have you any idea of the rents up there? Do you know the real estate prices for Park Avenue?' I thought that I wouldn't tell her that *Tiptop* was paying twice the going rate for Fred's apartment. It might upset her. But I was determined to visit her at her place of work. It had to be fun. And for someone in my business, you'd be surprised how few brothels I've been in.

I've sampled girls from the old Madam Claude's, in Paris, but I never actually visited the premises. She'd send them anywhere in the world, first class, if you could afford it. I've been to one in Jamaica. That's about it, I guess. Oh, sure, I've been to a hundred places where you can come to an arrangement with the management, and take the girls home with you. Nightclubs. Cabarets. Call them what you will. Remember Annabel? But actually going to a real brothel, of that I didn't have too much experience. June gathered her bits and pieces together, I paid the check, and we went our respective ways.

Back at the office, I looked in on Eileen on the way to my office. She raised a quizzical eyebrow. 'Traffic heavy?' she asked. 'Very funny,' I said. 'No, actually. I ran into an old friend. Someone from London that I used to know who lives out here.' 'Oh, great,' said Eileen. Then, 'All is quiet, generally speaking. Someone called Dee Dee keeps calling you. I said I didn't know when you'd be in. Dave from the art department wants to see you. I've put your mail on your desk. That's about it. I'll bring some coffee through in a minute.' I thanked her, and went along to my office. The air-conditioning felt as if it were running at about minus forty degrees. I turned it up a bit. I rang through to Dave, and said I was free if he was. He said he'd be right along. He and the coffee arrived together. Eileen poured for us both.

'I had a look at your friend Dee Dee,' he said. 'Terrific. Absolutely terrific. I told her we'd set up some test shots. But I was wondering. You remember your other friend? What was her name? Lucy. That's it. The bald black girl who kept wanting to show me her shaved pubes.' He grinned at me. 'I thought that was probably more up your street than mine. I'm more into enemas than shaved pubes.' I laughed with him. 'But there you go. I thought, what about getting them to do a lezzie set for the test? I just like the idea of the contrast. I mean, you couldn't get two more different chicks if you tried. Black and white. Bald and blonde. Beauty and the beast.' I looked at him, a questioning look on my face. 'Oh, you choose,' he said. 'I guess the black girl's got to be the beast. It's probably what she was born for. But I don't believe the blonde's all that innocent. But what the hell. What do you think? Do you think either of them would object? I think Lucy'd be photographed being shafted by a horse, as long as she was getting paid the going rate. But I'm not so sure about the blonde.' 'You can only ask her,' I said. 'Call her, and see what she says. You've got her number.'

'That aside, think of the way they'd look,' said Dave, 'with the black girl in sexy white, transparent lingerie, and the white girl ditto in black. Imagine a close-up shot of the black girl's shaved cunt – no doubt she's got great, big, fleshy, purply-brown cunt lips?' he asked. 'No doubt,' I replied, laughing at him this time. 'Just think of the white girl's face, with her sweet little luscious red lips over that lovely, big, juicy cunt, with her pale face and her blonde hair, looking as if she's just going to begin sucking it,' he said. 'Probably with the black girl's hands on top of her head, looking as if she was forcing the other girl's face down. I guarantee we'd have a sell-out issue.' 'Sounds good to me, Dave,' I said.

'Shall I set it up?' he asked. 'I thought of doing it in an apartment, if I can find a suitable one. Something more luxurious than we can reasonably build as a set down in Canal Street.' 'Please go ahead,' I told him. 'What would you think of Fred's apartment? Might that be suitable?' 'Oh, fabulous,' he said. 'Fred's always suggested that we use it for a shoot, but the problem has been, when you actually get down to it, that he's always there, usually still asleep, at the time of day we'd want to start shooting. Like in the morning. That, or he's got some girl there who he's shagging, and he doesn't want to be disturbed. But yes, while he's away. Fantastic. Why don't I tell the girls that it's a test shoot? Then if it doesn't come out well, we won't have to pay them. Not much, anyway. If it works, we'll pay them the full going rate, and use the pix. OK?' 'Great,' I said. 'Thank you. Can I be there? At the shoot, I mean?' 'Naturally' he said. 'What else? So, that's all I wanted to discuss. Many thanks.' He turned to leave, and then looked back. 'It's pretty warm in here, Tony,' he said. 'You can turn the air-conditioning to much cooler than this, you know.' 'Thanks, Dave,' I said.

I picked up the 'phone and called Dee Dee. She answered immediately. 'Hi,' I said. 'It's Tony. How are you, sweetheart?'

'Hey, Tony, darling,' she said. 'I'm good. I wanted to thank you. I saw Dave, your art director, and he liked me, I think. He's obviously gay, like you said, but he likes women too. He was sweet, and he's going to set up a test shoot. Isn't that exciting? And it's all because of you. Thank you, darling, thank you.' 'Actually,' I said, it's all down to a chap called Bill Carlson, whom you've seen, but you probably don't remember. But never mind.' 'Huh?' she said. 'It's not important,' I said. 'I'll explain it to you when I see you. Right now, tell me how you would feel about doing a lesbian test shoot with another girl? Do you have any hang-ups about that?'

'You do mean pretend lesbian, don't you?' she asked. 'I mean, it's not for real?' 'Well, no, of course it's not for real,' I told her. 'But you'll probably have to get fairly close to her, like with the odd kiss. That sort of thing. Pursing your lips together over her pussy, as if you were going to kiss it, and lick it. And vice versa, of course. And touching tongues is always big in those kind of sets. But nothing serious.'

'Hmmm,' she said. 'I guess that's OK. I've got nothing against girls, obviously, except that I'm not a dyke. And I don't want anyone to think that I am.' 'Don't worry about it, sweetheart,' I told her. 'It's all male fantasy stuff. And remember, around about twelve million readers will see your beautiful body, if the test works out. Some of them are editors and art directors and movie producers and theatrical agents and whatever. And they're always looking for new talent. You could be lucky. Even if it's simply more modelling work, that's what you're looking for. Isn't it?' 'Oh God, that's for sure,' she said.

It was true, actually. *Tiptop* was selling over four million copies a month. We reckoned that at least three people read each copy, at a fairly conservative estimate. Which equals twelve million readers. Research showed that a proportion of those were professionals of one sort or another, who were looking for new, pretty faces and bodies. It had happened to girls in *Playboy* and *Penthouse*. Why not *Tiptop*? 'In any case, Dee Dee,' I said, 'I shall be there. If there's anything that you don't like, you only have to say so. Oh, yes, there's one other thing. Dave will call you and ask you exactly what I've just been asking you. Don't tell him we've spoken about it already. It's his prerogative. I just wanted you to have time to think about it, rather than have it hit you out of the blue. OK?' 'Of course it's OK, darling,' she replied. 'You are a sweetheart. When am I going to see you again? I did so enjoy the other evening. When can we do it again? Please?' 'Soon, darling. I promise. Not today, if you'll forgive me. I'll be in touch. I said I'd set up the photographic shoot, and I have. I'm saying I'll be in touch, and I will. All right, sweetie?' 'Yes, of course,' she said. 'Forgive me. I don't mean to be a nuisance.' 'You're not,' I said. 'Bye for now.' 'Bye, darling,' she said.

I had thought, during our brief conversation, of telling her that Lucy was the other half of the soon-to-be-formed lesbian photographic couple, but then I thought that it was probably better to let Dave tell her about that. The thought of a six-foot-tall, bald, black girl with a shaven pussy might have been all too much. What turned me on just might appeal to Dee Dee. I laughed to myself. Whatever else anyone might think about Lucy, beautiful she was. Then I thought of Eileen's lesbian confessions of the previous night, and laughed again. She hated Lucy already. I felt that there was no point in telling her that Lucy was possibly going to feature in a lesbian girl set in *Tiptop*. She'd find that out soon enough herself.

I picked up the phone again, and told Lucy of the developments about the photographic session. She was as enthusiastic as I thought she would be. When we'd finished talking about the forthcoming shoot. and I'd told her that Dave would be in touch, probably later on in the day, she said 'Hey, baby, thank you. Come on downtown and I'll give you a thank-you fuck. I'm playing with my cooze right now, thinking about your lovely cock. It's getting all wet. Come and plug my hole, baby. Pussy needs you. Now. C'mon. How about it? It's not an offer I make to too many people, you know.' 'Baby, thank you. I much appreciate the offer. I really do. If I wasn't working, I'd be down there in seconds. I'll take a rain check, if I may. Keep it hot for me, honey. Save it for me. I'll be there. I promise.'

She was too much, that girl. I rang through to Eileen, and asked her for more coffee. When she brought it, she brought a cup for herself. 'OK if I join you?' she asked. 'Of course, sweet-heart,' I said. 'I could do with a break. Tell me something nice.' 'Nice,' she said, musingly. 'Nice. It's a strange word. It means all sorts of different things to different people. For me, for example, it would be nice if I had a steady guy. Someone who loved me.' I must have looked guilty, because she said, quickly, 'No, don't misunderstand me, Tony. I don't mean you. The fact that I've got hot panties for you, and that you like to fuck me – or at least, I think you do – doesn't mean that I've got illusions of grandeur about our relationship.

'However long you're out here – and the longer the better as far as I'm concerned – the fact remains that you'll be going home eventually. If you were staying out here permanently, well, things could be very different. But the word "nice" is epitomized, for me, by the thought of a steady, loving, ongoing relationship with some decent person.' She smiled at me. 'Yes, yes,' she said. 'I know you're basically decent. But you're not desperately, inconsolably, exclusively in love with me, now are you?' I had to admit that I wasn't. 'Or – as far as I can see – with anybody,' she said. 'Be that as it may. Now, "nice" for you probably means that you meet some pretty young girl, and you think to yourself, wouldn't it be nice if this young girl dropped her panties for me. Sorry, knickers, as you insist on calling them. And then you charm her knickers off her, fuck her in every orifice, and fuck off. You see what I mean? Now then, shall we start again? What would you like me to say that would be nice.'

'Put like that, sweetheart, I'm not sure,' I said. 'It wasn't actually a very serious suggestion. I just felt like a little light relief. But, since you ask, let me think for a moment. Nice.

What would be nice? It would be nice if no one ever fell in love with me ever again. It would be nice if women simply saw me as a reasonable, short-term fuck, rather than as a long-term, loving relationship. It would be nice if I never, ever was responsible in any way for anyone's continuing happiness ever again. It would be nice if I actually knew what to do about Annabel, who will soon be out here, probably in a few days' time. I am as near in love with her as I have ever been with anyone. But that's easy to say. I've felt exactly the same way about a number of other girls, recently. But something has always happened to change that. Perhaps I fall in love too easily? Perhaps I should never fall in love at all. I don't particularly want to get married. Why should I? I get more, better, prettier fucks than anyone else I know. How could I ever be faithful to one woman? For the rest of my life? I really like Annabel. I believe that I love her. But since I've been out here for – what is it? three weeks? four weeks? – I've fucked Pauline, I've fucked Dee Dee, I've fucked Lucy, I've fucked you. I've seriously thought about fucking Lisa. I'm not even particularly looking for it, apart from that first time, when I went to Daly's Dandelion. And I'm sitting here, trying to tell you that I'm in love with Annabel. I mean, what's the matter with me?'

Eileen got up, collected the dirty coffee cups, kissed me on the top of my head, and said 'The matter with you is that you've got a large cock, and you know how to use it. And you enjoy using it. Any woman who has spent more than ten minutes in your company knows that. And who the fuck is Lisa?' She didn't wait for an answer, but stalked out of the room, her head held high, slamming the door behind her. Oh, fuck, I thought. I really don't need this. I need something to cheer me up. And then I remembered June, and her brothel. That sounded like something that could cheer a chap up. I found her card in my wallet, and dialled the number.

A sweet little mid-Western voice answered the 'phone, simply with the number. 'Hi,' I said. 'My name's Tony

Andrews. Is June there, please?' 'Hold the line a moment, honey,' said the voice, redolent of fields of sun-ripened corn, hoe-downs, surreys with the fringe on top, short, fringed, pleated skirts, cowboy boots on cowgirls, and every other fantasy you've ever had about the State of Oklahoma. June came on the line. 'Hi,' she said. 'That was quick. What can I do for you?'

'You can cheer me up, darling, I said. 'I'm depressed. I need a little R & R.' 'You've chosen the right place, sweetheart,' she said. 'You know the address. Come on down. We'll all be waiting for you.' I didn't say goodnight to anyone in the office. I just left. Enough was enough. Fifteen minutes later, the cab dropped me off on Roosevelt Driveway at 34th Street. The block, as June had said, was large. Its atrium was impressive, and when I asked one of the three doormen for June's apartment, I watched carefully to see if he revealed the fact that he knew what went on up there. There wasn't a flicker of anything. 'I'll just call up and see if you're expected, sir,' he said. He spoke into the telephone, and then put it down. 'It's the nineteenth floor, sir,' he said. 'Take that elevator over there. You are expected.'

CHAPTER FIVE
ON THE GAME

I couldn't believe June's idea of a small apartment. It took up the entire nineteenth floor of the apartment block. It must have been a little early for the regular customers, or business was bad, I wasn't sure which, but I was the only man there. June welcomed me at the door, and took me through a short passageway into an enormous lounge, with floor-to-ceiling windows, and enormous, softly upholstered sofas everywhere. There was a large bar in one corner. She poured me a scotch and water, no ice, and then introduced me to her six girls. They were gorgeous.

First I met Charlene. She of the voice on the telephone. She was about five eight, blonde, and with a short, curly bob that framed her pretty, young face. She was wearing a black, virtually transparent chemise, that almost covered her snatch, but not quite. She wasn't wearing anything else, unless you count a black ribbon around her neck, and a jet bracelet. I could see her blonde pubic hair, which was luxuriant and bushy. Her breasts were full, and threatened to fall over the low-cut top of the chemise. Her nails were long, and painted a bright pink. She said 'Hi,' and kissed my cheek with the most matronly of kisses.

The next was Andrea. She was tanned, and black-haired, about five six, with her hair in a loosely-tied ponytail. She was wearing a tiny, cut-off tee-shirt top, and satin hot pants. The tee-shirt didn't hide full, firm breasts, with dark, erect nipples showing through the taut, white material. The hot pants were cut so tight, I wondered if she could actually sit down in them. Her legs were long and slim, and bare of tights or stockings, but she wore four-inch high heels in black patent leather. 'Hi, Tony,' she said, and gave me my second matronly kiss of the day.

Victoria was next. She was beautiful, with genuinely auburn hair, and the pale, white skin that so often accompanies it. It was dressed in a coif around her head, upon which she was wearing a black velvet headband. She was dressed in a black, satin miniskirt, and a black, lacy, see-through blouse. I could see her small breasts plainly, the nipples, as with Andrea, startlingly erect. I realized then that it was probably the air-conditioning which was having this effect on the girls. She reached out a hand and stroked my cheek, and then kissed me, just slightly more enthusiastically than the other girls so far. 'Hi,' she breathed in my ear. 'I'd love to fuck you.' I tried not to look as startled as I felt.

After Victoria came Louise. She was pushing five ten, with dyed blonde, streaked hair cut short boyishly in the fashion of the day. She wore a transparent white bra, which certainly wasn't designed to provide any uplift (something which I could plainly see she didn't need). This she wore with matching knickers – or should I say panties? – which revealed not blonde, but light brown pubic hair, which had been carefully trimmed into an attractive heart shape. 'Hello,' she said, kissing my cheek as chastely as the first two girls had. 'Welcome.' 'Thank you,' I said. The next one stepped forward even before June had pronounced her name. 'Hi, Tony,' she said. 'I'm Gloria. She had light brown hair with just a hint of chestnut, which she wore in short plaits. She was probably about five four. Quite short. She was wearing a baby doll nightdress which revealed everything, including pert little breasts with enormous nipples which, like those of the other girls, were hugely erect. She too kissed my cheek. 'Would you like to suck them?' she whispered, as she stepped away, smiling up at me. She puckered her rosebud lips and blew me a kiss. 'Naughty,' said June, smiling too. Five down, and one to go.

That was Rita. Rita was the third blonde of the three. She had long, straight, Veronica Lake-ish hair which fell over half her face in peek-a-boo style, just as the Forties film star's did. She was quite tall, about five nine in flat heels, and she was fully dressed in a smart black summer-weight cotton suit, and a shirt-style blouse, open at her throat. She wore a thin gold chain around her neck. 'Hello, Tony,' she said, and gave me yet another matronly kiss on the cheek. 'I'm Rita.' Her perfume was noticeably stronger than those of the other girls, a heavy, intensely sexy aroma, which appealed directly to my dick. Somehow, she seemed sexier than the other five together, despite their individually appealing, sexy outfits.

It had, I think, something to do with the strong aura of sexual confidence that surrounded her. Not that I'm trying to suggest that the other girls lacked confidence. Patently they didn't. It takes a lot of confidence to walk around dressed – or undressed – as they were. No, it was more a matter of Rita's acceptance of the fact that she was the most attractive woman in the room, without appearing even to think about it. Quiet confidence. That was it. It was difficult to put an age to Rita. She might have been a year or two older than the others, but that might just have been the contrast between being fully clothed, and not. June moved towards the bar. 'Come and have a drink,' she invited. 'There's champagne on ice if you fancy it. The real stuff. Not American.' 'That would be nice,' I said. 'Thank you.' I noticed that the six girls stayed where they were, out of earshot, over at the other end of the long room. 'I obviously told the girls that you were an old friend,' she said, as she stripped the foil from the bottle of champagne.

I could see that it was not only French – Mumm – but also vintage. Terrific. There are three kinds of American champagne. New York State champagne, about which the less said, the better. Californian champagne, of which there is good, bad, and indifferent, and champagne grown in California by partnerships between American growers and French champagne houses, in which French vines, and expertise, are used, and which produces perfectly drinkable champagne, which doesn't – in my opinion – hold a candle to the original. Disappointingly.

June unwound the wire and, using a linen napkin, she held the cork and twisted the bottle with a practised ease. She saw me watching her, and smiled. 'One tends to learn tricks of the trade in this business,' she said. 'And not only sexual ones. And speaking of tricks, if you'll forgive the pun, the girls all offered – and I do mean offered – entirely of their own volition, to give you whatever you fancied. On the house. It genuinely wasn't my suggestion, I promise.' 'You mean . . .' I stopped, not sure quite how to say it. 'Yes,' said June. 'Exactly that. A free fuck. Actually, rather more than that. They all six offered, and I know for a fact that if you were to choose just one of them over the others, that would cause more friction than I could stand. So I'm here to tell you that you are a very privileged young man. You have to fuck your way through all six of them. Not all tonight, of course,' she said, noticing my worried look. 'You can obviously take as long as you like. Do it by instalments. And by the way, it's a standing offer, for the duration of your stay. Free fucks. All I ask is that you spread them around evenly. Please? And the other thing is – and I haven't discussed this with the girls – but please suggest to them that you throw dice, or spin a coin, or something like that, to decide the order of preference. OK?' 'My God,' I said. 'What a fantastic present. Thank you. And, yes, of course. We can cut a pack of cards. Would that do?'

'Perfect,' she said. 'Now let's call the girls over. But just before I do, let me say one more thing, please, Tony. I'm sure you will have found one or two of the girls more attractive to you than others. You wouldn't be normal if you didn't. And no, I'm not going to ask you your order of preference. But I can guarantee you one thing. They're all terrific in bed. Honestly. And, oh, yes. There is one other thing. You are, of course, free to refuse their offer if you wish. You know, on moral grounds. Or whatever.' I grinned at her.

'You must be joking,' I said. 'I accept, with grateful thanks. But doesn't the offer include the guv'nor?' I asked. 'You don't mean, surely, that you're going to allow mere employees to offer me their all, and not offer something yourself?' She laughed. 'Fuck off, Tony,' she said. 'Unless you want a quick one off the wrist. Although, on second thoughts, no. I don't think I'll even offer that.' She leaned over, and gave me a kiss on my cheek. It was obviously a big day for kisses on the cheek. 'Just make do with what's on offer, and consider yourself lucky,' she said. 'Oh, I do,' I said. 'I really do.'

'Girls,' she called. The small group of six turned and looked across the room towards June and me. 'Come and join us,' she requested. When the girls had gathered around us, and June had poured us all champagne in beautifully elegant, cut-crystal flutes, June said, as she opened a second bottle, 'I've told Tony of your offer. I think he wants to say, thank you, himself.' 'I'm completely overwhelmed, girls,' I said. 'It is such a generous, and delightful offer, that I don't know how to thank you properly. The experience will, of course, end up being relived in the pages of *Tiptop*, but I shall naturally alter everyone's names, and there will be no question of addresses or telephone numbers, or anything that will enable anyone to know who, or where, you are.' 'What a shame,' said Charlene. 'It could have been so good for business.' We all laughed.

'And the other thing that I wanted to say,' I continued, 'was that trying to choose any kind of order in which to accept your generosity is quite beyond me. I have never seen six such beautiful, gorgeous girls together in one place before. So I thought that the only fair way to prepare, as it were, a list of engagements' (the girls all giggled, politely) 'would be to cut a deck of cards. Ace high. OK?' 'What a good idea,' said June. 'I'll go get a pack.' She went over to a bureau, and came back with a brand new, unopened pack. Whilst she opened it, I said 'The highest card will be the first person on the list, and so on. If there are two, or three, or whatever, cards of the same value, then those people will cut again. Any questions?' No-one said anything. June had finished stripping the cellophane off the pack, and she shuffled it expertly, and put it, face down, on top of the bar.

'OK, girls,' she said. 'From the left.' That meant that Titian haired Victoria went first. She drew a jack of spades. She smiled to herself, but didn't say anything. Gloria, in her baby doll nightdress, cut a ten of hearts. Charlene, her full breasts thrusting through her see-through chemise, drew a three of diamonds. She groaned. 'Just my fucking luck,' she said. 'Charlene. *Please*,' said June. 'Well,' grumbled Charlene. 'I might have known. Will somebody please sell me a high card?' She smiled at me, and licked her lips. I felt my cock twitch. 'Hush,' said June. 'Rita, you're next.'

I held my breath. She brushed her blonde hair back from her face, cut the pack, and turned up the ace of clubs. I couldn't believe my luck. There was a consensual moan from the rest of the girls. 'It must be my lucky day,' said Rita, smiling across at me. I smiled back, and remembered not to say 'Mine, too,' which was what I was thinking. Andrea was next, in her white tee shirt and black satin hot pants. She cut a five of diamonds, and slammed the cards back down on the rest of the pack. She didn't say anything, but: she was obviously displeased. Which left Louise, her breasts rising and falling with excitement in her transparent bra. I could see the cleavage of her buttocks through her sheer white panties as she turned her back on me to try her luck. I felt an irresistible urge to put a hand out to squeeze and feel them, but I managed to resist it. She cut a ten of clubs, the same value as Gloria's ten of hearts. 'That's you and Gloria to cut again, then,' said June. 'Shall I shuffle the pack first, or leave it as it is?' 'Shuffle it,' said both girls together. We all laughed. 'You go first,' said Louise to Gloria. 'OK,' said Gloria, and cut the king of spades. 'Oooooh,' said the rest of the girls, except Louise, who groaned. She closed her eyes, and cut the queen of diamonds.

'Close,' she said, when she opened them again, and saw what she'd drawn. 'But not quite close enough.' 'Right,' said June, who had been noting down the cards as they were drawn. 'This is how the list works out. First is Rita, with an ace.' Everyone cheered, including me, and Rita raised her glass towards me in a toast. I raised mine back. I could see what looked very like a twinkle in her eye. 'Next is Gloria,' said June, 'with her king. Followed by Louise with her queen. Then it's Victoria with her ten. Then Andrea with her five, and last – but not, of course, least – is Charlene with her three. So there we are. Now then, let's all have some more champagne. I certainly need some after all that.' She finished off what was left in the second bottle, and quickly and efficiently opened a third.

'So who's going to sell me their card?' asked Charlene. 'You, Rita?' Rita shook her head. 'Oh, do shut up, Charlene,' said Victoria. 'Don't be such a pain in the ass.' Rita came over and stood beside me. 'Let me take you away from these jealous, squabbling ladies,' she said. She drained her glass, and set it down on the bar. I did the same, and she then took me by the hand and started to lead me away. 'Let me give you the guided tour,' she said. 'You'll enjoy it.' We walked over to the other side of the room, and out through a doorway into a long passage with a lot of doors. I counted them. There were eight. 'Six of these door are bedrooms that are part of our workspace,' said Rita. 'I'll show them to you. They cater for pretty much every kind of taste.'

She opened the first door. 'This is our home-from-home bedroom,' she said. It was a large room, dominated (as were all of them, I was to discover) by an enormous, king-size bed. This one was a Louis Quinze, walnut four-poster, with hangings in white brocade. The bed was made with white, lacy, luxurious-looking sheets and pillows. It looked extremely well-upholstered. The rest of the room was expensively comfortable, and the whole was carpeted, wall-to-wall, in white, deep pile carpet. There were decent, well-framed, reproductions of French artists on the walls. Degas, Monet. That sort of thing. The whole concept was of tasteful comfort. There was a large bathroom leading off, with an enormous bath, more than big enough for two. 'Nice,' I said. 'Very pleasant. I like it.'

The next room was something of a startling contrast. The bed was large, but was little better than a sort of straw palliasse, and was laid on the floor across a corner, rather than in the centre of the room. There was a wooden construction that was obviously used for tying up people for whipping. There were implements of torture everywhere. Whips, canes, heavy leather belts, rubber masks and gags, the whole paraphernalia of S&M. Rita saw the expression on my face, and closed the door. 'Whatever turns you on,' she said. 'We cater for all tastes. But I'm personally glad that room doesn't appeal to you.' She looked me straight in the eye. 'You look to me like a man who simply likes a good fuck,' she said. 'Am I right?' 'Too right, darling,' I said. 'Why don't we get on with it? I seriously fancy you. I want to fuck you. I've been wanting to since I first met you, what? an hour ago? That first room looks comfortable enough to me. Unless you think I'm missing something?'

'Absolutely not,' she said. 'The other rooms are, first of all, one set up to look pretty much like a schoolroom. Then one that's very oriental. You know, lots of carved Indian furniture, with all those hand-printed materials studded with little mirrors. Plenty of incense. You know the sort of thing?' I did, and I said so. 'Then there is a futuristic room, made to look like the inside of a spacecraft,' she said. 'That's quite fun, if you're into that kind of thing. I've got a terrific space suit. Very kinky.'

She looked at me, and laughed. 'And the sixth is supposedly very sexy. It's all leather and rubber, with a chrome and steel four-poster, with disco lights running around the top. Heavy metal tapes playing. Pornographic pictures. Dirty movies projected on the wall. That sort of thing.' 'Hmmm,' I said. 'Sounds interesting. But I think I'll stay with the first room. If that's OK?' 'That's absolutely OK,' she said. 'With you, any one of them is absolutely OK. I'm sure I don't have to tell you that this isn't the greatest job in the world. But it's a great way to make a lot of money, fairly quickly. And the truth of the matter is that most of our customers here are knocking on a bit. We're extremely expensive. I've heard say we're the most expensive brothel in New York. Young men tend not to earn enough to come here. Old men are not a lot of fun, sexually. So you're a real treat.' She grinned at me, and I had to laugh. She was so natural. And very sexy. The fact that I had seen less of her feminine attractions than I had of those of the other five girls only added to her sexual allure.

The conversation about the contemporary room with its steel and chrome four-poster reminded me that a friend of mine, David Jones, who was to run Paul Raymond's American Publishing company – Fiona Press Inc – after Tony Power left, told me that he had stayed in Bob Guccione's house on a number of occasions, in the main guest bedroom, where there was also a contemporary steel four-poster, with miniature disco lights around the top of the bed. David said that he and his wife always assumed, rightly or wrongly, that there were video facilities for taking film of guests at their relaxation, and they always performed, sexually, to their very best, making their most athletic efforts, just in case. I wondered if June had her rooms wired for film and sound.

The Guccione house, in the low sixties, between Madison and Fifth Avenues, was originally two large New York town houses, which Guccione had gutted, and then rebuilt, from three floors below ground to five floors above. Other attractions in the house, according to my friend David, were an Olympic-size swimming pool on the ground floor, a gymnasium, complete with sauna, in the basement, a roof garden, a ballroom covering the complete area of both the original houses on the first floor, with specially imported Italian marble floor and matching columns – wherein reposed the original piano from Judy Garland's old New York apartment – and, of course, a permanent plethora of beautiful girls staying in the house whilst Bob took their photographs for his magazine *Penthouse*. One entire floor of the house was his workspace. On the downside chez Guccione, said David, were six Rhodesian Ridgebacks; pony-sized dogs with teeth rather akin to those of the sharks in *Jaws*, and with rather similar manners. The dogs roamed the house at will, night and day.

It was the only house in the street not to have been burgled, according to David, who swore that fact had much more to do with the dogs than with the armed ex-New York cops who minded the front door twenty-four hours a day. Coming in late to the Guccione residence after a night out on the town, and covering the hundred yards or so from inside the front door to the lift before the dogs did, used to keep David in good physical trim, he said. He used to pray that the lift was on the ground floor, and that he would not have to wait for it to come down from a floor above. The dogs lay on the steps of the huge, sweeping marble staircase, that rose from the ground floor of the building, up to the ballroom, from whence they had a direct view of the front door. David's wife, apparently, used to pat and fondle them as if they were pet corgis.

'So,' said Rita. 'What next? Is it back to the bar, for more champagne and conversation? If it's simply a drink you need' (this looking at my empty glass) 'all the rooms are fully equipped with a fairly extensive range of drinks. That certainly includes champagne. Would you like me to open a bottle? It would save us having to walk all the way back.' She smiled an enigmatic smile, and raised an eyebrow. 'That would be nice, Rita,' I said. 'Thank you. But let me open it.' We walked back to what Rita had described as the home-from-home room where she opened a white-painted cupboard door and selected a bottle of champagne from within. She handed it to me, and I took it over to a sort of catering area in a corner of the room, where there was a small, stainless steel sink, hot and cold water, a fridge, and various china and cutlery. I opened the bottle, and filled first Rita's, then my glass. 'Cheers,' I said. She raised her glass. 'Happy days,' she said. 'Why don't we make ourselves comfortable, and then I can give you some idea of what is on offer?' There were chairs, but they weren't exactly built for comfort, so I sat on the bed. Rita came and sat beside me. 'Please do,' I said. 'I'd like that.'

'May I be totally up front?' she asked. 'Yes, of course,' I said. 'I would much prefer that you did. 'Well,' she said, 'what I said earlier about you being something of a treat for us girls – bearing in mind the average age of our clients here – is absolutely true. And that, of course, guarantees you some of the best sex you have probably ever experienced.' She grinned at me. 'I think you've probably been around a bit,' she said, 'but even with your experience, I think you may be pleasantly surprised. Frankly, we're here because we're bloody good at what we do. June is a perfectionist. She keeps us on our toes.

'But what I'm going to say now is my professional – not my personal – advice. If you ran through all of us in turn, you'd have a lot of fun. I don't know specifically what your sexual preferences are, but you look pretty normal, as I said earlier. And any one of us will do absolutely anything that you wish. There are no restrictions. And no bill. But if you simply did that – fucked us individually – it would be like, oh, let me think. It would be like having the pick of any cars in the world to drive, and choosing a family Ford instead of Lamborghini, or a Maserati. So I want to point out some of the possibilities.' She took a long pull at her champagne, and I got up and went to fetch the bottle to give her a refill.

'Thank you,' she said. 'So, just think about this for a few moments. I am a great fuck. Victoria – she of the auburn hair,, with the black satin miniskirt and the see-through blouse is a great fuck.' 'I know which of you is Victoria,' I said. 'I noticed her nipples, amongst other things.' Rita looked at me again. 'But what you don't know is that Victoria and I do a fantastic lesbian scene on request – and, I must add, at great expense – for clients here. We really are very good at it.' She smiled at me, and leaned forward as she began to speak again. 'And what none of the customers know, is that the reason we do it so convincingly is that both Victoria and I swing both ways. We live together.' She grinned again. 'So we get lots of practice.' My surprise must have shown on my face, because she laughed out loud. 'Your face is too much,' she said. 'Surely you've heard of people swinging both ways before now?'

'Yes, of course I have,' I said. 'It's just that, on first acquaintance, I wouldn't have suspected that you and Victoria did.' 'Well,' she said. 'Be that as it may. But think about the three of us, in this room, with Victoria and me doing naughty things to each other while you watch, knowing that we'll be happy for you to join in at any time. Does that do anything for you? Does that turn you on?' Turn me on? I asked myself. I nearly fainted with excitement. 'Er, yes,' I said. 'It turns me on enormously.' 'Good,' said Rita. 'I can arrange it all quite quickly. You don't need to do anything. Just enjoy your champagne. Relax. I'll be right back. OK?' 'Sure,' I said.

Rita left the room, and I wandered about, idly looking at the pictures. You know how you do? She returned about ten minutes later, carrying a small suitcase, and accompanied by Victoria, who said 'Hi, Tony. So, I get my wish, rather sooner than I thought. That's great.' I didn't connect for a moment, and then I remembered that when we had met earlier, she had breathed 'I'd love to fuck you' in my ear. Naughty little thing.

'Terrific, sweetheart,' I said. 'It's obviously good news for me too.' 'I think we're ready,' said Rita, interrupting Victoria. 'Tony, since the chairs in here are rather small and hard, why don't you sit up against the headboard on one side of the bed here, and make yourself comfortable?' I did as I was bid. I took off my jacket and tie, and then made myself comfortable on the bed. Rita found a switch somewhere, and switched on some soft, bluesy, sexy music, playing gently in the background.
The two girls came close together, standing up by the side of

the bed, wrapped their arms around each other, and began kissing. Raunchily. Passionately. Enthusiastically. Tongues well into each other's mouths. Rita still in her cotton suit and blouse. Victoria in her miniskirt and black see-through blouse. They continued kissing, and then Rita's right hand started caressing Victoria's right breast and nipple through the thin material, and after a moment, Victoria's right hand found the hem of Rita's skirt and, lifting it up, she reached between her girlfriend's legs. Rita moaned slightly, and ground her crotch against Victoria's hand. Victoria took her hand away and started to undress Rita.

First she unbuttoned the jacket of the cotton suit, revealing a transparent, white, peep-hole bra, through which Rita's nipples jutted prominently. Such sexuality beneath her plain, business like suit was highly erotic. Victoria bent down and for a moment or two sucked each nipple in turn. Rita moaned again. Louder, this time. Victoria then found the zipper of Rita's skirt and, pulling it down, next pulled the skirt down Rita's legs, waiting for her to step out of it, which she did. She was left standing in transparent, white, crotchless panties which matched her bra, and the gap in which showed that naughty Rita had a shaven pussy. Bald as a coot. My favourite turn-on! She was also wearing black, hold-up stockings, with lacy tops.

I could see her swollen outer vaginal lips puffy with desire, with the colourless, sticky love-juice oozing from her slit and running down her thighs. Victoria knelt in front of her, and licked Rita's cunt slowly, running her tongue wetly down its full length, and then back up again. Rita grabbed Victoria's head and pulled it more firmly into her crotch. 'Oh, baby,' she said. 'That's good. That's really good. Please don't stop.' At that moment there was a soft knock on the bedroom door, and, without waiting for an answer, the door opened, and Charlene came in. In a quick glance, she took in what was happening. She tiptoed over to me and sat down on the bed beside me. 'I couldn't wait any longer,' she said. 'So here I am.' I didn't say anything. I was too busy getting my mental rocks off watching the other two girls. Rita was getting quite worked up as I watched.

As I did so, absolutely enthralled by what I was watching, Charlene leaned across and unzipped my fly, releasing my rigid John Thomas. 'Oh, wow,' she said, and bent forward and took its full length into her accommodating mouth. The pleasure, the sheer delight, of suddenly, unexpectedly, having one's erect cock (raised to full, firm hardness by the erotic sight of one beautiful lesbian licking another beautiful lesbian's pussy) taken into a soft, warm, wet mouth, and then sucked, tongued, and licked, with obvious enthusiasm and enjoyment, is something I shall long cherish and remember. I lasted no time at all.

I came. Strongly. It was no surprise to me, and it didn't seem to bother Charlene, who simply swallowed my come as I jetted it into her mouth. When I had finished, she licked her lips, and kept hold of my now flaccid prick, masturbating it slowly, more, I supposed, in hope than in anger. At that point Victoria stopped licking the length of Rita's lust-swollen labial lips, and pulled down, first, Rita's hold-up stockings, then her crotchless panties, leaving her standing there naked for a moment, her bald pudenda wet with love-juice. Victoria then guided her to the bed, where she lay down beside me, not more than two feet away. Neither of the other two girls took the slightest notice of Charlene, or acknowledged her presence in any way. Victoria next stripped off her black, see-through blouse, and then removed her short, black, satin skirt, leaving her wearing but the briefest of black, lacy panties. She bent down and took them off, dropping them on the floor beside the bed, exposing her auburn muff. It was shiny clean, and tightly curled. I could just see the thin, closed, wet, pink line of her pussy lips running downwards from the centre of it. Her rigid, pink nipples matched the colour of her cunt lips exactly.

Rita lay on her back on the bed, her head up at my end, and Victoria knelt over her head, with her own head down between

Rita's thighs. They then began to perform cunnilingus with well practised enthusiasm. Two pink tongues slurped. Two mouths kissed and sucked. Twenty fingers spread pussy lips and found clitorises, and then frigged them faster and faster, until both women started to orgasm together, shouting out their delight, hugging each other, still sucking and frigging and massaging, until finally they slowed to a halt, and then they simply lay there, their arms about each other, the perspiration gleaming wetly over their bodies.

The scent of aroused cunt permeated the room, mixed with that of three different kinds of perfume and two variations of sweat. It was a heady mixture. One that, along with Charlene's masturbatory attentions, had my cock rigid and looking for action. I'd had an arousing view of Victoria's rear as she went down on Rita, with wisps of golden red pubic hair running up, each side of her pinkly wet, swollen pussy lips, which were pressing down and working on Rita's mouth. Victoria's main pubic growth was, of course, largely hidden by Rita's mouth, face and head. But not at all hidden – in fact thrusting towards me, all too suggestively – was Victoria's pink, tight little sphincter, it too surrounded by a slight golden growth of curls, the hole glistening wetly, as if ready lubricated for the insertion of my engorged penis. Victoria's sexily tempting anus was set at the base of her lusciously rounded, full buttocks, forming a kind of isosceles triangle, of which the rectum was the round apex, the sides her lightly hirsute ass-cheeks, and the curved base itself formed by the lips and bag of her sex as seen from the rear. I could imagine my stiff prick fucking it.

Nothing was out of court, as I understood the situation. What had Rita said, not so long ago? 'There are no restrictions. Any one of us will do absolutely anything you wish.' That was it. Anal sex, patently, was on the menu. I leaned over and whispered in Charlene's ear. 'I want to have anal sex with Victoria. How do I go about it?' She stopped her lazy wanking action, and sat up. 'Oh, that's no problem,' she said.

'Victoria,' she called out. Victoria disentangled herself from

Rita, and sat up too. It was the first time she had acknowledged Charlene's presence. 'Yes, honey,' she replied. 'What's the problem?' 'No problem,' said Charlene. 'Our stud here wants to fuck you in the ass.' 'Oh,' said Victoria. 'Right.' She pondered for a moment. 'Well, OK. Let's make it a little amusing for him then, shall we, girls?' 'Sure,' said Rita and Charlene together. The three girls spoke quietly amongst themselves for a moment or two, and then Charlene stepped back a couple of paces, and pulled her transparent black chemise off over her head, leaving herself naked except for the black velvet ribbon around her neck, and her jet bracelet. Her breasts and nipples were eminently suckable. Next she lay on her back on the bed, spreading her legs open, her bushy blonde pubic hair the centre of my attention for that moment. As I watched, she put her hands down and spread the lips of her cunt, revealing a deep, pink, wet hole, into which she thrust two fingers, and she then started to frig herself. Neither of the other two girls seemed to notice. She looked up at me and smiled, her fingers busy.

'A girl has to do what a girl has to do, Tony,' she said. 'When there's no cock available, her fingers are a girl's best friend. Same as for fellas, I guess.' I didn't say anything, but just smiled back at her. Rita, I noticed, had gone over to the small suitcase that she had brought in with her when she originally went out to fetch Victoria. She opened it up and searched around in it for a moments, and came up with what she was looking for – a tube of KY jelly. 'OK, honey,' she said to Victoria. 'Time to get at it, baby.' Victoria grinned at me, and then got onto the bed, arranging herself so that her head was over Charlene's pussy, presently still occupied by Charlene's busy fingers. She knelt, making herself comfortable, her ass in the air, knees spread to give access, her pretty, puckered asshole presented as an offering. My prick got even harder.

'Come and watch,' said Rita. 'This will turn you on like nothing you've ever seen.' I went over to the bed, and watched as she took the cap off the tube of KY jelly. She squeezed out a length of the oleaginous lubricant onto her forefinger, and began to anoint Victoria's anus with it. She first circled the exterior, then inserted a finger, at first slowly, then more deeply, then withdrew it and, squeezing more of the colourless unguent out onto her finger, she reinserted it in Victoria's ass, twisting and turning her finger to ensure that the jelly was well spread around. 'There,' she said, after a while. 'That looks like a pretty well lubricated asshole to me.' She patted Victoria's bottom. 'Have fun,' she said. 'But first, let me lubricate you.' I then did something which I think surprised even these three experienced ladies. 'Hang on a second, love,' I said to Rita. 'I'm just going to give you a quick fuck, before I fuck Victoria in the ass. If that's all right with you?'

She positively grinned at me. 'It's more than all right,' she said. 'I'm delighted. But why?' 'Why' was because I knew that the moment I eased my cock into Victoria's tight little anus, I'd cream my lot. Instantly. I was almost doing it, just looking at her asshole. So if I had a quick fuck first with the lovely Rita, then I could be certain of my anal sex lasting long enough to get some real pleasure out of it. It made sense to me. I explained what it was all about to Rita. 'Whatever turns you on, baby,' she said. 'But let *me* fuck *you*. I promise you you'll enjoy it.' And why not, I thought to myself?

I lay on my back on the bed, alongside Charlene, who was still frigging happily away. Rita came and spread her thighs across me, and lowered herself down onto my rampant cock, spreading her cunt lips with her fingers as she did so. She was warm, tight, and very wet. She started to fuck me hard straight away, and it was no time at all before I shot my load up into her. 'Sorry, sweetheart,' I said. 'But I promise we'll do it again. More slowly next time. OK?' 'Sure, baby,' she said, raising herself up off me. 'Like I said, whatever turns you on. Your wish is our command. Let me get you ready for Victoria.' She went off for a moment, and came back again with the tube of KY, with which she started to anoint my flaccid prick. Under her gentle fingers, and with the added sensation of the lubricant being massaged into it, my cock was quickly reinstated into its erect condition, ready and willing for its next adventure.

'Thanks, sweetheart,' I said, as I stood up, and I knelt on the bed behind Victoria, who had just rearranged herself over the still supine Charlene, whose pussy she now bent down to and started to suck. I moved behind her, and was surprised when Rita came over and, leaning across the bed, took my prick in her hand yet again. 'Let me help you,' she said, and guided my stiff tool towards the tiny, puckered entrance that I had been thinking about for some time now. Rita reached out with her other hand, prised open Victoria's anus, and then pushed my tool firmly up against the open hole. I leaned into it with her, and it slid in with surprising ease. My compliments to the manufacturers of KY jelly, I thought. 'There you go, buster,' said Rita, as she let go of my cock. 'Enjoy.'

Not half, I thought to myself, as I eased my cock into Victoria's rectum. I watched excitedly, enjoying every tiny sensation as her sphincter muscles took my rod in their grasp, and my tool swelled even more as I watched the membrane of her anus stretching to accommodate its girth. I leaned forward and grasped Victoria's small tits, feeling her erect nipples stiffen further under my fingers. I twisted them, enjoying her gasp as she lifted her mouth from Charlene's twat for a moment. I squeezed and pulled and twisted some more. She gasped again, and then she reached down and plunged her fingers into Charlene's cunt, and then held them out to me over her shoulder, literally dripping with Charlene's sexual effluent. 'Have some pussy juice,' she invited. 'Taste Charlene's cunt. It tastes good to me.' I sucked her fingers, licking them clean. It did indeed taste good. 'More,' I said. 'Please. That's nice.'

Whilst Victoria fed me Charlene's vaginal juices, I fucked her asshole with intense, unflagging enjoyment. I was glad that I had worked off my initial sexual excitement with Rita, without which action I would have long since shot my load up Victoria's ass, to my extreme consternation.

The anus is a magical, elastic orifice. Victoria's had stretched from what had originally appeared to be a diameter of maybe half an inch at the very most, with a tiny – really tiny – hole at its centre, measuring certainly no more than the size of a small pea. Watching my member thrusting in and out of it, clenched tightly all the time, it now stretched to at least two and a half inches in diameter. Probably seven or eight inches in circumference. I appreciate that any woman's cunt stretches wide enough, when necessary, to allow the passing of a baby's head. Rather larger than the average penis. But what it doesn't do is grip with the tenacity of the female back passage. Hence, for me, the attraction of the latter. Speaking of which, I had heard much, since my arrival in New York, of the fashion amongst its gay fraternity for something called fist fucking. Rather like finger fucking, but with the clenched fist, and anally. It didn't sound – or look – possible to me, but then, since I had no intention of finding out whether it was or not, it didn't really matter, did it?

I could feel my imminent ejaculation building, getting itself together from the seriously erotic treatment it was receiving from Victoria's tight little ass. I began to pump faster, and then, suddenly, I was spurting my come up her anus. It was one of the most sensational ejaculations ever. I thought that it would never end. I *prayed* that it would never end. My prick spasmed and contracted and spasmed again. 'Oh, baby,' said Victoria, lifting her mouth up from Charlene's pussy. 'I can feel you coming. 'You're spurting your hot spunk right up my ass. That's lovely. Keep on spunking.' She thrust her bottom backwards, lasciviously, against my thighs, and I continued to jet my come up her for a few more seconds. And then, sadly, regretfully, it was all over. The one thing you want to do, before you have done it is come. The last thing in the world you wish you had done, once you have, is come. Such is life.

I pulled slowly, reluctantly, out of Victoria's sphincter. I went to the *en suite* bathroom, and washed myself. Even after that, my prick was still hard. I went back into the bedroom, and

Rita had opened another bottle of champagne. She poured me a welcome glass. Victoria smiled at me. 'I had the feeling that you enjoyed that,' she said. 'How was it?' 'It was terrific,' I said. 'It was something else. It really was. Thank you.' 'It was my pleasure,' she said. I wondered if it actually was. 'It's all right for you,' said Charlene. 'At least you got fucked in the ass. And Rita got fucked properly. I haven't been fucked anywhere.' She made an unhappy face. 'Oh, for God's sake, Charlene,' said Rita. 'Do shut up.' 'Why should I?' whined Charlene. She muttered on for a while, continuing to complain. Rita and Victoria took themselves aside, and had an animated, but to me quite audible conversation, over in the far corner of the room. They then went over to the suitcase again, and drew out what looked like a number of black silk scarves. Victoria, by far the taller of the two, went over to Charlene, where she was sitting on the edge of the bed, and took her firmly by the shoulders. Despite Charlene's vociferous complaints, Victoria took her arms and dragged her up to the top of the bed, until her back was right up against the four-poster's head-rail, where Rita tied her wrists – quite firmly, I could see – to the crossbar.

They both ignored Charlene's angry shouting, and then Rita found yet another black silk scarf. Using that, and with Victoria's discarded panties, rescued from where they had been abandoned on the floor, as a pad, she gagged Charlene, whose angry cries were instantly reduced to an indistinct mumbling. Rita then went back to the suitcase, from which, this time, she extracted an enormous black, rubber dildo, complete with harness. This she quickly strapped on. From her dexterity with the quite complicated strapping, I could see that she was more than familiar with the way the dildo fitted onto her body.

When it was finally in place, the huge rubber penis jutted out in front of her in proud fashion. She turned towards Charlene, whose eyes fell upon this monstrous implement for the first time. 'Here you are, honey,' said Rita, walking over to the bed. 'You wanted to get fucked. Now I'm going to fuck you. Where would you like it? Up your tight little ass?'

Charlene shook her head violently. 'Oh,' said Rita. 'Don't we like big rubber dicks up our ass, then?' Charlene shook her head yet again. 'Then I guess it's got to be our little pussy that needs fucking?' said Rita. Charlene once more shook her head. 'Oh, don't be so modest, baby,' taunted Rita. 'You can't have been making all that appalling noise, and now tell me that you don't want fucking?'

Charlene nodded her head, urgently. 'Tough shit,' said Rita. She picked up the tube of KY jelly, and applied it lavishly to the huge rubber cock. Victoria went over to one side of the bed, and took hold of one of Charlene's legs. She pulled it over to her side. 'Tony, honey,' she said to me. 'Do us a favour, will you, please? Come over here and pull this girl's far leg over to the other side of the bed will you? Rita needs a lot of room to get that great big dildo up our friend's tight little cunt here.'

I wondered if I should refuse to take part in this semi-rape, and then decided that discretion was perhaps the better part of valour. I did as I was told, after which Charlene's legs were splayed, obscenely, ready for Rita's assault. 'Now bend her knees up for her,' commanded Victoria. I did as I was told. The dildo was about twice as big as any human penis I had ever seen, and I wondered if it would, in fact, fit into Charlene's pussy. Bearing in mind her profession, it probably wasn't all that tight. But whatever its size, Rita certainly didn't try to ease it in. She climbed on top of Charlene's spread thighs, and then simply rammed the dildo home. Charlene moaned, in what must have been quite genuine pain. She tried to say something through her gag, but – unsurprisingly in the circumstances – it wasn't intelligible. Tears began to roll down her cheeks. 'I think you can probably let go of her leg now,' said Victoria, letting go of the one she was holding. I followed suit. Rita was thrusting the dildo in and out of Charlene like a rutting stag. I could see the thin membrane of Charlene's inner labia stretched so tight around the circumference of the dildo, it looked as if it might tear. Charlene was flinching with every stroke, and crying, insofar as the gag would allow it.

'Stop that noise, for God's sake,' said Rita. 'You were complaining that you hadn't been fucked. Now you're complaining that you *are* being fucked. There's no satisfying you, is there?' Rita didn't pause in her copulatory thrusting, but she turned to Victoria and said 'Take her gag off for me, will you please, darling?' Victoria took a few moments to do as she was asked, eventually untying the knots at the back of the black silk scarf, and pulling Victoria's black, lacy, balled-up panties out of Charlene's mouth. They were soaked through with her saliva. 'Now then,' said Rita, stopping what she was doing, but leaving the dildo hard up inside Charlene's stretched pussy. 'What's the problem? Speak up.' Charlene sniffed, and Victoria went over to the suitcase, returning with a tissue, with which she wiped Charlene's nose for her.

Then 'You . . . You . . . You're . . . hur . . . hurt . . . You're hurt . . . hurting me. Hurting me,' she sobbed. 'With . . . with . . . that . . . thing.' She broke down into painful sobs. Rita sighed, and slowly withdrew the dildo from Charlene's pussy. It was dripping with a combination of Charlene's juices and the remains of the KY jelly. Rita stood up. The dildo looked really obscene, standing there glistening proudly at an angle of forty-five degrees. I was sorry that it and its harness hid Rita's bald pudenda. I remembered how she had looked as she lowered herself down onto me, before I'd fucked Victoria in the ass. Victoria looked at the dildo, and started to finger her sex. 'Oh, I don't know,' she said. 'It looks quite amusing to me.' Rita laughed. 'No way, baby,' she said. 'Not right now, anyway.' And she began to lecture Charlene again as she unstrapped the dildo, dropping it casually on the floor when it finally became free. I tried not to stare at her bald pubis. A tiny stream of clear liquid trickled down from the bottom of her labia, and began to run down the inside of her thigh.

'Now listen here, baby,' she said. 'This really won't do. Tell me what it is that you really want.' Charlene looked up tearfully at Rita. 'Will you untie me if I do?' she asked. Rita thought for a moment. 'I tell you what,' she said. 'I'll untie you now. And then you can tell us what it is that is going to make you happy. If we don't like what you want, then we'll tie you up again, and do much nastier things to you than fuck you with a lovely big rubber dick. Do you understand?' Charlene nodded, tearfully. 'And stop that whining,' said Rita, as she started to untie the poor girl. Minutes later she was free, and she got up off the bed and began rubbing her wrists and ankles.

Rita gave her a little while to sort herself out, and then said 'Right, then. So what's it going to be, Charlene? What particular sexual indulgence would you like us to arrange for you? Would you like us to cane you? Or whip you, perhaps? How about us *really* tying you up? You know, serious knots, chains, nipple clamps, ball gags, the real gear? Then Victoria and I could take turns with the golden showers. Would that turn you on? Excite your hot little cunt? Make you all wet with anticipation, inside and out? Or would you prefer a really high enema? Lots and lots of hot, soapy water, and then you have to hold it for hours on end, on pain of serious punishment if you fail?' Charlene was looking horrified at this catalogue of fairly extreme sexual activities. She stamped her foot.

'Stop it, stop it,' she shouted. 'I'll tell you what I want. I want you two just to go away and leave me here with Tony, and I want Tony to fuck me. Fuck me gently. Lovingly. Excitingly. I want his real cock up inside me, making me come the proper way. I'm fed up with you lesbians and your nasty habits. Now go away, and leave me alone with Tony. Please?' 'Aaaah,' said Victoria. 'Isn't that sweet? Diddums wants a nice, old-fashioned fuck. Straight up and down, like ma and pa. Isn't that touching? Well, I guess that's entirely up to Tony. Tony? How do you feel about that? I mean, you've fucked both Rita and me. One way or another.' She giggled. 'It's a reasonable enough request, I suppose. What d'you think? Is that OK with you?'

'It sounds good to me,' I said. Little Charlene's face lit up. 'Oh, thank you, Tony,' she said. 'Thank you, darling.' 'No problem,' I said. 'My pleasure.' It was true. Most people would give their eye teeth to have half a chance of fucking this delightful little blonde, with her short, bubbly hair-cut, her large, firm breasts, crested, as they were, with large pink areolae, and tipped with big, pink nipples. She was still wearing her black velvet neckband and her jet bracelet. All she needed was to wash the tear-stains off, and she'd be as good as new. 'Oh, little Miss Hoity Toity,' said Rita. 'Let's us nasty dirty lesbians leave this dear, clean, straight, up-front lady to her romantic interlude.' She sounded quite vindictive about what she was saying. Patently there was a great deal going on behind the scenes in June's brothel that probably even June herself didn't know about.

'Thank you, girls,' I said. 'That was fun. I enjoyed myself enormously. We must do it again.' Victoria came over and kissed me. 'I'd like that,' she said. 'Is that a promise?' 'It's a promise, darling,' I said. Rita followed her. 'That goes for me, too,' she said. 'We'll be waiting. You hear?' She also kissed me. 'I hear,' I said. 'I'll be back. Don't worry.' 'Come on, then, Vee,' said Rita. 'To work, I guess. There should be paying customers about by this time.' She looked at me, rather apologetically. 'Sorry, honey,' she said. 'Take no notice. A girl has to earn her living, you know. *Au'voir*.' They took themselves off. Charlene came over and hugged me. 'Oh, what horrid girls,' she said. 'I hate them. And they hate me. Dirty dykes. I don't think girls like that should be allowed to work in a decent brothel, with normal girls like me and the other three. I really don't. And I daren't complain to June. They'd beat the shit out of me. They're so much bigger than I am. And there's two of them. Dirty cows.'

'Don't worry, sweetheart,' I said. 'They're gone now. It's just you and me.' 'How lovely,' she said. And she took my face in her hands, and gave me a long, deep, wet, French kiss. I almost came from the sheer excitement of being alone with this young Marilyn Monroe lookalike of the brothel world. My cock leapt to attention. She put a hand down, and grasped it. 'Oh, darling,' she breathed. 'You don't know just how good that feels.' She pulled my foreskin up and down a couple of times, reminding me of the earlier hand-job that she had so proficiently provided. 'I know how good it feels to me,' I said. 'I like it.' 'But this one's for me,' she said. 'I want to feel it throbbing in my cunt. I want you to fuck me with it.'

'Then I suggest that you leave it alone for the moment, sweet heart,' I said. 'Otherwise it simply won't last long enough.' She laughed. 'There's all the time in the world,' she said. 'It's the one thing we have plenty of. When we fuck – soon, dearest. Don't worry. Soon. But *when* we fuck, I want to be real, old-fashioned feminine for you. Sexy. Every man's fantasy. I want to dress up for you. You know? Sexy underwear. Black stockings. Garter belts. Stuff like that. Lingerie that makes me feel like a real woman. I want you to look at me, and say to yourself, wow! I really want to fuck that. OK?' 'Very OK, darling,' I said. 'Black knickers and suspenders are what my fantasy sex life is all about. Take as long as you like. I'll save this for you. I promise. Feel free.'

She went and found another bottle of champagne, and opened it, and poured us both a glass, leaving the bottle beside me. 'Here's to us, baby,' she said. 'To us,' I agreed. We clinked glasses, and drank. 'I won't be long, honey,' she said. 'Don't go away.' 'Don't worry, darling,' I said. 'I'll be here.' She was back inside fifteen minutes. She was, as she had more or less promised, tarted up like every red-blooded man's fantasy fuck. She was wearing a flimsy, black, satin-and-lace, see through bra, which almost contained her ample bosom. Her teats showed large and erect through the thin material. She was also wearing matching, tiny, see-through black satin-and-lace knickers, pulled tightly up into her crotch. I could see the shape of her cunt-lips outlined in the shiny material between her legs. Over these, she wore a small, black garter belt, with long suspenders reaching down to the opaque, lacy tops of her fine-denier nylon stockings.

Silk stockings are a big turn-on for me, but the kind of black nylon stockings in this very fine gauge have a glossy sheen that somehow silk never manage to produce. 'What do you think, baby?' she asked. 'Do you like it?' 'Like it, darling?' I said. 'I love it. My fantasy fuck. Black stockings, black knickers, black suspenders, and you inside them. What more could a man want? Come here. I want to fuck you. Now.' She laughed, I think genuinely and happily. 'Just do whatever you want, baby,' she said. 'If you need to tell me what to do, then tell me. I'm yours. Fuck me long and hard. Please?'

'For a start, sweetheart,' I said, 'just lie on the bed, and spread your legs. I want to kiss and suck your pussy through those lovely black knickers.' 'You're a pantie freak,' she said. 'I can tell.' 'Tell me about it,' I said. 'Did you go about, when you were in grade school, sniffing little girls' bicycle saddles?' she asked. 'No,' I said. (I didn't, actually. We didn't have little girls – or big girls, either – at my public school, more's the pity.) 'At that age, I wasn't aware of the delights of sniffing girls' knickers. It's something I've come to enjoy as I've grown older. I see it now as a gourmet sexual experience. But for me, doing it while the owner is still wearing the knickers is fantasy time indeed.'

'Then come enjoy yourself, baby,' she said. So saying, she lay down on the bed, and spread her legs. The crotch of her knickers was still embedded in her pussy lips. I knelt over her, from her left-hand side, and buried my nose and mouth in her knicker crotch. She smelt of woman. A woman whose sex had been aroused to fever heat. Over the scent of that, there were other aromas melding in, combining to produce the most sexually arousing fragrance known to man. That of wet pussy. There was, of course, her perfume. A strong, exotic, musk-based, animal scent. Then there was the odour of fresh perspiration. The scent of fresh sweat has always, to me, been sexually arousing. To these fragrant smells I could add the tactile sensation I received from the silken, lacy material of her knickers, softened already as it was by the dampness flowing into her crotch as I began to kiss her down there. I nuzzled, and kissed, and sucked, enjoying the excitement of satisfying four of my five senses; those of sight, taste, feel, and smell. Her knicker crotch was, by now, very wet indeed.

Charlene began to move her hips under me, and I suddenly remembered that there was another party to this – so far – rather one-man sexual adventure. I felt quite guilty, for a moment. Then I began, unselfishly, to pull her knickers down. She lifted her hips, and I slid them carefully down her thighs, noting with growing excitement how that part of the crotch that was embedded in her cunt lips disengaged itself as I pulled. Her lips were swollen and puffy with lust. I held her knickers while she pulled her stockinged legs and feet out of them. I pressed their crotch to my nose, and inhaled their now slightly acrid tang for one final, ecstatic moment, and then turned back to the serious business of the day. I now sucked those puffy lips, without the protection of her silky knicker material, and the contrast between the smoothness of the knickers, and the swollen, slightly ridged, naked fleshiness of her labia was tremendously sensually exciting. I spent quite a few minutes at this delightful activity, during which time I found her clitoris with my tongue, and I licked it into an even more erect little knurl than it was when I first discovered it.

Eventually, I felt that the time had come to put my cock where both of us now wanted it to be. I raised myself up from between her spread thighs, and bent down to kiss her mouth. As I kissed her, I reached behind her with both hands, and raised her upper body sufficiently far to unhook the fastening of her flimsy bra. I pulled the straps down and she shrugged her arms out of them, then lay back as she had been before. I took one of her firm, globular breasts in my right hand, my fingers finding her tumescent teat at its tip. I played with it gently, twirling, squeezing and pulling, feeling it become even more protuberant, enjoying my power to affect this woman's seemingly ever-sensitive body.

She slid her warm, wet tongue into my mouth as I kissed her, then withdrew it, and said 'I can taste my pussy juice on your lips and in your mouth. I love the taste of my own pussy.

That's naughty, isn't it? Often, when I've been playing with my pussy – you know, jerking myself off – I suck my fingers when I've finished. And I keep putting my fingers up my pussy, to get them wet with my juices again, and then suck them clean, over and over, until I get so excited that I have to jerk off again.' 'I don't think that's at all naughty,' I said. 'I love the taste and flavour of your pussy juice. Why shouldn't you?' I didn't tell her the truth, which is that I love the taste of *any* girl's pussy juice. It didn't seem necessary, somehow.

'I've never thought of it that way,' she said. 'I suppose that's true. But enough of that. If you like, I'll jerk off in front of you one day soon, and you can watch me, and then we can both push our fingers up my pussy, and share my pussy juice, afterwards. Would you like that? Most men seem to enjoy watching me jerk off. But right now, please fuck me. Pussy's wet enough now. Pussy needs a good fuck. Please.' 'No problem, sweetheart,' I said. At which I climbed on top of her, and thrust my rampant prick into her wetly waiting sexual orifice.

It slid in easily, to its full length, to the accompaniment of 'Oooohs' and 'Aaaahs' and finally an 'Oh, yes. That's it. That feels so good. That's what I've been waiting for. Now fuck me,' from Charlene. Her cunt muscles wrapped around my girth like a tightly fitting skin around a thick sausage, and began to massage my prick as I fucked her. I rammed it fully home, then withdrew, almost to the tip of my prick. Slowly at first, and then increasingly quickly. Charlene picked up my momentum with her hips, and I could feel her clitoris rubbing against the top of my cock on the downwards thrusts. We soon settled down to a rhythm which suited us both, and each of us was revelling in the sensations that an enduring fuck with a stiff prick in a tight, well-lubricated cunt can produce.

I held back deliberately, which wasn't difficult, bearing in mind the sheer amount of sexual activity in which I had been involved this particular evening. After a little while, Charlene began to have a series of orgasms, building up from, at first, quite small ones, to increasingly larger ones to, eventually, an enormous climax that wracked her with vaginal contractions that finally had her shouting with ecstasy. 'Oh, God, yes,' she shouted. 'I'm coming. I'm coming. Your huge cock is fucking me, and I'm coming. I'm coming for you. You're making me come. I like it. God. God. God. Fuck. Oh, fuck. Yes. Fuck.'

I kept on with deep, strong strokes, trying to keep the final orgasm going for as long as possible, enjoying the litany of lust that was being shouted into my ear, taking it as a compliment to my ability to satisfy Charlene sexually, and pleased that she was, after so much earlier angst, now actually enjoying herself. Eventually she came down from whichever particular erotic heaven she was in for the moment, and gave me a big squeeze. 'Hey, baby' she said. 'That was something else. That was worth all that nonsense with those two bitch lesbians. That was a seriously acceptable fuck.' She leaned over and kissed me. Fiercely. I returned her kisses. Eventually she broke away. 'Thank you, baby,' she said. 'Thank you. Thank you.' 'My pleasure, sweetheart,' I said. I seemed to have been saying that rather a lot today. 'What would you like to do now, baby?' she asked . 'Would you like a French necklace? That's something I do rather well. She held up her two impressive tits in explanation. For those few of you who may not know, a French necklace is when a girl tosses you off with her breasts. Normally, you kneel across her chest, and she takes your cock between her two boobs, and massages it with them until you come. Girls with long necks can often accommodate the end of your cock in their mouths at the same time, which adds considerably to the attraction of this – minor and extremely enjoyable – deviation.

Another version is to lie on your back and have the girl kneel over your mouth, so that you may suck her pussy whilst she engages your prick in her breasts from above. Girls with small tits can't do it. Big, soft, all-encompassing bazzooms are what French necklaces are about. Charlene was considerably over qualified. She was probably world champion. I thought for a moment, considering the plumply pneumatic attractions that she was offering. And then common sense prevailed. 'Dearest, darling Charlene,' I said. 'May I take a rain-check? I'm shagged. Worn out. Exhausted. Done. I couldn't fuck my way out of a paper bag at this particular moment. Much as the idea of a French necklace, brought about by those quite superb tits of yours, fills me with excitement, I think I'd be well advised to take myself off home and have an early night, with a big mug of hot, strong, steaming cocoa.'

'Hey, baby,' she said. 'Where's your staying power?' I had to laugh, and – give credit where credit's due – she laughed with me. She accompanied me into the *en suite* bathroom, and we bathed together in a bath probably big enough for four. She carefully washed my prick with the expensive French soap and the designer flannel supplied, and then – just to make sure – she sucked it thoroughly, from base to tip, and back again, taking it out of her mouth from time to time to examine her handiwork . It got sort of half hard, but nothing to boast about, and I eventually, and gently, withdrew it from her mouth. 'E for effort, sweetheart,' I said. 'But enough's enough. We'll catch up another time. OK?' 'OK, baby,' she said. 'That's a promise.'

I got dressed finally, and Charlene kissed me, and departed, I know not where. When I made it back through to the lounge, there were six or seven other men – obviously customers – sitting and standing around, chatting to the girls. June was over at the bar. She saw me coming, and waved me over. I looked at my watch for the first time since picking up the phone, back in the office, to telephone her, which seemed now like a hundred years ago. I couldn't believe it, but it was almost midnight.

'Hi, sweetie,' she said. 'Did you have a lovely time? And what would you like to drink?' There was now a barman behind the bar . 'I think I'll stay with the champagne, if I may,' I said. 'Of course you may,' she said. 'Alvaro, a glass of champagne for Mr Andrews here.' 'Coming right up, madam,' he said. 'Good evening, Mr Andrews.' 'Good evening, Alvaro,' I replied. He was a smooth, pleasant, attractive Italian in what? his mid-thirties? Somewhere around there. There was no one else at the bar at that moment. All the girls were there, talking to customers, bar Charlene and Andrea. As I took a sip of my champagne, Charlene came back into the room, this time wearing a long, black, evening skirt, ostentatiously split high up on her thigh, and a transparent black voile blouse. She looked as if she had just gotten herself ready for a fashion shoot. Her hair, her make-up, her apparel – indisputably sexy, as it was – were all perfect. She saw me, and raised a languid finger. I waved back. She smiled. You would never have guessed how she had spent the past few hours. 'Yeah,' I said. 'All thanks to you. I had the most fantastic time. I don't think you would believe what I've been doing, even if I told you.' She laughed. 'I suspect I might,' she said. 'But all I want to know is that you enjoyed yourself.' 'That I most certainly did,' I said.

'What would you like to do now?' asked June. 'Rest up a little, and start again? Eat something? We have an excellent chef. Play a little poker? One or two of our clients have got a game of stud poker going in one of the back rooms. I'd be happy to introduce you. The stakes are high, but I guess you can afford them. Or perhaps you'd just like to sit and talk to me about the old days? Relax over the bottle of champagne? There's plenty more where that came from.' I explained that I had decided that my best plan was probably to go home, and have what I originally thought was going to be an early night. Right now, it was just going to be not an early morning. I could see Rita and Victoria, both looking totally demure, talking to a couple of elderly punters across on the other side of the room. They didn't see me.

I thanked June, very genuinely, from the bottom of my heart. 'You're more than welcome, Tony,' she said. 'It's been lovely to see you here. Now, don't forget. First of all, there are still three of the girls who haven't had the pleasure, as it were. And then, they're all six here for second helpings. And thirds, and fourths. Whatever. As often as you like. It's my pleasure. And theirs. You take care now.' She gave me a big kiss. 'See you soon, darling.' She saw me out, and I took the elevator down, and asked the doorman to get me a cab. He was back in moments. 'It's waiting for you outside, sir,' he said. I gave him five dollars, and thanked him. The journey home took just fifteen minutes, at that time of night. I was asleep the moment my head hit the pillow.

CHAPTER SIX
TIT FOR TAT

I slept soundly that night, as you might imagine. At the office in the morning, Eileen smiled, her apparent ill temper of the previous evening seemingly gone. She brought in my mail, and some coffee, with a bright, happy smile. 'You've got a fun invitation here today, Tony,' she said. 'Oh, yes,' I said. 'What's that?' 'Do you know Peter's TV Theatre?' she asked. 'Its downtown. Somewhere in the Village, I think.' 'Well, I've heard of it,' I said. 'But I haven't been there. Isn't that where a certain Ms Peter, queen of the New York transvestite world, showcases female impersonators?' 'That's the one,' she said. 'You've got it. So she's sent you an invitation, as an editor of *Tiptop*, to be a member of the judging panel at this year's Miss TV New York, run by the disco G.G's Barnum Room. How about that?'

'Hey, terrific,' I said. 'But why me?' 'God knows,' said Eileen. 'But if you haven't been to either place, then you've got a real surprise coming. These transvestites are *gorgeous*. You'd never know that they were men, if someone didn't tell you. I mean, Danny La Rue they're not.' 'How do you know about Danny La Rue?' I asked. 'I've been to London,' said Eileen. 'I've been about a bit. You're not the only person in the world who's been on an aeroplane, you know.' I held up my hands in submission. 'OK, OK. So you've seen Danny La Rue. So what's so different about these girls? Chaps? TVs?'

Eileen said, 'Look, the only way to find out the answer to that question is to go. Shall I accept for you?' 'Sure,' I said. 'When is it?' 'Tomorrow,' she said. 'Six thirty.' 'Great,' I said. 'Tell them I'll be there.' I wasn't at all sure what to expect as I stepped out of the cab outside G.G's Barnum Room. Inside, it was sumptuous, and the place was packed. I proffered my invitation, and was shown up to a raised dais on the stage. I sat down next to a reasonably normal looking guy, who held out his hand, and said 'I'm Phil Driver. Who're you?' When I told him, we shook hands, and he said 'So you like drag queens, huh?' There's no answer to that, really, is there? Just then, the show started, so I escaped having to answer the question.

I'd been handed background information when I arrived, explaining what was going on. Apparently, throughout the previous week, New York's most stunning transvestites had competed in talent and swimwear segments, yielding, at the end of the week, nine finalists. They were the contestants that we were to judge this evening. Ms Peter appeared, to uproarious applause from the audience, in a gown that would have made Corporal Klinger's heart flutter. She was the evening's emcee, as they say in America, and she had a nice line in bitchy humour. She introduced the 'girls' as they came on, individually. They were dressed in an amazing collection of the most fantastic evening dresses.

There were satins and chiffons, maribou and ermine. You name it, someone was almost certainly wearing it. The one thing that the dresses – and the contestants – all had in common, was the fact that the dresses were all extremely low cut, exposing some of the prettiest bosoms it has been my pleasure to drool over for a very long time. The girls (?) themselves were too much. If I hadn't known that they were actually fellas, I'd have fucked any one of them, given the opportunity. They were simply beautiful. And so feminine. The winner, a Puerto Rican lady – Ms Channel Perez – was a popular choice with the crowd. At the end of the competition, having been announced as the winner, she stood there, her rhinestone tiara askew, dropping tears of pleasure onto an armful of red roses, her mother at her side. 'I'm thrilled,' she gushed, in broken English. 'This is wonderful. We're all human beings, no matter how we choose to live.'

Right on, baby, I thought. Interesting subject, that of transvestites. I mean, what exactly are they? Men? Women? Homosexual? Bisexual? All these pretty girls, I was reliably informed, had cocks. They just preferred to dress, act, and live, as women. Hormone tablets – and sometimes implants as well – produced the pretty breasts. But what did they do for sex? Presumably they did whatever it was with men? I've never heard of a transvestite having a sexual relationship with a woman, despite the fact that they obviously have the equipment for such an affair. Transsexuals are something else.

One transsexual getting her fifteen minutes of fame in New York at that time was Liz Eden, a gentleman – now a lady – who went the whole way and had the operation. For operation, read three operations (the first two were unsuccessful, for one reason or another), hormone therapy and silicone implants. The silicone implants were followed by water-bag implants, after the initial ones sagged. She's now a 40DD, and says she comes when she's fucked. Her claim to fame was to have a Warner Brothers movie – *Dog Day Afternoon* – made about her story, in which one of her lovers, John Wojtowicz, attempted to rob a bank in order to raise the money for her sex change operation. When last heard of, Liz was living with an air-conditioning and refrigeration mechanic in an apartment on Manhattan's Lower East side. I saw some colour transparencies that had been taken of her nude at that time. She was certainly no raving beauty, in my opinion, but yes, she looked like a woman, and yes, I guess that glimpse of pink peeping out of the mass of her brown pubic hair *could* be a cunt. According to an article that she wrote for the magazine *Club* around then, her new female sexual organ was made from '. . . the hollowed (out), still-connected cock (which) was tucked up inside me, inside out, creating a vagina from the sensitive skin. The scrotum was then used to form the lips of the vagina. It sounds – and apparently was – extremely painful. I wonder what she's doing now?

But enough of that. The Miss New York Transvestite competition would make a perfect item for *Tiptop*'s next monthly sexual diary pages, and I went back to the office at the end of the evening to write a piece whilst everything was still fresh in my mind. There had been a number of photographers at the event taking pictures, and I had asked a couple of the more professional-looking ones to bring me their transparencies to look at when they had been processed.

Since I was there, I went through the mail that Eileen had left on my desk, together with various telephone messages, and a small, neatly wrapped parcel. When I opened the parcel, I was touched – and delighted – to find revealed inside the wrapping a small, perfectly sculpted female torso. It was anatomically correct in every detail, and was a gift from the sculptor Doug Johns, who had liked, he said in his accompanying note, the piece I'd recently published about his work. I still have the sculpture, which sits, these days, in my study in Hampstead.

That afternoon I went off to visit the Erotics Gallery, downtown at 316 Fifth Avenue, at the invitation of artist John Squadra, who was exhibiting some of his work there. When we met, he told me that he had been selling paintings to buyers as far away as Europe and Australia, as well as to New Yorkers, and to art lovers in his home state of Connecticut. Most of these, however, bought his popular surrealist paintings, and the owners of these were probably unaware of another, quite different, aspect of his work – his erotic oil paintings and collages. The Erotics Gallery had quite a selection, of which more in a moment.

John was both a graphic and an industrial designer. His interest in producing erotic works of art was something that 'just happened,' he told me. My own favourite, from those on display, was the aptly named *Fur Piece*, an excitingly realistic oil painting of an exquisitely formed naked female rump, sensually raised in the air, due to the fact that its owner was kneeling upon a fur carpet (bedspread?). Next to that, I loved the painting of a lady's nude body, from the waist down, and from the rear, seen through a window. She was clad only in the sheerest of fine net stockings, both of which, lacking any visible means of support, are falling down the lady's legs, in wrinkled, cock stiffening distrait. This model had the finest buttocks – complete with cleavage and anal hair – that it had ever been my privilege to view. The collages were three-dimensional, and a lot of fun, if not exactly my cup of tea. One, entitled *Miami*, was of an attractive woman who appeared to be wearing a pair of saucepans as a brassiere. More to my taste was *Espresso*, a colour photograph of a young girl's spread legs, her snatch partially hidden by a real, brilliantly blue-green peacock's feather, while her right leg was adorned with a coffee cup as an anklet. Talented, highly original work. And a lot of fun. I made arrangements to send a photographer down to take pictures to accompany the piece that I would write for *Tiptop*'s diary, and then took my leave of John Squadra. He was eventually to become a firm friend.

It was early yet, so I took a cab back up to the office. Eileen brought me coffee, and more messages. She poured us both a cup, sugared mine, and sat down. She looked at me, and raised her eyebrows. 'So can you phone Annabel?' she said. 'She's got the time and date of her arrival.' 'Oh,' I said. 'Great.' 'For you, maybe,' said Eileen. 'For me, no.' 'Oh, come on, Eileen,' I said what's your problem?' 'It's not that much of a problem, really,' said Eileen, flatly. 'It's just that I've fallen in love for the first time for what seems like a lifetime, with someone who finds the world and her wife more attractive than me. It took me weeks to get this asshole into bed, and then, when I do, the next thing he does is to invite one of his London fucks over to stay with him. I tell you, there's no justice in this world.' There's not a lot to say to someone feeling as Eileen was feeling, right at that particular moment, so I didn't say anything. She finished her coffee, and got up. 'Shall I get Annabel on the phone for you?' she asked. 'That would be kind, Eileen,' I said. 'Thank you.' Two minutes later Annabel's mellifluous, well-remembered voice was telling me excitedly that she was arriving, courtesy of British Airways, at Kennedy Airport at eleven a.m. the following Wednesday. 'Have you been missing me, my darling?' she asked. 'You've not exactly been burning up the telephone lines between London and New York.' 'Of course I've been missing you, sweetheart,' I said. 'And I'm sorry about the lack of contact. I'll make it up to you when you arrive. Don't worry about a thing. I shall be there when you get off the plane. I'm so looking forward to seeing you.'

'What do I need to bring?' she asked. 'What's the weather doing?' 'It's seriously hot,' I told her. 'Bring summer clothes. And swimsuits and stuff. That's all. We'll go out to the Hamptons, or Fire Island, or somewhere, at the weekends. Or we can drop down to the Caribbean. Or Florida. Whatever turns you on. I'll take some time off. OK?' 'Oh, that sounds lovely, darling,' she said. 'I can't wait. Will I really see you next week? For two whole weeks?' 'Of course you will baby,' I said to her. 'I'm looking forward to it as much as you are. Probably more.' 'Not possible,' she said. 'But thank you for saying it. See you next week. Bye for now. I love you.' 'I love you too, darling,' I said. 'Goodbye now.'

When I'd put the phone down, I sat for a while, thinking about the implications of what I'd been saying. I *did* love her. I was sure of that. But that didn't stop me enjoying my relationships with other women. Leaving aside anyone else in London, I mean, what about Lucy? Eileen? Dee Dee? Pauline? What about Charlene, Victoria, and Rita, the girls at June's brothel? What about the other three girls there, Andrea, Louise, and Gloria, whom I had undertaken to fuck in the not too distant future? What about the list of women that my old friend John Lane had given to me, all of them guaranteed, he had said, to drop their knickers? At that moment, Dave, the magazine's art director, knocked on my door, and put his head around it. 'Come in, Dave,' I said. 'What can I do for you?'

'I just wanted to tell you that I've set up the lesbian set with your two friends Dee Dee and Lucy,' he said. 'George Barter is going to do it. I've told him that it will be in Fred's apartment, rather than down at the *Tiptop* studio on Canal Street. You've been down there, haven't you?' 'Yes,' I said. 'I met George there, with Betsy.' 'Good,' said Dave. 'I've briefed George, and he and I have worked together for so long now that I don't feel there's any need for me to be there. He knows what I want. And I told him you'll be there, at least for part of the shoot, so if there are any problems, you can sort them out for me,' he said. 'OK?' 'Sure,' I said. 'My pleasure. When is it?' 'Tomorrow,' said Dave. 'Unless that's a problem with you?' 'Not at all,' I said, thinking *shit! This is all I need*.

Oh, well. I *had* offered Fred's apartment for the shoot, and I *had* told both Dee Dee and Lucy that I'd be there. I didn't have to stay until the bitter end, I thought. Probably the sooner I left, the better. I looked at my watch. It was just after six-thirty. Too soon for Dee Dee to have left the Bottomless Pit. I felt like amusing myself, so I quit the office, remembering to say goodnight to Eileen as I left, and walked the three blocks up to the topless, bottomless bar where she worked. I took a seat right up at the bar, ordered a scotch and water, straight up, and looked around for Dee Dee. She was over on the other side, and hadn't seen me yet. I waited for her to bump and grind her way around to my seat, and then waved a five-dollar bill at her, keeping my head well down. 'Show me your split beaver, baby,' I demanded. 'Oh, come on, buster,' she said. 'For *five* dollars?' I looked up at her, and said 'I bet you'd show it to me for nothing, if I asked you nicely.'

Her face broke into a great big grin. 'Baby,' she said, squatting down in front of me. 'What a nice surprise. Is this what you want?' she asked, reaching down to her honeypot with the fingers of both hands, and pulling her labia wide apart until her pussy looked like a wet, pink, miniature version of the

Midtown Tunnel. My prick tried to get up, out of my trousers, to get a better view. 'You can fuck it if you'd like to,' she offered. 'No charge. But you'll have to wait until just after seven, when I finish.' 'You're on, sweetheart,' I said, my earlier philosophical self-examination disappearing at the sight of this gorgeous girl, with her firm, young, fabulous body, and the sight of her wet cunt, with its pungent, aroused aroma, just inches away from my eyes and nose. 'I'd better move on,' she said, 'or I'll be in trouble. 'I'll see you in the bar at P.J. Clarke's at seven fifteen. Just like last time. OK?' 'OK, darling,' I said. 'I'll be there.'

She pranced off to the music, my five bill tucked into her garter, as usual her only apparel. She must have had two hundred dollars tucked in there. Worth every cent, I thought. So too, apparently, did the other men sitting around the bar. Just then a big, strapping redhead squatted in front of me, and handed me a twenty-dollar bill. 'Hey,' she said. 'Tuck that in my garter. Then I can sit and rap with you for a couple of minutes.' I did as I was told. 'I'm Rhoda,' she said. 'And you're Tony Andrews, from London, England. You're the editor of *Tiptop*, aren't you?' She smiled at me. 'Dee Dee's told me all about you. She says you've got a big dick, and that you love to fuck. How would you like to fuck this?'

She reached down into her red pubic bush, and spread her fanny for me. That close, I must admit, it looked pretty good. And that close, I find, they're difficult to say no to. It had really big, long, purplish pink labia, and was a genuine shocking pink inside. 'All same Princess Margaret inside,' as the Arabs say about their teenage sisters in Cairo. Did you ever refuse the offer of a wet, open cunt, six inches in front of your face, and owned by a big, busty redhead who looked as if she knew a million different ways to use it? Just as with Dee Dee, minutes earlier, I could smell the strong scent of wet pussy, but Rhoda's had that extra pungency that redheads all seem to have. I felt my erection becoming an embarrassment.

'It certainly bears thinking about, darling' I said. Why don't you call me at *Tiptop*'s office sometime? It's in the phone book. Then we could arrange to meet, and maybe work something out?' 'Now you're talking, honey,' she said. 'You can have a quick feel, if you like. It's all hot and wet, thinking about that big prick of yours. Here, feel it. Imagine putting your stiff cock into that. It's like fucking a teenager. I promise.' I would have loved to have done exactly as she asked, but I was afraid that Dee Dee, or even one of the other girls, would see what was going on, and report back. 'I'd love to, sweetheart,' I said. 'Feel it, *and* fuck it. But I don't think this is either the time or the place, all things considered. But thank you for the offer. I much appreciate it. Just call me. OK?' 'You can bet on it,' she said. 'See you.' She took off, sashaying along the bar, her short, curly red hair standing out amongst the black and blonde and just plain brown of the other girls.

I finished my drink, waved at Rhoda, and took off for P.J. Clarke's. I got there before Dee Dee, and found a space at the bar to lean against. She arrived not long after, and I ordered her a vodka martini, on the rocks, with a slice. 'Cheers, sweetie,' I said. 'Cheers Tony,' she said. 'What a nice surprise. What's new?' 'I just felt like a little company,' I said. 'Is that OK?' 'Sure,' she said. That's very OK with me.' 'How much did Dave tell you about tomorrow morning's job?' I asked her. 'Did he tell you that it was a test run for a lesbian set?' 'Yes,' she said. 'He did tell me that. Why do you ask?' 'I just wondered,' I said. 'And did he tell you that the other half of the so-called lesbian couple is a tall, black lady with a bald head and a shaved box?'

'Good God,' she said, laughing, 'no, he certainly didn't mention that. What a gas.' 'Does that cause you any angst?' I asked, curiously. 'No, honey. Why should it?' she asked. 'Oh, I don't know,' I said. 'Some people in this city are quite racist. Others don't seem bothered by colour at all. I just thought that maybe coming to close quarters with a black girl might embarrass you in some way.' 'Lord, no,' she said. 'I have no problems of that kind. I usually get on with other girls OK, unless there's some reason not to.' 'This one is something of a character,' I said. 'But I reckon you'll get on OK. But changing the subject, if you'll forgive me, are you hungry?' She smiled. 'I'm starving,' she said. 'How about you?' 'I certainly am,' I said. 'What do you fancy.' 'Do you like Chinese?' she asked. 'Love it,' I said. 'Where do you suggest?' 'Let me take you to a place I know down in SoHo, on West Broadway. It's called the Oh Ho So. It's really nice. I think you'll like it. What do you say?' 'Sounds good,' I said. 'Lead on, McDuff.' 'Huh?,' she said. 'Oh, nothing,' I said. 'Forgive me. I was just rambling on.' We finished our drinks, and found a cab right outside to take us down to SoHo. The Oh Ho So turned out to be a converted warehouse, as were so many of the smart, downtown restaurants.

It had been elegantly – and expensively – converted, and there was much naked ironwork, and vast expanses of exposed brick. It sounds awful, but it was a popular style of conversion in the Big Apple in those days, and if you were ever fortunate enough to see it you will know just how good it can look. Its only slight incongruity, to my mind, was the plethora of intensely populated aquaria that were everywhere, but I think fish were fashionable with New York interior designers that year.

The food was something else, and we gorged ourselves on some of the finest Chinese food I've ever had, before or since. I was never greatly impressed with the Chinese restaurants in New York's China Town (unlike, for example, the Italian restaurants in New York's Little Italy, which are excellent) but the food at the Oh Ho So was genuinely (that over-used – in America – word gourmet). I was pleased when Dee Dee asked if I would forgive her for not coming back to the apartment with me, because she wanted an early night, in order to look her best for the photographic session the following morning. I dropped her off at her studio apartment on the Upper West side, not exactly on my way home, but it was a pleasure for me so to do. A lovely girl. When I got home, I watched Home Box

Office until I almost fell asleep in front of it, and decided, not before time, that I should go to bed. It was the best decision that I had made that day. I remembered to set the alarm, to allow myself sufficient time to get both me, and the apartment, ready for the morning.

Friday dawned. I could see out of the window that the ConEd chimneys were belching forth their daily insult to the world's ecologists. Another New York day. I remembered that the photographic shoot was due to arrive by 10 a.m. and got myself together rather more quickly than was my usual procedure. The morning promised to be more amusing than for a normal, end-of-the-week Friday. To my surprise, Lucy was the first to arrive. 'Hi, baby,' she cried, as I opened the apartment door. 'What's for breakfast? Have you got any prunes?' I looked at her, perhaps rather sourly. 'Prunes?' I said. 'You've gotta be kidding. There's coffee, tea, cereal, and/or toast. Anything else you can order from the neighbourhood deli. The number's by the kitchen telephone.'

Dee Dee arrived about fifteen minutes later. She looked absolutely amazing. A different girl from the one that I knew, either from the topless/bottomless bar in which she earned her daily bread, or from the quite different, delightful lady that I knew from my bed. 'Hi, baby,' she said as I opened the door, having cleared her arrival with the doormen downstairs. 'What a lovely start to the day.' She looked fresh, beautiful, and astonishingly young. She was wearing an absolutely minuscule white cotton mini-skirt, and a crisp, freshly laundered and ironed white cotton blouse. Butter, as you looked at her, wouldn't have melted in her mouth. I introduced her to Lucy, and vice versa. Lucy blew her a big kiss, which Dee Dee returned.

'Hey,' said Lucy to me, 'You didn't tell me that this lady was somtin' else.' 'You didn't ask me,' I replied. 'Nor did I tell her that you were somtin' different.' She had the grace to fall about laughing. It wasn't that funny a joke, but she made the most of it, bless her. 'Hey, baby,' she said, to Dee Dee. 'Come over here, sweetheart.' Dee Dee hesitated for a moment. Then she went over to Lucy, and took her in her arms. 'Hey,' said Lucy. 'This girl's got guts.' And she gave Dee Dee a big kiss. Dee Dee seemed to hesitate for a moment, and then she wholeheartedly grabbed Lucy, and began to kiss her back. The two girls together began to take whatever it was that they thought they were doing together rather more seriously, and then suddenly Dee Dee said 'Hey, hang on a moment there, Lucy, sweetheart. This is fine. Not to say extremely pleasant. But there isn't a camera in sight. Beautiful as you are, let's save the kisses for when there's a reason for them. What do you say?'

Lucy grinned her cheeky grin. 'I say whatever you wanna do is fine with me,' she intoned through her large, white teeth. 'You need a reason, a camera, whatever, that's fine with me. You just enjoy doin' it, you know, for the fun, for the enjoyment, that's fine too. No problem. No hassle.' She turned to me. 'What time's the crew gettin' here, honey?' she asked. 'We got time to send out to the deli for some prunes?' I had to laugh. It wasn't possible to take the lady seriously. She was too much. 'No, Lucy love,' I said. 'No prunes. Have some juice, and some coffee, and forget about the goddamn prunes. OK?' 'OK, baby,' she said. And she busied herself making a big pot of coffee, whilst chattering to Dee Dee. She was fascinated when Dee Dee described how she was earning her living. 'Wow, baby,' she said. 'That is one tough way to earn a living.'

Right then the doorman rang through to tell me that George Barter and Betsy were on their way up, with an assistant called Bob. They arrived a few minutes later, and as I let them into the apartment, I could see the reason for the assistant, who was almost hidden beneath the lighting equipment that he was carrying. George introduced him to me, and I did the rest of the introductions all around. Betsy was carrying two largish cases. When she opened the first of these, I could see that it was full of lingerie. The second proved to contain jewellery, scarves, gloves, shoes and so on. Betsy took over the two would-be models, and after getting them to sign the usual release form, she took them off into the bedroom, together with the two cases. When they emerged, Lucy was in white, Dee Dee in black, as Dave had originally suggested. They made a marvellous pair. Standing beside Lucy, the diminutive Betsy looked rather like a midget.

While the girls were getting dressed, George and Bob had set up the camera tripod and lighting equipment around one of Fred's larger sofas, one upholstered in a textured white material which would act as a good, but not over-assertive, background for the two girls. Having had their outfits approved by George, the girls then went away and took them off again, and they both came back wearing gowns, to wait for the elastic marks from the lingerie on their skin to wear off. George would, as was usual, begin the shoot with shots of the girls naked, and then slowly dress them, the reverse of the way the photographs would be laid out in the magazine. That, of course, was assuming that the photographs would be of publishable quality, that again depending on the suitability of the girls as models, rather than of George as a photographer, he having proven his skills over many hundreds of girl sets over the years.

George filled in the time waiting for the girls' elastic marks to fade by fine-tuning his lighting, and taking a series of test shots with a Polaroid camera. The rest of us sat around and chatted, and drank copious amounts of coffee. Finally the girls proclaimed themselves ready, and the serious work of the day began. Both girls entered into it enthusiastically, and there were no problems that I could see, as the shoot progressed. Watching Dee Dee kissing the inside of Lucy's satin-textured black thigh, her tongue only centimetres away from Lucy's bald pudenda, with its central pink gash, now oozing her juices, was a fantastically erotic experience, as was watching Dee Dee sucking Lucy's nipples. After ten minutes or so of such sucking, Lucy's nipples looked as erect and as hard as if made of blue-black iron.

But the real fun began, for me at least, as the girls started, under George's instructions, to don their underwear. They began, of course, with their knickers; Lucy's of filmy white, gauzy, totally transparent material, and Dee Dee's of black shiny satin, trimmed with little red bows. George had them both doing the obligatory this-is-me-pulling-my-knicker-crotch-aside-so-that-you-can-see-my-pussy shots, which I found totally enthralling, especially since I'd had, as we say, the pleasure of both of them. Their contrasting pussy lips, Lucy's of purply black, fleshily swollen, Dee Dee's of palest pink, and slightly less fleshy, both now wetly shiny with their sexually engendered lubrication, were a sensual picture in themselves.

George had, at the beginning of the shoot, rather been concentrating on pictures of Dee Dee doing sexually explicit (or, perhaps I should say, *apparently* doing sexually explicit) things to Lucy. Now he began to concentrate on shots of Lucy apparently doing naughty things to Dee Dee. But, very shortly, those of us watching could discern a subtle difference in approach. Where Dee Dee's tongue had stopped perhaps millimetres short of Lucy's luscious black cunt, Lucy's tongue took a number of serious licks at Dee Dee's pretty pink one, before settling down the requisite short distance away for the benefit of the camera. Dee Dee obviously was aware of what was being done to her, but made no audible objection. But the tremors that ran through her body when it happened left no doubt in my mind that she was actually enjoying the contacts as they were made.

When it came to photographs of Lucy kissing and sucking Dee Dee's breasts and nipples, Dee Dee suddenly grabbed Lucy's bald head and pressed it more tightly to her bosom. Looking at her spread thighs at that moment, I could see her love juice literally running down her legs. All of which made for extremely erotic photographs, but I wondered, at the end of the day, just how many of them we would be able to publish.

But Betsy quickly came to the rescue, noncommittally wiping down Dee Dee's wet pussy lips and thighs with a warm, damp flannel, her face as void of expression as a stone statue as she did so. It was obviously something she'd coped with many times before. Dee Dee was obviously embarrassed by the need for this treatment, but forbore from commenting on it. A wet pussy is a wet pussy is a wet pussy, her expression seemed to say. If you play sexual games, you must expect to get sexual results.

Just then George called for a break while he changed from photographing the girls on and around the sofa, and asked for time to set up in one of the bedrooms. I suggested Fred's bedroom as being the largest and, having had a look at it, George was in agreement. Looking at my watch and, seeing that it was after twelve, I suggested that in fact we stop for lunch. Betsy rang the local deli for a selection of sandwiches, and I opened a bottle of Fred's champagne as what I thought would be a pleasant way of us all relaxing together.

In what seemed like no time at all, the sandwiches were delivered, and we all took time out to partake. If you've never eaten an American sandwich, you've missed a new, exciting experience. American sandwiches are a way of life. They come in such variety, in such generously filled plenitude, in such mouth-watering variation, that I cringe with shame whenever I see an American ordering a sandwich in London. That apart, one bottle of champagne, as you know, doesn't go far amongst six. One glass each, to be pedantic. So I soon found myself opening first another, then another, then another, until we had consumed four without even thinking about it. It is also very difficult to change to something inferior – even to a decent white wine – once you have begun on champagne. So I opened two more before we declared ourselves sufficiently replete. I made a mental note to restock Fred's supply of champagne before he returned. And back to work we went.

The stage reached in the schedule after lunch required both girls to be wearing panties, stockings, and suspender belts.

Nothing else. Lucy in her white, transparent knickers, with her hairless black pudenda showing through the crotch, and with her fleshy, blue-black cunt lips squashed, half open, against the thin material, was also wearing white, sheer stockings, and a white, minuscule garter belt. She looked sensational. When she turned around, I could see the crack of her ass all the way down to her anus. Dee Dee wore flimsy black voile knickers, which were entirely see-through all the way from the elasticated top down to the crotch at the front and rear. The sides, perversely, were opaque, and threaded through with pale pink, narrow ribbon. Dee Dee's cunt lips could also be seen through her black knickers, their pinkness matching that of the decorative ribbon.

For his first post-prandial shot, George had the girls pretending to masturbate themselves. You'll know the picture I mean. It's the one where the girl's facial expression tells you that she knows that she's entirely alone – or, as in this case, alone with her best girlfriend – and they both have been talking about men so much and for so long that they've gotten themselves seriously horny. So it's knickers down or pulled to one side, forefingers delving into pussies, find clitorises, and, by numbers, from the left, frig. And very pretty it always looks too. Not to say sexy. But, of course, naughty Lucy couldn't simply *act*, could she? She had to go the whole hog. I couldn't believe my eyes. She slid her fingers deep inside her pussy, felt around for her clitoris, and began to masturbate. And I do mean *masturbate*!

She had the crotch of her knicks pulled right over to one side, her legs and thighs spread, her head thrown back, her eyes closed, and her fingers were going like an electric toothbrush. They were just a blur. Bob – the lighting assistant – was standing there with his mouth hanging open. He simply couldn't believe what he was watching. George raised his head up from his view through his camera lens, as if to check that he really *was* seeing what he thought he was seeing, and just stood there, amazed. After a few moments, when it became obvious that Lucy wasn't going to stop – at least, not until she achieved the orgasm she was working so hard for – Betsy once more came to the aid of the party. She disappeared into the kitchen for a few moments, and then came back with a tray on which she had put a large jug of orange juice, and half a dozen glasses. She reached out and took hold of Lucy's arm. The one she was masturbating with, and shook it. Hard.

Lucy opened her eyes, but before she had a chance to say a word, Betsy had thrust a glass of juice into her hand. 'Here you are, Lucy,' she said. 'Juice.' And having given Lucy hers, she gave each one of us a glass of orange juice too. 'Mmmmm,' she said, finally taking a long pull from hers, 'how delicious. There's nothing like a glass of cold juice on a hot, sunny afternoon, is there?' George announced that he was happy with what shots he wanted from the bedroom, and we all heaved a sigh of relief as we took ourselves out of it. Quite frankly, after that, I'd had enough. First of all, patently the photographic shoot was basically going well. I'd seen enough to know that we were going to get some excellent pictures. Of both girls. And it had occurred to me that at the end of the shoot, I was either going to have to choose between Dee Dee or Lucy as my companion for the evening, or take the whole damn crew out to dinner. Neither of which possibilities really appealed to me.

So I decided to make myself scarce. I looked at my watch. It was just after three. I could be in the office in fifteen minutes. I took my decision, and made my departure. In answer to the girls' questions, I asked them to contact Dave in the office in a couple of days to find out how the photographs had turned out. George gave me a grateful look, since it was he who would receive them back from the processors long before anyone else saw them.

I looked in on Eileen as I went past her office. 'Hi,' she said. 'How did it go? Did you get to fuck Lucy in the closet? Or should that be did Lucy get to fuck you in the closet?' I grinned at her. 'Very funny,' I said. 'No one got to fuck anyone.' 'What went wrong?' Eileen asked. 'Perhaps I should rephrase that,' I suggested. 'Perhaps I should have said, no one had fucked anyone, up to the time I left the apartment, but if I was Dee Dee, I wouldn't half keep my hand on my halfpenny.' Eileen laughed. 'I can imagine,' she said. 'Go look at your mail. I'll bring some coffee through, momentarily.' 'Thanks, honey,' I said. She was a good girl. Nice, too. And terrific in bed. What early women's magazines used to describe coyly, back in the Fifties, as GIB. That, as I remember being told, stood for Good In Bed. Funny how the world changes. People would die laughing if anyone described someone else as good in bed these days. Terrific? Certainly. Good? I don't, somehow, think so. Eileen came in with the coffee.

'Is there anything of interest in the mail, before I start wading through it?' I asked. She thought for a moment. 'There's an interesting letter from someone who claims to run an S&M club downtown somewhere,' she said. 'It sounds horrible to me, but you might find it makes an amusing piece for your new monthly sex diary.' 'That's a thought,' I said. 'Can you find it for me?' I asked, pushing the pile of paper across my desk. She found it quite quickly. The writer, a woman, said that she was running a club that she had originally started for friends with a mutual interest in S&M. It had been very successful initially, and she had finally given in to suggestions that she went commercial with it. She had just moved into much larger – and much more expensive – premises, and she needed more members. Quickly.

At least she was being honest. She wondered if anyone at *Tiptop* would like to go and have a look at the place. They apparently did an evening show Wednesdays through Saturdays, at eight p.m. admission $25 (gratis to any representative from *Tiptop*). After the show, there was a bar, light refreshments, and members could get up to anything with each other that turned them on. There was a good supply (she said) of whips, canes, manacles, chains, leather straps, gags, restrainers, straitjackets, whipping posts, facilities for golden showers, and associated water sports, enemas, rubber gear, and so on. All the things that I personally abhor. Oh well, I thought. I have a duty to my readers. I picked up the telephone. 'Fancy an evening of S&M?' I asked Eileen. 'Are you serious?' she said. 'You've got to be kidding.' 'Well, up to a point,' I said. I was in the midst of explaining to Eileen what it was all about, when a pleasant female voice answered the number I had dialled. I explained who I was, and why I was telephoning. 'Oh, hi, Tony,' said the voice. 'I'm Rene. It's my letter to *Tiptop* you're talking about. I just love your magazine. It really turns me on. Which is why I wrote. Say, this is terrific. Are you really interested in coming down to have a look at us? See our show? When would you like to come? How about tonight?'

'Hang on a second, will you, please?' I asked, putting my hand over the mouthpiece. 'How about this evening, Eileen? We can grab a bite somewhere, and be downtown by eight. No problem. What do you say?' 'Oh, sure,' said Eileen. 'Yeah. It could be fun.' I went back to Rene. 'Yes, thank you. This evening will be fine. Eight o'clock, isn't it?' 'You've got it,' she said. 'Ask for me at the door. You've got the address, obviously?' 'Yes, I have,' I told her. 'Thank you. We'll see you later.' They were way downtown, just off West 14th Street, down on the Lower West Side. 'How about the new One Fifth restaurant?' I asked Eileen. 'Have you been there? Do you like it? It's roughly a block away from the S&M place.' 'Oh, terrific,' she said. 'I just love it. That would be really great.' Eileen had always been everywhere.

We got ourselves together, and took a cab down to the restaurant that had opened recently down at number one, Fifth Avenue. Hence its name. It wasn't a million miles away from the Bowery, but Manhattan is like that. One end of a street can be a slum, the other end a really smart address. Greenwich Village was no distance away either, with its sophisticated, Christopher Street shops and hangouts, and its sleazy leather bars, with their notorious back rooms.

The interior of One Fifth was like the first-class dining room on an elegant, luxurious 1930s ocean liner. Indeed, much of the panelling had come from great liners of the past: the *France*, the *Queen Mary*, and the like. The food was upmarket American, and good. Eileen went for the grilled tuna special, I ordered the New York sirloin. I was hungry. We both had the soft-shelled crab to start with. 'So what's the attraction of this S&M place,' asked Eileen, as I poured the chilled Californian chardonnay. 'You're not into any of that stuff, are you? Because if you are, let me tell you now, before it's too late, that I'm not. If you had any thought of tying me up and whipping me, I'm simply not on for it. OK? I don't want there to be any misunderstandings, once we get there.' 'Don't worry about a thing, sweetheart,' I told her. 'I hate all that stuff too. I've never been able to relate sex with pain. I just thought it might make a fun piece for the monthly sex diary that I'm just starting. You know, tongue in cheek stuff.'

'Thank God for that,' said Eileen. 'You had me worried there for a moment.' She then changed the subject away from our impending visit to the S&M club, and I spent an intriguing dinner listening to the latest hot office gossip, upon which Eileen was the expert. Much of it centred around the magazine's art department, and the gays who mostly staffed it. They were a promiscuous lot, and always rowing with each other in the office about who had been unfaithful to whom – and how – the previous night. We spoke of Annabel's impending arrival, and Eileen confirmed that she had ordered a stretch limo for me to meet Annabel with at the airport. 'It's not a question of status, or anything silly like that,' I said. 'It's just that we don't have stretch limos in England' (at that time, we didn't: we do now, of course) 'and they're a gas for anyone who's never seen one before. Annabel will have hysterics.'

I looked at my watch. It was seven thirty. 'If we left now,' I suggested, 'we could walk gently up to Seventh Avenue and 20th Street, which is where we're going. Does that sound all right to you? The serious heat of the day has pretty much gone now.' 'Sure,' she said. 'I'm on for that.' I paid the check, and we went out from the restaurant's air-conditioning into the warmth of the summer evening, walking slowly west and north.

When we got there, we found that the club was housed in the basement of a well kept brownstone. There was no suggestion of the club's name. Simply a small brass plate with the address, and beside it the push-button of a bell. I rang. The door was opened almost immediately by a large, unshaven gentleman, who could only have been a bouncer. 'Yus?' he said. 'My name's Tony Andrews,' I said. 'The young lady is with me. I was told to ask for Rene.' He looked at me, menacingly, I thought. 'Hoh, yus,' he said, opening the door rather wider. 'Won't you come in?' We went inside, to find a sort of small foyer, with a desk, some chairs, a decent carpet, and little else. The bouncer picked up the telephone, and pressed a button. 'Miss Rene?' he asked. 'Your guests is here. Mr Andrews and a young lady. Right.' He put the phone down. 'She'll be right out,' he said. Moments later an extremely attractive, dark-haired woman came out from behind a curtain, which partly concealed the entrance to a corridor. She was dressed in what I can only describe as the full dominatrice outfit. She was wearing a closely-fitting black velvet body and black net tights, with a black velvet ribbon around her neck. She wore leather wristlets, studded with chrome spikes, and high-heeled, black leather boots. Her body was large, voluptuous, and well-proportioned. Her eyes were a soft brown. She was very beautiful, and she was carrying a vicious-looking, black, leather-bound, bone-handled whip, with a number of longish, knotted thongs. She smiled at Eileen and me, and stretched out a hand.

'Tony Andrews?' she said. 'How very good of you to come. And . . .?' I introduced Eileen. Rene looked at her watch. 'There's about ten minutes before we start the show,' she said. 'Let me show you where the bar is, and get you a drink.' *What a good idea*, I said to myself. When we got there, the bar was at the back of a large room, which had been turned into a small theatre. There were five rows of comfortable-looking seats, each row with room for twelve people. They faced a smallish, raised dais at the other end of the room, presently covered by a curtain. Some sort of canned music was playing, and there were about twenty people standing about around the bar, talking and drinking quietly. Rene didn't introduce us to anyone, other than to the barman. 'This is Frank,' she said. 'Frank, look after the guests of mine, will you, please? Everything is on the house.' He nodded his agreement. She faced back towards Eileen and me. 'The show will start at any moment now,' she said. 'I do hope you enjoy it. I'll catch up with you afterwards. I'll answer any questions you may have then. OK?' 'Fine,' I said. 'Excellent. Thank you.' She smiled once more, and took herself off backstage. A few minutes later the canned music faded and a man's voice said, 'Ladies and gentlemen, we are about to begin our presentation. Will you please take your seats.' There was a click, and then silence. We finished our drinks, and sat down towards the back of the small theatre. Even there, the stage was only about thirty feet away. Then the house lights went down, and I could hear the curtain being raised.

The stage lights came up, and there was Rene, in her costume, this time complete with stage make-up. She was standing centre stage. 'Good evening, everyone,' she said. 'It's good to welcome old friends, and nice to greet some new ones. To begin with, I'm going to show you around some of our facilities here.' She turned away from us, and more lights came on, lighting up what looked like a large dog kennel at the rear of the stage. As my eyes became accustomed to the light, I could make out what looked like a naked man, on all fours. And then I could see that, not only was it indeed a naked man, but he had a leather collar around his neck, and a lead which tied him to the kennel.

Rene cracked her whip. The noise was startlingly loud in the surroundings of the theatre. Rene looked back towards her audience. 'This is Kenneth,' she said. 'He's here to learn obedience.' She cracked her whip again, this time rather too close to Kenneth for his comfort, I would have felt, had I been him. 'What are you here for, Kenneth?' she asked him. He hung his head and said, 'To learn obedience, mistress.' 'That's right,' she said. 'Now go and get me your water bowl, and bring it to me. Quickly, now,' she barked at him. 'I haven't got all day.' Poor Kenneth scurried around to the side of his kennel, and brought back a white, enamelled metal bowl that had the word 'Dog' painted on it. He was carrying it in his teeth, and he placed it carefully onto the floor, by Rene's feet.

Rene then put down her whip, and undid a previously hidden zip that appeared to run from just below her navel at the front of her costume to up around the top of her ass at the back. She pulled the now-open legs of the costume apart, revealing the fact that she wore nothing beneath it. I could see her hirsute pudenda. 'Bring your water bowl to me, and hold it for me,' she commanded of Kenneth.

He had obviously been through this routine before, for he squatted on his ass in front of Rene, and held the bowl in his hands, carefully positioning it between her legs. He held it there, not moving, until suddenly the sound of pissing told the audience that Rene was, in fact, pissing in Kenneth's bowl. She stopped, eventually. 'Now put it down and lick me clean,' she demanded, picking up her whip again as she spoke. Kenneth took hold of Rene's hips, and pulled her groin towards him until he was able to lick away at her pussy lips, which he now did. Rene let him go on doing this for some time, until she finally said, 'All right. That's enough.' An enormous erection told those of us in the audience that Kenneth was thoroughly enjoying himself. 'Good boy,' said Rene. Now you can have your reward. Bring me your riding crop.'

She walked away from where she had been standing, and the spotlight followed her, lighting up a whipping horse that was standing against the back of the stage. Kenneth reappeared from the darkness, carrying a wicked-looking riding crop in his mouth. Rene took it from him, and then put down both the crop and her whip. Kenneth stood in front of the whipping horse, his back to the audience, and put up his hands, to where we could now see there were metal manacles, which Rene clipped around his willing wrists. He then spread his legs, as Rene clipped his ankles to two more manacles at each side of the bottom of the horse.

She next turned to the audience, and said, 'I'd just like to say one thing to you all, before I carry on with this next part of our demonstration. Kenneth is a member of this club. He asks me to make clear to you that what he does here – and what we do to him – is at his request, and for his pleasure. And, of course, at his expense. Is that right, Kenneth?' Despite the awkwardness of his position, Kenneth managed to nod his head. 'Yes,' we heard him say. 'That's absolutely right.' Rene then positioned herself carefully about four feet behind Kenneth's buttocks and, measuring the distance between them and her crop precisely, she began to beat him. Mercilessly. She beat him with steady, well-timed, well-placed strokes. His buttocks were soon pink, then red, then scarlet. I heard Eileen gasp again, and she put out a hand and gripped my knee. She leaned over and whispered in my ear, 'I'm not sure I can take much more of this.' 'I'm not sure I can, either,' I said. 'But I'm going to try and stick it out, so that I can write about it in the magazine. If it gets too much for you, just leave, and wait for me in reception. OK?' She nodded.

The beating continued for what seemed an awfully long time, and then, at last, Rene put down the riding crop, and unbuckled the unfortunate (to my mind) Kenneth, who hadn't made a sound throughout. Rene left him standing there, and walked over to the far left-hand side of the stage. The light followed her as before, and this time it illuminated what looked like an ordinary wooden table of the kind one used in kitchens before the invention of plastics. Upon the table, right over to one side of it, was a block of wood, about a foot square, and three inches deep. Rene faced the audience once more.

'I would like to repeat that what you are about to see is again performed at the specific request of Kenneth,' she said. 'You will understand why I am being so emphatic about this, when I tell you that I am going to pierce Kenneth's foreskin with a nail, by literally nailing it to this block of wood.' A concerted gasp went up from the twenty or so of us in the audience, and Eileen, and one other woman, got up and left the theatre hurriedly. Rene waited for them to leave, and then picked up a hammer and a nail. At that moment Kenneth entered into the circle of light, still naked. For the record, his penis was completely flaccid. It soon became obvious that this was something both Rene and Kenneth had done many times before. The block of wood on the table was at exactly the right height for Kenneth to lay his flaccid penis upon. This he did, and then he pulled his foreskin away from his body, so that the skin itself was free of the penis inside.

Rene then held up what looked like a steel nail, about three inches long, and of the normal sort of thickness that you would expect in a nail of that length. 'Would someone please come to the edge of the stage and just check that this is a genuine nail, please?' she asked. A man from a group of two men and two women near the front of the small theatre got up, and took the nail from Rene's hand. He turned around to the rest of us. 'It's real enough,' he said, handed it back, and resumed his seat.

Kenneth was still holding his stretched foreskin in place upon the block of wood. Rene went back to the table, placed the nail in the centre of the stretched skin, and tapped it with the hammer. When she let go of it, the nail stayed firmly in place. Kenneth didn't flinch. Rene tapped it firmly again, twice, and then stepped back. 'If anyone there can't see to their complete satisfaction that Kenneth's foreskin is now properly nailed to the block of wood, they're very welcome to come and examine it,' she said. No one moved. She looked at Kenneth, who nodded, and she then took up a pair of ordinary pliers from the table and pulled out the nail. Kenneth turned to face the audience. He was smiling, as was Rene, and someone started to applaud. I joined in, I'm not sure why, and then everyone there was applauding. The curtains closed for a moment or two, and the house lights came up. The curtains then quite quickly reopened.

The house lights stayed up, revealing Rene sitting on an upright, upholstered chair, of the kind you see in dining rooms. She was still wearing her dominatrice outfit, and she had been joined by a young girl of around eighteen or nineteen, who was pretty, blonde, and dressed in a short, red, cotton summer skirt, and a white blouse. Rene introduced her. 'This is Jean,' she said. 'Jean has been very naughty, and needs spanking. I'm just going to demonstrate the kind of spanking that she deserves. Jean. Come over here.' Jean moved nearer to Rene. She was either genuinely sulking or putting on a very good semblance.

Rene patted her knees. 'You know what to do,' she said. Jean didn't say anything, but if looks could kill, as they say, Rene would no longer have been with us. Jean then lay across Rene's knees, in the classic spanking position. Rene pulled Jean's short skirt up over her waist, revealing tightly fitting, transparent white knickers. She looked at the audience. 'Panties up or down?' she queried. 'Down,' said all the men in the audience, in unison. Rene pulled Jean's panties down her thighs, leaving them around her knees. Then looking up to ascertain, perhaps, that she had our complete attention – she had – Rene began spanking Jean's rounded little bottom with her bare hand. She spanked sharply, her hand making a sharp slapping sound each time it landed. This went on for some five minutes, after which Jean began to sniffle, then cry, at which point Rene stopped. 'Now, then,' she said, 'who's going to volunteer to carry on with Jean's punishment?' I'm ashamed, on reflection, to say that I was the first of a number of men in the audience to put my hand up. 'Ah,' said Rene. 'Tony. Great. Come along then.'

I went up to the stage and climbed the small steps at the side to get onto the stage proper. Jean got up off Rene's knees, and stood up for a moment, her knickers still down around her knees. Her breasts looked even more suckable from close to than they had from my seat at the back of the theatre. Her nipples were enormous from a couple of feet away, and I began to get a hard-on just looking at them.

Rene got up and took my arm, leading me over to the chair. I sat down. She then brought Jean over, and arranged her across my knees, the gorgeous globes of her bare bottom less than a foot below my face. I could smell her pussy, aroused – presumably – as it was by the spanking she had already received. I could see her tight little pink anus winking up at me from between her buttocks, and below that the beginning of her cunt, a pink gash at the centre of her dyed blonde pubic hair, which curled thickly around its centrepiece. I put down a tentative hand, and stroked and squeezed her bottom. I let a finger stray, for a moment, just far enough down to slide over her pussy, feeling its moist warmth. My erection was becoming uncomfortable.

'So OK,' said Rene. 'Let's get on with the punishment. 'This isn't the feel-a-quim-for-Christmas campaign. It's the spank-a-bottom-for-fun crusade. Do I make myself clear?' I actually felt guilty. I should have stood up and told the woman to fuck off. Nevertheless, I raised my right hand and brought it down sharply on those beautiful, curvaceous buttocks. I could feel myself getting a hard-on. Jean turned her head towards me (and away from the audience) and said, 'How would you like to fuck me after this? I give great head, too, and I love Greek. And I'm not expensive. A hundred bucks buys me for the night. Imagine putting your cock where your finger was a few moments ago! How about it?'

I smacked her even harder, probably out of sheer frustration. 'I'd love to, baby,' I said. 'But I've got a girl with me. How about some other time?' 'So get rid of the girl,' suggested Jean. 'I can meet you anywhere you like. Just give me an address.' I was carrying on spanking her whilst this rather one sided conversation was going on. I was very tempted indeed to accept her invitation. 'I tell you what, sweetheart,' I said. 'If you hang on here after I've gone, I'll get rid of the girl, and then I'll telephone you here, and come back and pick you up.

In the unlikely event that I don't call you within, say, fifteen minutes, then I'm not coming. How about that?' 'Done,' she said. 'And by the way, my real name's Jenny. So ask for Jenny when you call. OK'?' 'Sure,' I said. 'I can't wait.' 'Now do me a favour,' she asked. 'Will you stop beating the fuck out of my ass? I only do this because I need the money, and the money's not that good either. I don't actually enjoy it. It's just that it beats going hungry.' I stopped spanking her, and looked around for Rene, who suddenly appeared from the wings. 'That was terrific, Tony,' she said. 'Thank you. Did you enjoy it?' 'I most certainly did,' I said. 'Great,' said Rene. She beamed out at the audience. 'So let's hear it for young Jean here, folks. And not forgetting Tony, of course. How about a round of applause?' The audience responded, generously. Jean/Jenny took a bow, smiling at the audience, and we both left the stage, me back down the steps that I'd come up by, Jenny going off back stage. Rene took up her position centre stage once more.

'Now is the time for all of you to enjoy yourselves,' she announced. 'It's spanking time. After Jean's exquisite demonstration with Tony, you can all feel free to spank, or be spanked. You can come up here and spank each other. Or any of you – man or woman – can come up here to be spanked by me. Now who's going to start things off? 'I am,' said a large man sitting next to a small, rather pretty young girl. 'I'd like you to spank Renata here, while we all watch. And definitely with her panties down.'

Renata didn't argue or quibble. She simply stood up and made her way up onto the stage, via the same steps that I had used. When she got to Rene, she lay across her knees, and Rene lifted up her long, black evening skirt, to reveal shiny black satin knickers, black suspenders, and black silk stockings. One or two of the men whistled, and someone called out 'Let me know when you've finished with her, honey. I'll come up and take over. But it's not my hand I'll be hitting her with.' One or two of the audience laughed. Rene slowly pulled down the black satin knickers, exposing a tanned, muscular, very healthy-looking bottom indeed. As she started to spank the poor girl, I got up to leave. I felt that this was where I came in. Enough was enough. As I walked to the back of the theatre, and out through the entrance door, Kenneth – he of the mutilated foreskin – was sitting in a chair at the back of the room. He was fully dressed, but his fly was open, and he was masturbating his rigid prick with fervent enthusiasm. He was looking straight ahead. As I passed, his eyes didn't waver. It was almost as if he was in a trance. Perhaps he was.

Eileen was waiting patiently in the foyer, talking to the bouncer. They seemed to have struck up rather a better rapport than that which had greeted us upon our arrival. 'Hi, sweetheart,' I said. 'I'm sorry to have kept you waiting.' 'No problem,' she said. 'Did I miss anything?' 'Absolutely not,' I said. 'Unless the sight of Kenneth pulling his battered plonker as I came out would have done anything for you.' She shuddered. 'No way,' she said. 'No fucking way.' We bid the bouncer goodnight, and left. Back up on street level, I waved at the first cab I saw, pulled out a ten, and thrust it into Eileen's hand. 'Forgive me, sweetheart,' I said. 'But I want to go and talk to that Rene for a while. I know you've had more than enough of this S&M rubbish. So have this cab on *Tiptop*. Thank you for keeping me company. See you in the morning. Bless you, darling. Ciao.'

I gave her a big kiss, and helped her into the cab, waving as she and it disappeared into the distance. I looked around, and saw a bar a few hundred yards up the street. I walked slowly up to and into it, ordering myself a Budweiser. It was that sort of bar. I didn't want to draw attention to myself with my British accent, or my usual order of a scotch and water, no ice. I took my drink, went over to the public telephone, and dialled the number of the S&M club. I asked for Jenny, and she was on the phone in moments. I told her where I was. 'I'll be right with you, honey,' she said. 'Don't go away.' I put the phone down, and went and sat at the bar. There were just three other customers, all men, each one sitting on their own.

She arrived about ten minutes later. She was still wearing the red cotton miniskirt and the white blouse. She looked terrific. She looked even younger close to. 'Hi, Tony,' she said. 'Hi, Jenny,' said I. 'What'll you have?' 'Oh, a white wine spritzer, please,' she said. 'So what did you think of your evening at the club?' 'D'you want an honest answer?' I asked. 'Sure,' she said. 'Always.' 'Well, I have to tell you that, first of all, sado-masochism isn't my bag. Never has been. So my only reason for being there was to cover the show for *Tiptop*. You know I'm from *Tiptop*?' I asked.

'Doesn't everybody?' said Jenny, grinning. 'After your telephone call earlier on, Rene hasn't stopped talking about it.' 'Fine,' I said. 'That's OK. But, having said that, the show didn't do anything for me at all.' I grinned at her this time. 'Except that I enjoyed feeling your bum,' I said. 'And the rest,' she replied. 'You got a real fingerful of my pussy, as I remember.' She actually blushed. 'And I enjoyed it,' she said. 'You can finger my pussy any time you like. Oh, and yes,' she said. 'There's one other thing. I said something about a hundred bucks.' She smiled at me, and then looked down, as if embarrassed. 'I'm not really on the game. It's just that I'm out of work. I'm an actress, you see.' I didn't laugh. It would have been cruel. 'So I do what I do down at the club to keep body and soul together. But since every man I meet down there wants to fuck me, and since they've all got to be loaded to be able to afford all that rubbish, I don't feel guilty about making them pay for it. Do you understand what I'm saying? It just plain beats going hungry.'

'Of course I hear what you're saying, darling,' I said. 'And I quite understand. Have you eaten this evening?' She looked at me. 'I haven't actually eaten today, apart from some biscuits with my coffee at the club this evening,' she said. 'If you're asking me if I'm hungry, I'm starving.' She grinned her little girl grin. 'We can't have that, now, can we?' I asked her. 'Drink up your wine, and we'll go get something to eat.' I looked at my watch. It was almost eleven o'clock. 'I was hoping you might say that,' she said, laughing with pleasure at the thought of eating. She swallowed her spritzer rapidly. 'Right,' she said. 'I'm all yours.' 'Promises, promises,' I said. Where to go? It would need to be an evening place, rather than an ordinary restaurant. There were plenty of restaurants still open, all over Manhattan, but they were knocking on towards their last orders, and that's never a good time, in my opinion, to begin a meal. Probably the cabaret room at one of the hotels would be as good as anywhere. And since I had already eaten, it would give me something to do whilst young Jenny filled her face with much-needed food.

In the end I decided on the Drake Hotel, on Park Avenue and 56th Street. It served good food, and it was on the way home, and I didn't think they were starring anyone in their cabaret this week that would preclude us from getting a table at the last minute. We left the bar, and found a cab after a few minutes.

I was right about the Drake. We had no problem getting a table in their cabaret room, and it was worth the effort to see Jenny's face as she looked at the menu. She was so pretty, I spent most of the time looking at her as she ate, rather than watching the cabaret, a rather sultry torch singer, with an extremely pleasant voice. Her name didn't mean anything to me, but then I wasn't up on New York cabaret acts at that time. Jenny had started with seafood cocktail, and then chose a steak. When it arrived, it was enormous, in the American manner. It must have weighed at least a pound. She accompanied it with a huge baked potato, and demolished the lot in record time. Well, she *did* say that she was hungry! I had chosen a decent burgundy, for a change, and I helped Jenny to drink it while she ate her meal. She finished up with some kind of exotic ice-cream, covered in nuts and maple syrup. I often wonder how pretty young girls stay so slim.

When we got back to Fred's apartment, I got the usual knowing look from the doormen, which I ignored. Fred's cleaning woman had done her normal first-class job, and there was no sign of the photographic session that had been taking place earlier in the day. Jenny was greatly impressed with the apartment, and I gave her the guided tour before we ended up in the bedroom. There were still a couple of bottles of champagne left in the fridge, so I opened one, and took it and two glasses into the bedroom with us. I sipped mine as I watched Jenny undress, seeing her transparent white knickers for the second time that evening. That was all she was wearing beneath the white blouse and the little red cotton skirt, apart from little white socks, I stripped off quickly, and joined her on the bed. I had been wanting to suckle those over-sized teats since I first saw them earlier on, and now I did, sucking and licking at them until they were firmly erect, as was my cock by the time I had finished suckling. 'Were you boasting about giving great head, back at the club?' I asked. 'Absolutely not,' she said, sliding down the bed and grasping hold of my stiffened prick.

She enveloped it with her mouth, and started teasing it with her tongue, at the same time moving her head up and down, so that her soft, warm lips were encircling my shaft, and moving up and down its full length. I was in heaven. I love to watch my cock disappearing into and then reappearing, wetly covered in saliva, from the full red lips of a pretty young girl, and Jenny fulfilled all of these pleasurable requirements. She sucked strongly and steadily, and I could feel the spunk gathering in my scrotum as she worked at me. I could reach her breasts in the position that she was in, and I played with those elongated teats as she sucked me, until suddenly I knew that I was going to come at any second, and I held her face in my hands and fucked her mouth as I spurted my hot come down her throat. She sucked firmly on, and kept at it until there was nothing left to suck, at which point I withdrew my cock, and lay back on the bed, exhausted for the moment. As she lay beside me, she began to frig herself, her fingers moving idly inside her pussy lips. She was completely unselfconscious about what she was doing. So much so, that I might as well not have been there.

'So you tell me, honey,' she said, as I lay there, fascinated by her finger exercises. 'Was I boasting?' I grinned at her. 'Let me put it this way, sweetheart,' I said. 'If you were, it was fully justified. You were terrific. Thank you.'

I paused for a moment, wondering whether I should now ask the second question that was burning its way into my subconscious. What the hell, I thought. Faint heart never won fair lady. 'And do you really like Greek?' I asked. 'I love it,' she said, immediately. 'Do you?' 'Not half,' I said, my prick already standing to attention. 'I just love to get fucked in the ass,' she said. 'Would you like to do it to me now?' 'Yes, please,' I said. 'Have you got some KY jelly?' she asked. 'Something like that? I'm quite tight. I don't want you to hurt me. My ass is still sore from that spanking you gave me. In a different place, of course.' She laughed 'Are you really a spanker? Or were you just doing it to make up a story for *Tiptop*?' I laughed too, at the memory of it. 'Frankly, I just wanted to get as close to you as I possibly could,' I told her. It was true. 'The more especially when you took your clothes off. You've got a sensational body. You do know that, don't you? You could model for *Tiptop* any time you wanted to. And to answer your question, yes, I do have some KY jelly I'll go and get it.' I walked next door, to the en suite bathroom, got the tube of KY out of the bathroom cabinet, and took it back into the bedroom.

'Are you serious?' she asked. 'About the modelling, I mean?' 'Absolutely,' I said. 'I never spoke a truer word. 'Crazy,' she said. 'How much would I get paid?' 'It depends a bit,' I told her. 'Partly on who's paying you. If we paid you – the magazine, that is – you'd get rather more than if a photographer paid you himself. We'd pay you somewhere around five hundred dollars for a day's work. A photographer would probably pay you three hundred. But you ought to have an agent, really. Both to find you work, and to negotiate your fees. It's worth the percentage that they charge, if they're any good.' 'Wow,' she said. 'Just think; I've been selling myself for a hundred bucks a night. And that's hard work. With never a wink of sleep. Not often, anyway.'

My cock was so stiff, it was hurting. I didn't want to talk about modelling fees, I wanted to fuck Jenny's tight little asshole. I waved the tube of KY at her, and without saying anything, she knelt down on the bed, her pretty bottom towards me. I squeezed an inch of jelly onto my forefinger, and inserted it up her anus. God, she *was* tight. She felt hot inside, and she closed her sphincter muscles tightly around my finger. I could hardly wait to get my cock up her. I greased the inside of her rectum as far as I possibly could, and then pushed a big splodge of jelly up her as far as I could reach with my finger, on the principle that my cock would push it further into her, given an opportunity. I then rubbed jelly all around the entrance to her asshole, and finally, I rubbed my prick all over with the stuff. I went quickly back into the bathroom to wash the jelly off my hands, and then, at long last, I was ready.

She was looking over her shoulder at me when I walked back into the bedroom. 'Let me put it in, will you, Tony?' she asked. 'That way, there shouldn't be any problems. And if I say stop, please stop. OK?' 'OK, baby,' I said. I grabbed hold of her thighs, and poised my throbbing cock centimetres away from her puckered little anus. My engorged cock, by comparison, looked impossibly swollen, as if it could never penetrate such a tiny orifice, but I knew, from happy experience, the elasticity of the female asshole. She reached behind her and took hold of my cock. Holding it firmly, she pushed herself backwards, at the same time guiding my prick into her. There was a moment of strong resistance, and then, suddenly, my cock-head was inside her, and she let go of me. 'Just ease it in gently, for a moment,' she said. 'That feels good.' *It feels fucking good to me too, baby*, I said to myself, resisting the urge to ram my cock up her as hard, and as far, and as fast as I could.

Instead, I eased it gently up her, and I could feel her

sphincter opening up and expanding, to accept me. She was hot, and the KY jelly made her wonderfully slippery, and in no time at all, I was in her up to the hilt. 'OK, baby,' she said, suddenly. 'That's it. Fuck away.' I did as I was told. It was magical. She had the tightest asshole ever. Her sphincter muscles massaged my prick like nothing I had ever experienced before. She was hot and wet, and wonderfully tight. I slowed my rhythm down a bit, suddenly realizing that if I continued at the present rate, I would ejaculate very quickly.

I tried to fix my mind on boring things, whilst my prick was experiencing the most beautiful sensations. If this was what anal sex was all about, I was a convert. Forget cunts. Jenny put her right hand between her legs and began to wank herself. I let go of her thighs, and reached out and took hold of her firm breasts. I felt her teats grow large in my fingers, and Jenny began to moan quietly to herself. It was a strange sound, somewhere between a groan and a deep, sustained musical note. 'Oh, yes, baby,' she said. 'Fuck my asshole. Come inside my ass. Spurt your hot come up my ass.' Her hand began to move faster, and I could see that her orgasm was approaching rapidly. As did hers, so did mine, and then, within an instant, we were both coming, shouting out our pleasure, writhing and bucking as we came, until at last, panting with exertion, I withdrew from her tight little ass, and fell asleep, one arm across the lovely Jenny's slim waist.

When I awoke the following morning, it was to realize that it was Saturday, and that there was not the usual inducement to get up. Jenny was asleep beside me, her face angelic in sleep. The face of total innocence. I got up nevertheless, put on a robe, and went to collect the paper from outside the apartment door and put some coffee on. It was soon made, and I sat down with a cup and the *New York Times*. It has always intrigued me that in America, everywhere in the world is basically America. The largest, richest nation in the world does little to recognize that there are any other countries, or peoples, outside of the

United States. The Queen of England being murdered in her bed might just make page three of the *New York Times*.

Israel is perhaps the one exception, the reason being that there are actually more Jewish people in New York than there are in Israel. Thus Jerusalem becomes their alma mater, whether they have been there or not. They have an interest in Japan that stems from a paranoia that says that the Japanese are buying up America, piece of real estate by piece of real estate, and that it is all part of a plot to take over the nation. Britain and Europe are thought of rather as a not particularly worthwhile theme park, rescued by America from two world wars which we couldn't handle on our own. South America is simply the place where cocaine is grown. Africa is where every Harlem black believes his ancestors came from, and Australia is where they make quaint films about strange Australians from the outback visiting New York. Scandinavia probably doesn't exist. Reindeer come from Canada for Americans. Canada is a nation of poor relations who live up north. The less said about them, the better. Caribbean islands are OK for holidays, but for no longer than a week at a time. China and Russia are enemy countries left over from the Cold War. To many Americans, they are still enemies. Don't mention Vietnam.

In a different way, Americans are charmingly nationalistic. They don't need a reason to fly the Stars and Stripes. Many homes have flagpoles, and fly it all the time. Certainly on holidays. Always on the Fourth of July. (Remember? It's the date of the anniversary of the Declaration of Independence, made in 1776.) The bicentennial celebrations in New York in 1976 were wondrous to perceive. All Americans are fiercely defensive of their independence, and fiercely protective of their freedom of speech, thought, and acts. They all think that we British (to Americans we're not English, we're British. They are, of course, right.) speak quaintly, and they all just *lurve* our accent.

We think that *they* speak quaintly, of course. They say

TIT FOR TAT

'gotten', instead of 'got'. Actually, they're quite right. As you will know, it is the past participle of the verb 'get', and was used as such in this country up to around the turn of the eighteenth century, after which it fell into disuse. But then they use words like, for example, 'momentarily' to mean 'in a moment', as in 'Mr Cornfed will be with you momentarily,' which is quite incorrect. I guess it would be a dull world if we all spoke the same way. There are differences that we British simply have to become accustomed to if we live in America for any length of time. It is absolutely vital to learn these differences if you are a Briton writing for an American magazine, which is what I was doing. Pavements are sidewalks. Lifts are elevators. Car boots are trunks. Windscreens are windshields. The underground is the subway. Holiday is vacation. Films are movies. And so on. *Ad infinitum*. There are many differences, too, in the way some words are spelt. Tyre is tire. Centre is center. Rumour is rumor. Humour is humor. Traveller is traveler.

At this point in my reverie, Jenny appeared, rather charmingly wearing a big, fluffy bath towel. 'Hi, honey,' she said. 'You're up early.' 'Hi, sweetheart,' I said. 'Have some coffee. Would you like some breakfast? There's most things.' 'No, thank you, ' she said. 'Just some juice and coffee, please. Regular coffee. Hold the sugar.' I got the orange juice out of the fridge, and poured a cup of white coffee.

Jenny grabbed one of the *New York Times* Saturday supplements, and buried her nose in it. We sat there quietly for a while, reading and drinking coffee, relaxed together. I checked the time. It was just after eleven. 'I think I'll take a shower,' I said to Jenny. Then maybe it would be fun to go for brunch somewhere. What do you say?' 'Oh, that would be fun,' she said. 'I'd love that. Where shall we go?' 'How about the Rainbow Room?' I suggested. 'Hey, terrific,' said Jenny. 'In all my time in New York, I've never been to the Rainbow Room.' 'Then it will be a fun place to go,' I said. 'Let's do that.' The Rainbow Room is at the top of the Rockefeller

Center, at Rockefeller Plaza, on Fifth Avenue, between 49th and 50th streets. It's an enormous room, with a raised gallery, which has windows offering amazing views out over the city, and looking down, inside, onto what was originally a dance floor, while at the far end of the room there is a stage. In the evenings, they often have star cabaret acts. The decor was beautifully maintained, original art deco, with much use of gilt and red damask. I had telephoned before we left, and a crisp five dollar bill to the *maître d'* guaranteed us a good table in the raised gallery, right beside one of the windows.

We ordered from the brunch menu. Jenny ordered Eggs Florentine, while I went for my old favourite, Corned Beef Hash. We drank some excellent red Californian wine. Sunday is the traditional day for brunch if you are a New Yorker, but some of the larger restaurants serve it daily for tourists who want to sample the menu. Jenny was easy to talk to, and fun to be with. She asked me if I had been serious when I had said that she would make a good model for *Tiptop*, and I told her that yes, I had. 'Leave it with me, sweetheart,' I said. 'I'll set something up, and I'll get back in touch with you. I'm not making any promises, but I'm reasonably certain that I can arrange it for you.' I took her address and telephone number, and we parted outside the building, on Rockefeller Plaza. With the sun blazing down, it was difficult to imagine that there was a skating rink here in the winter. I walked a block to Madison, and took the bus home.

CHAPTER SEVEN
THE FOURTH OF JULY

Just after three the next day, Sunday, I was amazed – and delighted – to hear Fred's voice on the telephone when I answered it. And then I realized that, with the five hours' time difference between New York and London, it was just after eight p.m. at home. 'Hey, Tony,' he said. 'How goes it? Are you getting your fair share?' I laughed. You can always rely on Fred to get down to basics. 'No complaints at all, Fred,' I said. 'All seems to be going well, thank you. But how about you? What gives with Wally?' 'Oh, shit, don't ask,' he said. 'Except that he seems pleased with what you're doing out there. But I'm distinctly out of favour, right now. I think I'm going to have to stay here in London for a bit longer. Does that cause you any angst?' 'God, no,' I told him. 'I'm loving every minute of it. Stay in London as long as you like, as far as I'm concerned.'

'Hey, that's cool, man,' he said. 'It's nice to know that you're out there keeping an eye on things. Any problems in the office?' 'None that I'm aware of,' I said. 'They seem a nice bunch of people. Eileen basically keeps me on a level footing. She's worth her weight in gold. This coming week – on Wednesday – I've got a girlfriend from London coming over for a couple of weeks. I thought I might take some time off. Would that be OK with you?' 'Of course it would, Tony,' he said. 'Whatever you want to do is fine with me. Just make certain that Eileen knows where you are, and that she can get hold of you if needs be. If you're thinking of travelling, book your tickets through the office, and charge them. Draw some expenses money for the trip, too. Put it all down as research for a feature. You might just as well get some personal benefit out of your trip to the States.' He paused for a moment or two. Then 'Hey, that's a thought. How would you like to move over to New York permanently? You know, be my deputy editor? What would you think about that?'

'In principle, I'd love it,' I said. 'But I'd need to sort one or two things out with you before I gave you a definite "yes". You know, salary, cost of living here. That sort of thing. Can I have a little time to think about it?' 'Sure,' he said. 'When I fix a date to come back to the States, why don't you arrange to stay on with me for my first week back, and then we can sort everything out? OK?' 'OK,' I said. 'And thanks for the travelling expenses. I appreciate that.'

'Don't thank me,' he said. 'Thank Wally.' He paused. 'No. On second thought, don't thank anybody. Just do it. OK?' 'OK,' I said. 'Cheers now then, Tony,' he said. 'Cheers,' I said. And then he was gone. I put the phone down, thoughtfully.

Personally, I knew I'd love to move over to New York permanently. I couldn't think of anything I'd rather do. But. Various 'buts'. But what about my flat in Hampstead? But what about the Porsche? But would I earn enough to be able to live as I would want to live in New York? Right now, I wasn't actually paying any rent, staying, as I was, in Fred's apartment. He wouldn't want me to be there on a permanent basis, nor would I want to be, once he returned. But New York rents were high. I guess that these were the things that I would have to sort out with Fred, on his return. But the biggest 'but' of all was, but what about Annabel? *The hell with all that*, I thought. *Let me concentrate on what's in hand right now*. Annabel would arrive on Wednesday. It was July, and during her first week here, it was the Bicentennial. The two hundredth anniversary of the Declaration of Independence. The President was going to make a speech.

In New York, there was to be Operation Sailing Ships, 1976 (abbreviated, as was everything, by the American media to Op Sail '76). From approximately eleven in the morning on, some twenty or thirty of the world's great sailing ships were to sail in from the Atlantic, around Battery Park, and up the Hudson River. At night, there was to be a tremendous firework display, from barges moored in the Hudson River. And there were parties, parties, everywhere. I had been invited to a lunchtime party in an apartment block overlooking Battery Park, right down at the bottom of Manhattan, to watch the sailing ships as they sailed in. They were to be welcomed in the traditional New York Harbour manner, with Fire Department tugs playing huge jets of water up in the air from their mounted hoses. And then, in the evening, I had been invited to another party over on the West Side, in an apartment block overlooking Riverside Park, and the Hudson River, to watch the firework display. It was going to be quite a day.

Which meant that if Annabel and I were going to go away from New York for a few days, it would have to be for her second week. Well, she wouldn't mind that. But it rather precluded staying, as I had thought, rather loosely, with my old friend John Lane in Kingston, Jamaica, simply because we wouldn't have enough time to both stay with John and spend much time on the beach, even if we only went as far as Port Antonio. It seemed a shame for Annabel to come this far, and not see a real Caribbean beach. But there were other places. If we weren't going to stay with John, then I wouldn't bother to go to Jamaica. There were, after all, some three thousand other Caribbean islands to chose from. And then I remembered Charles.

Charles Dainton. He was an old school friend who now lived in Puerto Rico. In an apartment block literally on the beach, just on the outskirts of San Juan. He was married, and worked for one of the larger international advertising agencies' San Juan office. Unlike John Lane, who was a creative director, Charles worked on the client service side of the business. I had never been to Puerto Rico, but we'd always kept in touch since he first left London some six or seven years ago, and I'd seen pictures of his apartment block. It – and the beach upon which it stood – looked magical. Whenever he wrote, he always ended by inviting me to go stay, and to bring whomsoever I wanted, so I went and found his telephone number, and called him. He was delighted at the prospect of Annabel and I going down there, and he looked forward, he said, to introducing his wife to us. Jo was an American girl he'd met in New York whilst working there, and they had got married as soon as he knew that he'd been posted down to Puerto Rico. So, subject to discussing it with Annabel, I said, we'd be there with him the week after next. I'd call him with flight times and so on as soon as I could.

I always remembered one rather strange thing that he had told me in his first letter to me in London from San Juan. Along with the photographs of the apartment (and some beautiful ones of old San Juan itself) his letter had said that one of the stranger habits of the male Puerto Rican beach habituté was to lie on the beach, masturbating, in full view of the girls whose presence brought on this apparently urgent need for sexual relief. The Puerto Rican girls, he had said, were very beautiful. The masturbatory habit was thought, by its practitioners, to be extremely macho. Well, I thought, it should serve to give Annabel some amusement.

Next, I called Annabel, to explain about the Bicentennial, and to see if the thought of a week with Charles and Jo on the beach in Puerto Rico sounded like a good idea. 'It sounds like Paradise, darling,' she said. 'Will it be very hot?' 'Sort of high nineties, sweetheart,' I told her. 'In which case, I'd better go and buy a couple of new bikinis,' she said. 'Small ones.' 'Sounds good to me,' I said. 'See you Wednesday.' 'I can't believe it's really happening,' she told me. 'It seems like months that you've been gone, rather than the weeks that it actually is. Is there anything that you want me to bring with me? Anything that you need?' 'I can't think of anything, sweetheart,' I said. 'Just you. OK?'

I was really looking forward to seeing Annabel. I realized that, despite my busy sex life since I'd arrived in New York, I did seriously miss her. She was, I was beginning to understand, more to me than just good sex. Don't misunderstand me. I'm not knocking good sex. I was, after all, getting plenty of that. But with Annabel, I got good sex, plus. Plus what, exactly, I asked myself? Plus friendship. Plus affection. Plus understanding. Plus conversation. Plus liking the same things. Plus happiness. Plus not feeling complete when she wasn't there. That would do for a start. I would have to get Eileen to monitor my calls and messages, things like that, both when I was in the office, during Annabel's stay, and when I was out of town. I would also have to give Annabel Eileen's name as someone to contact, if she needed help when I wasn't around. And I would have to explain to Eileen that I really was very fond of Annabel. To the exclusion of anyone and everyone else. Even her. Especially her. But then, I'd said that much already. Hadn't I? I thought that I had.

I was up in good time the following morning, and, for once was one of the first into the office. There's nothing like an early night to make you feel on top of the world. I even beat Eileen in. When she arrived, she brought me coffee, and settled down to go through the morning's mail with me. 'What's the matter?' she asked. 'Couldn't sleep?' 'Not a bit of it,' I said. 'I just went to bed early, like a good boy. By myself, I hasten to add. And you know what they say? Early to bed, early to rise, makes you healthy, wealthy, and wise.'

'Heaven preserve me,' said Eileen. 'You'll be giving blood next. Did you telephone Miss Hot Panties?' I looked at her. 'And who might Miss Hot Panties be?' I asked. 'Excusing the vulgarity, of course.' 'Of course,' said Eileen. 'I expect it's just my jealousy. You know who Miss Hot Panties is. Miss London. Miss "I'm Arriving On Wednesday." What's her name? Annabel. That's it. Annabel. Did you telephone

Annabel?' I looked at Eileen. Long and hard. 'Now, look here, Eileen, sweetheart,' I started, but she interrupted me. 'Don't you "Now, look here" me,' she said, raising an accusatory finger. 'You need me this coming couple of weeks. And if I get any of that "Now, look here" nonsense, you're going to be in serious trouble. To start off with, I want a firm promise from you.' 'What's that?' I asked, a sinking feeling in my stomach. God preserve me from stroppy women.

'When Miss Hot Panties goes home . . .' I opened my mouth, but she put up a warning finger. I shut my mouth. 'When Miss Hot Panties goes back to London,' she said. 'I want a firm promise from you that for the following three days, I will get fucked from here to the breakfast table. And back. Whenever I want it. All day, and all night, if that is what I feel like. By you,' she added. As if there had been some doubt. 'Do I get what I want?' She looked at me. Quite belligerently. 'What if I say no?' I asked. Eileen actually laughed. 'Then Miss Hot Panties gets a personal letter from me. Detailing what you have been doing ever since you arrived here. And a list of who you've been doing it with. Including me,' she said. 'And that's just for starters. I'll get trannies from the art department, and I'll send her pictures of that dirty bald black cow. And of that Dee Dee. Topless model, indeed. And bottomless. And with a bottomless cunt. From what I hear. Do I have to go any farther?'

'No, Eileen, sweetheart,' I said. 'A chap knows when he's beaten. You've got your promise. Three days. OK?' 'That'll do for a start,' she said, grinning at me like a demented woman. 'I may extend it nearer the day. I'll see how I feel. But that's a firm promise, for now. Three days. Right?' 'Right, darling,' I said. 'Would you like a down payment this evening?' 'Are you serious?' she asked, looking positively startled. 'Yes,' I said. 'Of course I am.' I'll play the cow at her own game, I thought. 'Nah,' she said. 'No. Thank you. I don't think so. Annabel is due here the day after tomorrow. I'd worry about it all the time she was here with you. No. I'll wait until she's gone.' She looked at me, askance. 'Were you really serious?' 'Of course not, Eileen,' I said. 'Come on. A joke's a joke.' *Fuck you, baby*, I thought. *Two can play at your game*.

Wednesday morning, at ten, Eileen rang through to me in my office to tell me that the stretch limo that had collected me from Kennedy on my arrival in New York was waiting outside for me. I went down, and we made our leisurely way out to the airport. Annabel was due to land at eleven, which meant that it would probably be pushing twelve by the time she had cleared Immigration and Customs. The limo driver said he'd park in the car park, and wait for us by the exit doors from the British Airways terminal. I found a bar, and ordered myself a Bloody Mary. It reminded me of that morning – it seemed ages ago – in Daly's Dandelion, where I met Pauline. I found a bookstall and bought a paper, and went back to the bar for another Bloody Mary, and thanked God that I didn't have to spend too much time waiting for people to arrive at airports.

Finally the tannoy pinged, announcing that Annabel's flight had landed. I gave it half an hour, and took up my position by the passengers' arrival gates, joining that strangely mixed throng of people always to be found in position there. And then there she was. Looking adorable, her face lit up by an enormous smile, her eyes sparkling, her whole appearance saying I'm here, I'm alive, I'm happy.' She had a porter trundling along behind her. She saw me, and came running, flinging herself into my arms. 'Hallo, darling,' she said, nibbling my ear. 'Hallo, sweetheart,' I said. 'You look absolutely terrific.'

And so she did. She was wearing a beautifully-cut, navy blue, summer-weight suit, with a cream blouse, and a red, white, and blue silk scarf. Her blonde hair shone with health, and hours of brushing, and her face was exquisitely – and delicately – made up. Her blue eyes were clear and bright, her figure firm and trim. I directed the porter to the door that the chauffeur had indicated, and when he saw us coming, he waved at me and went off at a trot to collect the limo.

He was back within ten minutes, to Annabel's great amusement. I had asked Eileen to make certain that the drinks cabinet in the rear of the limo was fully stocked, and amused Annabel even more by opening a bottle of champagne as we drove back into Manhattan. I had asked that we drive back through Queens, and over the 59th Street Bridge, enabling Annabel to enjoy that fabulous view of the Manhattan skyline suddenly appearing, as if from nowhere. It is instantly recognizable, whether you've been to New York before or not. It must be the most instantly recognizable view in the world; even more so perhaps than Big Ben and the Houses of Parliament. I got more knowing looks from the apartment block's doormen when I arrived there with Annabel and her luggage. Almost as if to say 'Jesus – as if he didn't have enough women in, and out of here already. Now he's moving them in.' *Fuck them*, I thought. *They should be so lucky*. Annabel loved the apartment, of course. How could she not? I simply dropped her bags off, gave her a quick guided tour, as much time as she wanted to freshen up, and then took her off to lunch at the Tavern On The Green. It is one of New York's most beautiful restaurants, at Central Park West and 67th street. It is actually right in Central Park, 67th Street being one of four streets that cross the park – from the south, going north, 67th, 79th, 86th, and 96th. It is a large, airy, one-storey building, surrounded by trees and flowers, and with views across the park, which make it the perfect place for lunch in the summer. It's all white paint, enormous, sparkling glass windows, and glittering crystal chandeliers. Native New Yorkers have a tendency to look down their noses at it, describing it as rather touristy, but that's because it's always been there for them, and they have become accustomed to it. You'll notice, when you get to know them, that it is one of the first restaurants that they take out-of-towners to. The Tavern On The Green is, in its own way, just as unique as, say, Windows On The World, or Maxwell's Plum, or P.J. Clarke's.

All four are very different, and all four are very New York.

The food is excellent, as you would expect. We both started with huge, plump, juicy oysters, from Chesapeake Bay. Don't ask me to explain how or why, but you can eat fresh oysters all the year round in the States. It might have been July, but there is no question, there, of there needing to be an R in the month.

They came as they should, on the half shell, with half lemons – carefully sewn into little muslin covers, lest we should squeeze a lemon pip onto our oysters – and accompanied by a bottle of Tabasco hot pepper sauce, and vinegar, in which were marinating chopped shallots, and served with freshly cut brown bread and butter. If you like oysters – as Annabel and I both do – there is no finer way to start a lunch. I chose a decent half-bottle of French chablis to accompany them.

For the main course, we both chose the dish of the day, since neither of us had ever heard of it, never mind eaten it. It sounded interesting, and was called Chicken Tetrazzini. It was named, according to the menu, after Luisa Tetrazzini, the Italian coloratura soprano. It was basically chicken, stewed with onion, celery, cloves, carrots, mushrooms, spaghetti, Parmesan cheese, toasted almonds, an egg yolk, dry sherry, and cream. Who could possibly resist that?

When it came, we could see that layers of chicken had been placed between layers of the spaghetti, sprinkled with the Parmesan cheese, covered with a sauce, and browned in the oven. It was served with the almonds toasted. It was delicious, and we ate it accompanied by a good French burgundy. Californian wines are excellent, but if you can afford good ones, French wines are superb. It is cheap French wines that are so disappointing. If you cannot afford expensive wines, the Italians, in my opinion, make the most drinkable ordinary table wines available, and at extremely reasonable prices. But this was a day for sheer extravagance. The Chicken Tetrazzini came with simple new potatoes, served freshly cooked, and smothered in butter, and fresh peas, also cooked to perfection.

Crisp. For pudding we both had Tangerines En Surprise; tangerines hollowed out and filled with a tangerine sorbet and tangerine flesh mixture, which is then frozen. (For some reason best known to themselves, the Americans call sorbet 'sherbet'.) The sorbet came as described, garnished with a sprig of fresh mint. It seemed silly not to do something which I love to do, despite the horrendous cost, and I ordered a half-bottle of Chateau d'Yquem to drink with our dessert. Twenty years ago, that half-bottle cost me the dollar equivalent of forty-five pounds. Today, you simply can't buy it. There are other pudding wines, of course. But nothing – ever – to compare with d'Yquem. It is sheer nectar.

Annabel was feeling sleepy. Whilst it was only just after three in the afternoon New York time, it was eight in the evening by her body clock. A combination of ordinary tiredness, jet lag, and an ample sufficiency of good food and wine were taking their toll. I ordered a cab, paid my bill, took her home, helped her to undress, and tucked her up in bed. She was practically asleep before her head touched the pillow. I was greatly moved to see that marvellous body once more. Those beautiful breasts. Those firm, but ample, buttocks. The slim waist. The long, long legs. Most of all, perhaps, that beautifully shaven, smooth, unwrinkled pussy, its pink lips shining wetly from between her legs. I had an erection big enough to trip up a kangaroo, but I don't believe she even noticed it. I didn't mind in the least bit. She wasn't going to run away. I left her in bed, her angel face relaxed and happy, and – shutting the bedroom door quietly, in order that any noise I might make wouldn't waken her – I settled myself down in front of the television.

The amount of food and drink that I too had consumed at lunchtime eventually caught up with me, and I awoke in front of the TV set at midnight, watching a rerun of the Gong Show. Something I would normally pay money not to have to watch. I switched it off, took a quick shower to wash away the cobwebs, and joined Annabel in bed. She was still there, sleeping the sleep of the innocent. I crept into bed beside her, and minutes later I, too, was fast asleep.

Annabel awoke first, not unreasonably, since New York's eight in the morning was one o'clock in her afternoon. When I finally woke up, at eight-thirty, she was sitting, propped up on the bed beside me, reading the *New York Times*, and drinking a cup of coffee. She looked across at me. 'Good morning, darling,' she said. I groaned. 'What's the matter?' she asked, looking at me with a worried expression. I grinned at her. 'Nothing that a cup of coffee, a shave and a shower, and a loving fuck wont cure,' I said. 'Probably in that order. How did you manage to find the paper?' 'I heard the thump as it was delivered,' she said. 'Hang on, while I get you some coffee.' She disappeared, presumably into the kitchen. She came back, moments later, coffee in hand. 'How do you feel, sweetheart?' I asked. 'How's the jet lag?' 'I feel fine,' she said. 'I feel really good. I think the jet lag's gone. At least for now. I don't remember getting into bed. I'm so sorry. I so much wanted you to make love to me. I nearly wet my knickers in the cab coming back here after lunch, just thinking about it. Then I just plain fell asleep. Can you ever forgive me?'

'Of course I can, my darling,' I said. 'Consider yourself forgiven. If you're ready, let's shower together. What do you say?' She smiled at me, that lovely, beautiful, urchin-like grin that had so entranced me when I first saw it. And still did now. 'I say yes, please,' she said. I drained my coffee, and put down the cup. Sitting up properly, I could see that Annabel had unpacked her cases, and that she was wearing a pretty, summer weight, silk gown. I got out of bed, and she dropped the gown on the floor, revealing her naked body. I wanted to leap on her right then, and fuck her. Seriously fuck her. But I restrained myself. I'm not sure how.

'Come and talk to me while I shave,' I said. 'Tell me what's been happening in your life.' She came and sat beside me, on the side of the bath, while I shaved. 'Not a lot, really,' she said.

'Work goes on. Business at the club has been pretty good, all things considered. I've been missing you, of course.' She held up her right hand, the middle finger extended. 'I've practically worn my finger out, masturbating,' she said. 'I'm wet, and willing, and ready. Just as soon as you are.' She moved a little closer, taking hold of my semi-stiff prick. She pulled my foreskin backwards and forwards a few times, very slowly. She looked up at me. 'Am I distracting you?' she asked. I smiled down at her. 'Yes,' I said. 'But don't stop.'

She got down on her knees and took my cock in her mouth. Her lips were warm, soft, and wet. She teased me with her tongue, and bobbed her head up and down so that my now rigidly stiff prick was sucked in, then withdrawn, then sucked in again, between those lovely, soft, wet lips. I put down my razor, and took her head between my hands, and she sat back on her heels as I began to fuck her mouth. Within seconds I was spurting hot come down her throat, which she swallowed without taking my prick out of her mouth. 'Mmn,' she said, when I had finished. 'It tastes just like caviar. I love it. Is there any more where that came from?' I had to laugh.' Of course there is, my darling,' I said. 'But not for a little while. OK?' I gave her a big, wet kiss, and then picked up my razor again, to finish what I had been doing when my ejaculation had suddenly become my number one priority. Then I cleaned my teeth, gargled with mouthwash, and pronounced myself ready for our shower.

The shower in Fred's apartment was big enough for four people, never mind two, and we had plenty of space in which to enjoy ourselves. We soaped each other in all the naughty places that we could think of, and eventually I found myself kneeling before her, sucking that beautiful, shaven cunt. After a few enjoyable minutes, I stopped, and got up, saying to her, 'I think we'd both enjoy this better if we dried off, and went back to the bedroom.' 'I'm sure you're right, darling,' she said. We came out of the shower, and I dried Annabel with one of Fred's huge, fluffy towels, and then she dried me. From time to time we would stop our drying activities so that I could thrust a finger up her pussy, or she could take my penis in her mouth. Anything to keep the excitement going. And then we were all dry, and I picked Annabel up and carried her off to the bed. I placed her down upon it, and she spread her legs immediately. 'I think I can remember where you left off,' she said. She stuck a finger deep down into her quim. 'It was right there, I think. In fact, I'm pretty sure.'

I grinned at her, and bent over her, spearing her moist pussy with a stretched tongue. I wiggled it about a bit until I found her clitoris, and then I took it out again. Just for a moment, you understand. 'About there, darling?' I asked. 'Exactly there,' she said. 'Yes. Thank you.' I knelt over her, arranged myself comfortably, and set about sucking her pussy seriously, to our mutual advantage and delight. The feel of her silken, closely shaven pudenda was one of the most erotic sensations in this world. The sight and feel combined was almost too much for me to bear. I ran my tongue over the satiny surface, wetting it with my saliva, rubbing my lips across it, tasting it, and wondering at how anyone could shave off hair – however silken in texture – and leave such a completely smooth surface. Perhaps she used some kind of chemical hair-removal process, rather than the razor of my imagination.

The skin of her *mons veneris* was pure white, and her labial lips, now puffy with sexual desire, were a darkly pink contrast against it. I could taste the slightly acrid, slightly sweet flavour of her juices as I delved with my tongue between those velvet lips, and I found her rampant clitoris again without any trouble at all. I concentrated on it with my tongue, massaging its erect, hard little nub, until Annabel started bucking her pelvis up against my mouth in her orgasmic enjoyment. I stayed at it until she relaxed, spent: from her exertions, and then, giving her pussy lips a (strictly temporarily) final kiss, I lay down beside her. We lay quietly in each other's arms for a while, comfortable in each other's silence, and then Annabel took an arm from around my neck, and the next thing that I felt was her cool hand on my flaccid cock. It didn't stay flaccid for long, and soon it was fully erect. She turned to face me.

'Your cock feels rather dry, and rather cold, my darling,' she said. 'I know a lovely warm, wet place where you could put it that would make it feel much better. Shall I put it there for you?' 'That would be nice, sweetheart,' I replied. There are times for me when there is nothing more pleasurable than just lying back and enjoying it. Not even thinking of England. Just plain enjoying being fucked, instead of fucking.

It's an offer I never refuse. Annabel climbed on top of me, her legs spread wide. I watched, fascinated, as she fed my newly rampant prick slowly between those well-loved lips at the centre of her bald pudenda. Its engorged, purply head disappeared with an audible little plop, and she then eased herself slowly down the full length of it, until my John Thomas was swallowed, right up to the hilt. She was, as she had said, both warm and wet.

She was also as tight as the proverbial mouse's earhole, and as such, her cunt imparted incredibly intense, totally wanton, unspeakably profligate sensations. I lay back, as is my wont, and enjoyed them. To the full. I did nothing to hasten their conclusion. Nor, to be fair, did I do anything to prevent the natural sequence of events. I simply let nature take its inevitable, delightful course. As I lay there, I could not but help comparing Annabel's bald accoutrements with those of Lucy, since they were, respectively, both similar, and so very different. Annabel's lips so full and pink, Lucy's so puckered and purply black. The skin texture of their pudenda was, in both cases, exceptionally smooth. And I had to admit to myself, as I lay there, that the feeling of being fucked in this way by either woman, was something that I enormously enjoyed. Thinking of naughty Lucy's black cunt as I lay beneath the pale white Annabel was the final thought, of many such comparative erotic thoughts, that for me, on that occasion, began the process of my orgasm. I could feel my eventual ejaculation coming from a long way off. The

THE FOURTH OF JULY

exceptionally satisfying blow-job that Annabel had performed on me earlier patently caused me to take longer the second time around, and I was glad of that.

Annabel looked down at me, smiling 'I can feel your ejaculation getting itself ready,' she said. 'Do you mind if I play with myself now, in order to keep company with you?' 'Of course not, darling,' I said. 'Feel free.' It has always excited me to see – and feel – girls playing with themselves in order to bring about their orgasm, either whilst they are fucking you, or you are fucking them.

Some men see it as an insult. I'm not sure why. Perhaps the implication that the man himself (or perhaps that should be the man's cock itself) is insufficient to bring about the necessary orgasm, is seen as derogatory? Who knows? All I know is that I find it extremely erotic, as I said, to see and feel this activity whilst indulging in sexual intercourse. Thus I enjoyed immensely the feeling as Annabel slipped her hand down between her legs, and between her groin and mine, and then as I felt her finger against my rigid cock as she searched for, then found, her clitoris, and began masturbating herself towards orgasm. These additional sensations, added to her already generously offered vaginal contractions, and her naturally tight pussy anyway, quickly brought about my excited ejaculation which, I was happy to see (and feel) brought Annabel to her orgasmic spasms too. 'Oh, how beautiful, my darling,' she said. 'I had almost forgotten how your hot come felt, spurting up inside me. Don't stop. Please don't stop.' Eventually, of course, I was compelled to stop. But, all in all, a happy, loving, satisfying, delightful fuck, for both of us. I sucked Annabel's beautiful nipples as she came, ensuring that she produced every possible, final, orgasmic contraction, before sliding off me, totally enervated by her magnificent efforts.

Checking my watch, I saw that it was after eleven. I had remembered, before Annabel's arrival, to replenish Fred's supply of champagne, which I had rather seriously depleted since my arrival. I had also made sure – purely because of

Annabel – that I had replenished it with Louis Roederer Crystal. I went now to the fridge in the kitchen, where I had put three bottles, in case of such an emergency as now presented itself, and I took one out and opened it. I poured two glasses, and took them into the bedroom. Annabel was delighted. 'Oh, darling,' she said. 'So I still rate a glass of champagne? That's really nice. Really good news. I thought that, with all the competition that there must be here in New York, I might have dropped down a category or two' She smiled, and raised her glass. 'Or even three,' she said. 'Cheers.'

'Cheers, sweetheart,' I said. 'You know, darling,' she continued, 'I don't seriously mind who you fuck whilst you're out here. Does that surprise you?' I mentally shuffled my feet for a moment or two. 'It's not something I'd thought about,' I said. 'Not really.' 'Then let me explain it to you, if I may?' she said. 'Of course,' I said. 'If you really want to.' 'I do,' she said.

'Since you and I first met in the club, what seems like a hundred years ago now, for what was then, for me, a rare and unusual sexual experience – rare and unusual, because I felt that I'd grown out of that kind of one-night stand relationship – I realize that I have fallen totally, completely, and utterly in love with you.' I was about to say something, but she put a hand up. 'Let me finish, darling, if I may.' 'Yes, of course,' I said. 'For the, what is it? five weeks that you've been here? I've realized that being without you is something that I can live with. Your fucking other women is something I can live with too. And I never thought that I'd hear myself say that. But so long as it's only me that you *love*, I don't mind what you do, sexually. As long as you come back to me in the end. Fucking other girls, whilst you're away, is just like your needing to eat in a restaurant, simply because I'm not there to cook you a meal. Does that make any kind of sense to you? Do you understand that?' She didn't give me time to reply. 'It's something that I've learned since you've been away from me. Personally, I think it shows a rather more grown-up attitude to life than the one that I had before I met you. Certainly to the one that I had before you came out here. But it does depend, I suppose, if I'm honest with myself, upon my belief that there is, in fact, some kind of a long-term relationship ahead of us. I don't mean marriage. Not necessarily. I mean, if you wanted to, then that would be good. But it's not conditional. I just mean something that is as ongoing as anything can be, in the strange world that we both live in. What do you think, Tony?'

Oh shit, is what I think, I thought to myself. But that's just because you're a frightened, selfish, uncaring, unthinking, nasty human being. For God's sake, try and say something nice, some thing loving, something that gives hope to this adorable girl, who deserves so much better than you. Something, for the same God's sake, that gives you some hope. Something that gives *you* a chance of survival, some kind of belief in the future. Something that actually qualifies you for the kindness, the love, the affection, the unstinting loyalty, the genuine friendship, that this gorgeous woman is offering you.

'I think that I'm a very lucky person,' I said, eventually. I may have hesitated a little bit too long for it to sound believable, but it was the best I could do in the circumstances. Suddenly I could hear Pamela's voice saying 'Just please don't turn into a frog.' I felt consumed with guilt. 'I do love you, you know, sweetheart,' I said. 'I really do love you. And I'm sure that there is a future for us together. It's just that, at this particular moment in my life, I spend more time thinking about my financial future than I do about my emotional future. I'd agree with you that that's probably the wrong order of priorities, but I find it difficult to separate them out any differently. For example,' I told her, 'Fred is now suggesting to me that I join him out here as his deputy editor. Permanently. You know, as permanently as anything is permanent these days. I'd love to do that. I'd earn approximately twice as much as I earn in London, I'd live about twice as well, and my future would look a lot more attractive. As far as I can forecast. Taxes are lower out here, too.

'But how would that affect us? Would you want to give up

your job at the club, and join me out here? I've got no right to ask you that question, but I'm asking it. And then, if you said that yes, you'd like to join me, that would mean marrying me, as far as the company was concerned. We wouldn't *have* to get married, but we would if we wanted the company to pay your fares between here and London, and pay me enough – in their opinion – to support a wife out here.' I took a deep, mental breath. 'And in any case, I would want you to. But leaving aside the question of marriage for the moment, would you want to give up your job? I mean, how would you feel about that? Hmmm?' She gave me a long, lingering, loving look. 'Is that a hypothetical question?' she asked. 'Or are you asking me to join you out here?' I took a deep breath. 'It has to be hypothetical for the moment,' I told her, 'because I haven't got the job yet. But I'm confident that I will, within a few weeks. I don't know, right now, when Fred's coming back. But the moment that he does, we will either work out the situation to our mutual satisfaction, or we won't. If we do – and I believe that we will – then I would want to come back to London for a matter of weeks. Mostly to sort out things like the Hampstead flat, and the car. Stuff like that. But most of all, under those circumstances, I'd want to ask you to marry me. And live life happily ever after.' I grinned a big grin at her. 'If I *did* ask you that,' I said, 'what would your answer be?'

She looked at me in a way that I can only describe as bemused. 'Are you serious, Tony?' she asked. 'Of course I'm serious,' I said. 'Why would I not be?' She thought for a moment, and then laughed. 'Since you ask, I'm not sure,' she said. 'But if you are, then the answer would be – is – yes. Firmly, definitely, unconditionally, yes. Thank you.' She smiled at me. 'Does that answer your question?' I kissed her, soundly. 'Yes, sweetheart, it does. And thank you. But what about the club, for example? What about the penthouse?'

'No problem, either way,' she said. 'I'm a partner in the club. My contract requires me to give three months' notice of wanting to stop acting as its manager, but that's all. I remain a

THE FOURTH OF JULY 199

partner, and continue to receive my share of the profits.' She smiled at me. 'If all else fails – God forbid – those will keep us in luxury until our old age. And as far as the penthouse is concerned, well, I guess we need to talk about that. Probably at some other time. It would be my thought that if we came to live out here in New York together which, incidentally, I would love to do. Live in New York, that is. You already know about the other. It would be my thought that we should keep a home in London, whatever else we did. Yours or mine, it wouldn't really matter. We could rent out whichever one we didn't want to live in, if we ever came back. Or we could rent out both. Or sell both. But it's not really important. Not to me, anyway. Does that answer your questions?'

I kissed her again. 'Yes, sweetheart, it does,' I said. 'Thank you.' We chattered on for a while, talking about the future, as engaged couples do. And then it suddenly occurred to me that I should buy an engagement ring. I didn't say anything about it to Annabel at the time, but I started working out in my head what kind of a ring it should be, how much I could afford, and where I should buy it. And then we got ourselves out of bed and up and dressed – eventually – in time for lunch.

I chose a little Italian restaurant on Lexington Avenue, at 61st Street, that I had been introduced to by David Jones, who had recently come over to New York from London to work with Tony Power on Paul Raymond's *Club* and *Quest* magazines. I rang down to the doorman, and ordered a cab, and we took off. The restaurant is called Gino's, and David was introduced to it, he told me, by Margie McClean, at that time Macy's public relations person. Margie was an attractive, vivacious, black-haired, New York Italian, with a lot of style. Gino's was opened in 1945, and was the kind of excellent, basic, seriously good New York Italian restaurant that is getting more and more difficult to find. (It's still there, if you're interested. It celebrated its 50th anniversary in 1995). Gino is Gino Circiello, who saw a rental sign outside premises on Lexington Avenue, not far from Bloomingdale's, whilst he was working as a waiter at a restaurant on East 59th Street. There was no competing Italian restaurant nearby, so he got together with two partners, and took out a five year lease on the premises. According to Gino, little has changed over the years. (Except of course, costs. In fifty years, the rent has increased from $400 a month to $20,000 a month. A starter that used to cost 60 cents when the restaurant opened now costs $7.20, while a main course that used to be $2.50 is now $25.

The restaurant still boasts its original mahogany bar, and the walls are still decorated in the same, slightly garish wallpaper, which features rows of zebras on a soft red background, which has, says Gino, been reproduced at least once, after a fire in the 1970s. I must admit that on my first visit there, with David, the whole place had, for me, the atmosphere of the kind of Italian restaurants depicted in every American movie about the New York Mafia that you've ever seen, but I guess all that says is that it is a genuine New York Italian restaurant. It is a very welcoming restaurant.

The food is exquisite. Annabel and I both had the Parma ham and fresh figs, followed by the lamb chops, served with spinach and spaghetti, with a tomato sauce. We drank Sicilian Chianti Superiore, and finished with cassata, followed by strong espresso coffee, and Annabel had a Sambuca – with the full coffee beans on fire treatment – whilst I had a Strega. One of the better lunches. Very different from London's Italian restaurants, whilst to my mind, neither New York nor London Italian establishments have any kind of relationship, in real terms, with the many different varieties of restaurant that are in Italy itself. But then, it's difficult to compare lunch at a smart trattoria in Porto Cervo, on the Costa Smeralda, in Sardinia, with, say, lunch at Gennaro's in Soho's Dean Street, in London, or with lunch in Harry's Bar in Venice. Or, of course, with Gino's, in New York. All have their appropriate place in the scheme of things.

Feeling replete, relaxed, and happy, we wandered slowly (mainly because of the heat) in the brilliant July afternoon sunshine across town, westwards for three blocks, from Lexington, across Park, and Madison, until we came to Fifth Avenue, window-shopping all the way. At Fifth we turned left and started to wander downtown. It wasn't long before we came to Tiffany's, probably New York's best known jewellery store, at 727 Fifth Avenue. (Although if you're seriously rich, you'll probably know and prefer Harry Winston's emporium, slightly north of Tiffany's, at 718 Fifth Avenue). I've long been a fan of Tiffany's who, apart from selling items of jewellery and a whole range of things made from precious metals, sell greetings cards, stationery – personalized or otherwise – and glass and china. Their exquisite pale blue, beribboned boxes, are always a promise of the ultimate in expensive good taste.

Annabel was happy to concur with my suggestion that we take a look inside the store, and we started off on the ground floor, which mainly carries the stationery, cards, board and card games, and so on. Grateful for the air-conditioning, we progressed up a floor, which mostly offers sterling silver, for which Tiffany's is justly famous, from the kind of things that you would expect, including trays, plates, jugs, mugs, and cutlery, down to things, like photograph frames, key-rings, bracelets, money-clips, and tie-clips and pins. There's something for everybody. The last time I was there, the cheapest thing you could buy was a beautifully made and presented, high quality, double pack of cards, in that unique Tiffany blue, with the company's name in gilt. Magic. Annabel bought various trinkets as presents for friends and business chums, and a pretty key-ring with a small heart attached for herself. I suggested that she perhaps have the heart engraved with the words 'New York,' and the year – 1976. She agreed, and we left the key-ring there for the engraving. It would take two weeks, they said.

The next floor was exclusively glass and china which, unless you actually want to buy some glass or china (and we didn't), has limited interest. So we progressed up to the next floor, where the serious jewellery was on display. Diamonds, emeralds, sapphires, rubies, turquoise, pearls, whatever your personal preference, Tiffany's stock it.

It was at this point that I told Annabel that I had deliberately arranged for us to get to this particular floor, in this particular store, because I wanted to buy her an engagement ring. To my surprise, she burst into tears. In answer to the courteous member of Tiffany's staff who came to ask if she was all right, and if there was anything that she, the attendant, could do to help, Annabel smiled through her tears, and said no, thank you. She was simply crying because she was so happy. The Tiffany person had obviously seen it all before, and went away, smiling. Annabel settled down after a few minutes, and she finally decided (having asked, rather sweetly, I thought, if I could really afford it) that what she would really like was a diamond engagement ring. A *small* diamond engagement ring, she emphasized. We wandered about, looking in showcases, and at counters, seeing many beautiful diamond rings. Eventually we wound up at a particular counter, where a charming sales lady asked how she could help us. After some discussion, Annabel said that what she was looking for was probably a small – emphasis on the small – solitaire diamond engagement ring. The sales lady asked us to kindly wait for a few minutes, and she went away, out through a door at the far end of the floor.

I know a bit about diamonds. After I'd done my national service with the RAF, I went to work as a diamond buyer for De Beers in Sierra Leone, West Africa. Buying rough diamonds from the native diggings. In those days, De Beers controlled the sale of ninety-four per cent of the world's production of rough diamonds, either by owning the mines, or by contracting to purchase, and subsequently sell, the production from mines that they didn't own. These days, that ninety-four per cent has shrunk, I'm told, to somewhere around sixty per cent. De Beers have, nevertheless, operated a cartel on the sale of rough diamonds to the trade – those who cut and manufacture jewellery from diamonds – for over a hundred years.

Back in the days when I worked for them – the early 1950s – Sierra Leone was one of the few places in which De Beers didn't control either production or sales. That was because diamonds were only discovered in Sierra Leone as recently as 1948. They were alluvial, i.e. they were roughly ten or fifteen feet below the surface of the ground. They would have been washed there, millions of years earlier, from some long dried-up river bed, that had itself, in its day, swept away the diamonds from the effluent of a so-called 'pipe,' through which a volcanic eruption had originally brought up the diamonds from miles below ground. They would first have been formed, eons earlier, from carbon probably originally from fossilized forest trees – crystallized by the intense heat and pressure near the earth's centre.

A perfectly formed rough diamond, as a matter of interest, is an exact octahedron. The diamonds from Sierra Leone are spectacularly fine quality gem stones. The problem with these alluvial deposits was that they were spread over many square miles, and which in themselves were subdivided in hundreds – literally – of tribal plots, thus negating the possibility of De Beers negotiating an overall contract for the purchase and disposal of the stones. Hence the flourishing proliferation of an illegal diamond trade, which eventually brought the Sierra Leone government to approach De Beers, asking them to set up a government buying organization. This was what I was part of: it took us three years to set up, and then we handed over to the local people. (There were only eight of us, manning altogether three up-country locations, plus a manager in Freetown.)

We used to go off into the bush (for bush, read jungle) individually, with a dozen native bearers and a tin trunk with ten thousand pounds in West African pound notes in it, and stay out there until we had spent all that money on rough diamonds. We had one Sierra Leone policeman, with a .303 Short Magazine Lee-Enfield rifle, a cook boy, and an interpreter, while the rest of the natives carried the necessary supplies, which included, apart from food and drinking water, a camp bed, a portable mosquito net, and an Elsan chemical lavatory. Water was in short supply, and during the three to four weeks that we were out in the bush, we seldom enjoyed the luxury of a wash or a shave. Serious British Empire stuff. Fascinating. It was out there in West Africa, all those years ago, that I saw my first unclothed women. Every day. And very beautiful they were, too. But enough of this colonial rubbish.

The main thing that my time as a diamond buyer with De Beers taught me was that I was never likely to be able to afford a good-quality diamond. Not of any size, anyway. And not much liking second best, despite the fact that I have, in my day, bought a lot of pretty jewellery for a lot of pretty women, I had never, until that day, bought a diamond for anyone. So this was going to be a first. And I was going to do it properly.

Lesson one. Never judge either the colour, or the quality, of any kind of gem stone, in artificial light. The facets with which the stone has been cut reflect artificial light – intentionally – to such a degree, that you really cannot see what you are looking at. Lesson two. Unless you are so rich that you don't care what you buy, so long as you like what you are looking at, do not buy a diamond that is anything other than brilliant cut. If it's heart-shaped, pear-shaped, emerald-shaped, or anything other than the classic brilliant (cut from the afore mentioned perfect octahedron) then it will have been cut from a stone that was originally malformed,. It will have been – at best – a piece of cleavage, i.e., a piece of broken diamond. At worst, it will have been what is called in the trade a *maccle*, or a *naat*. This is a serious malformation, producing a flat, often triangular-shaped, rough stone, with a visible herring bone-like join around its centre. By the standards of really good diamonds, these are practically worthless. Not that you'll ever find a diamond retailer to agree with that statement.

There are four things by which experts value diamonds: colour, quality, shape, and size. Colour to the expert means a brilliance that is actually no colour at all. De Beers call it finest blue-white. Much of what you see in the way of diamond jewellery in the ordinary high street jeweller's window is what I would call yellow, almost the lowest colour in a long list of high-quality colours. You'll never find a retail jeweller describing any of his diamonds as yellow, even if you can clearly see that they are. Some of them even stock pieces that are brown – strictly a colour that any serious jeweller would discard as fit only for industrial use.

To help you see both colour and quality, never buy a stone unless you have examined it in natural daylight, and preferably with a jeweller's magnifying glass, called a loup. If you don't feel confident of doing this yourself, and you haven't got a friend in the business that you trust, don't buy diamonds. Diamond dealers, in my opinion, are like second-hand car dealers. They are totally unscrupulous. Many diamonds set as jewellery – rings, bracelets, necklaces, whatever – have serious flaws in them. Spots – usually black. Cracks. Malformations. Clever cutting can hide many of these improprieties. The usual place to find a spot in a brilliant cut stone is right down at the base, in the point, right at the very bottom. Shape and size are self-explanatory, but they won't help you to put a real value on anything. If you can afford it, and you like it, buy it. But insist that you buy it with a full, guaranteed description, signed by the dealer who sold it to you, and including his valuation of the stone. It's not foolproof, but it might help.

I told the sales lady at Tiffanys that if Annabel chose a ring, I would want to look at it in natural daylight, using my loup. It was not a problem, she said, immediately. It is fortunate, perhaps, that magazine publishers, editors, production people, and printers, use loups to look at print and paper quality. They are exactly the same items that jewellers use, and I had made sure that I'd brought mine with me. The sales lady asked me if I had a particular amount in mind that I wished to spend, and I said no, not really. Patently I couldn't afford a million dollars. Or even half a million dollars. But then I didn't think Annabel was likely to choose a ring at that sort of price. I would guess that she was looking for a pretty ring that would please her to wear, to mark the fact that she had agreed to marry me. She wasn't looking for an investment for the future. I had no idea how much money Annabel *did* have, but she had more than I did, that was for sure.

She eventually said that she was very much attracted to a small, solitaire, brilliant cut diamond, which the sales lady said was a carat and three-quarters. She didn't mention colour, but it looked a reasonable colour in the artificial lighting of Tiffany's, and I asked the woman if I might have a look at the ring in daylight. She said yes, of course, and if I'd follow her, she would take me to a room nearby with good natural light. She asked me to hang on for a minute or so, whilst she got someone else to take over her counter. Annabel said that she would wait where she was, and that if she wasn't at the counter when we got back, she wouldn't be far away.

I eventually followed the woman into a room in which there was a bench running along in front of the windows, covered in blue baize, with the baize covered with stiff, white cartridge paper. She explained that this was a room normally used by those Tiffany's staff whose job it was to make an offer for any jewellery brought in for sale. The sales woman then passed me the ring, which she had brought from her counter, and I sat down at a chair at the bench, got out my loup and had a good look at it. It was what I would call 'clean,' which is a diamond trade category, denoting that, whilst not absolutely perfect, the stone has no obvious imperfections. The colour I would describe as 'white,' also a trade term. It is a perfectly acceptable colour for a stone of reasonable quality, but is some way off the top qualities. The ring would look beautiful to anyone not an expert in the subject. I asked the price, and whilst it was rather more than the month's salary that the De Beers television advertisements imply is what you might expect to pay for an engagement ring, it seemed reasonable enough, accepting that my inside knowledge of the trade prices per carat for the three hundred-odd qualities that exist for diamonds was long out of date.

Back at the sales woman's counter, I could see Annabel wandering about some distance away, looking at the various displays. She looked over towards me, and I waved. She waved back. When asked how I wanted to pay, I asked if a cheque (check to Americans!) would be acceptable, and she said yes, but that, unless it was a cashier's cheque, I would have to wait for it to clear. I asked her to hang on for a moment, and went over to ask Annabel if she wanted me to go to the trouble of going all the way to the bank where the company had helped me to open an account in New York, getting a cashier's cheque, and then bringing it back to Tiffany's, in order to be able collect the ring today.

Happily, she seemed relaxed about waiting the three days that the woman said it would take. I went back to the counter, wrote out my cheque, collected a ticket which identified my purchase, and the woman said she would telephone me the moment the cheque was cleared. I gave her both my home and my office telephone numbers. Annabel squeezed my arm as we took the elevator back down to the ground floor. 'What shall we do now, sweetheart?' I asked. 'I think you should take me back to the apartment, and fuck the living daylights out of me,' she said. 'How does that sound?' 'Sounds good,' darling, I said. 'Let's get a cab.'

Twenty minutes later, I was unlocking the door to the apartment. 'I think this calls for a little champagne,' I said. 'Does that sound all right to you, sweetheart?' 'It most certainly does, my darling,' she said. At which point Fred's cleaner – whom I had met, but whose name I couldn't remember – came out of Fred's room, the vacuum cleaner in her hand. 'Oh, hello, Mr Andrews,' she said. 'I thought I heard somebody. Hello, madam.' 'Hi' I said. 'Good to see you. This is my fiancée, Annabel Crighton.' The woman smiled at Annabel. 'Hello, Annabel,' she said. 'What a pretty name. My name's Rose.' They shook hands. 'I'm nearly finished, sir,' she said to me. 'I'll be out of your way in a few minutes.' 'No hurry, Rose,' I said, lying in my teeth. I carried the bottle of champagne that I'd taken out of the fridge through into the living room. Rose was black, around fifty, incredibly overweight, and she had emigrated to New York from London many years ago. Her American husband had abandoned her a couple of years back, and she worked all the hours God sent as a cleaner, to bring up her two boys. She was a delightful woman, and an excellent cleaner. As far as Fred was concerned, she came with the apartment block.

I found a couple of champagne flutes, opened the bottle, and filled them, handing one to Annabel. 'Cheers, darling,' I said. We clinked glasses. 'Cheers, darling,' said Annabel. She put her glass down, took mine out of my hand, put that down too, came back and, wrapping herself around me, started to kiss me, her tongue half-way down my throat. She disentangled one arm, and slid it down between us. The hand found my trouser zip, and slowly unzipped it, Annabel continuing to kiss me meanwhile. I felt her hand inside my fly, and then inside my underpants. She took hold of my cock, her hand cool and firm, and began to masturbate me, very, very slowly. She disengaged her mouth from mine. 'When did a woman last give you a decent wank, darling?' she asked. 'Or shouldn't I ask?' I actually couldn't remember, and said so. Just then Rose called through from the corridor 'Goodbye now, Mr Andrews. Goodbye, Miss Annabel.' We both called out goodbye, without moving from where we were.

'If it's so long that you can't remember, then I think it's high time that I gave you one,' said Annabel. 'Would you like me to give you one off the wrist?' I laughed at the long-forgotten teenage expression. 'Yes, please,' I said. 'Let's do it here,' she said. 'That's much naughtier than going into the bedroom for it, isn't it? Let's just stay like this, fully dressed and standing up and kissing while I wank you. OK?' 'Sure, sweetheart,' I said. 'Just one thing,' she continued. 'You'd better get your hankie out to come into. I don't want come all over this suit, if

THE FOURTH OF JULY

you don't mind.' I did as I was told, and found my handkerchief. I held it, ready when needed, in my hand.

Annabel went back to kissing me, and her obviously practised hand went back to jacking me off. She was an artiste. She masturbated me slowly, gently, salaciously, at the same time doing what I can only describe as kissing me off while she was tossing me off. Her tongue, in my mouth, had a life of its own. It added intensely to the erotic sensations that her fingers were bringing about in my cock. She built my mounting lust, my increasing need for sexual release, deliberately, gradually, until I was almost on the point of screaming, when she suddenly squeezed my prick much more firmly, and with confident strokes, took me over the top, into one of the finest, most memorable ejaculations that it has ever been my pleasure to experience. I held my handkerchief to my pumping tool until all was spent. She kept up her ministrations until I was quite, quite finished.

'There you are, kind sir,' she said. 'Was that good?' 'That was terrific, darling,' I said. 'Absolutely terrific.' I was quite breathless from the efforts of the lengths to which she had taken me. When I had my breath back, I said 'And thank you, my love. Thank you. That was, without doubt, the finest wank of my life. Bar none.' 'From you, Tony,' she said, smiling at me, 'that has to be a compliment. Thank you.' 'My pleasure,' I said. 'Very genuinely my pleasure.' We both laughed. 'What now?' I asked her. 'Would you like me to return the compliment, or would you rather be fucked?' She looked at me for a moment before replying. 'Actually, if you don't mind, neither,' she said. 'I had something slightly different in mind, if you've no objection.' 'Tell me all,' I invited. 'I can't imagine anything that would upset me. Surprise me.'

'What I'd really like to do,' she said, 'is for us to go into the bedroom, get undressed – both of us – and for me to masturbate, with you watching me. I mean, really watching me. From close. That would turn me on tremendously. It's been a fantasy of mine all my life, and I've never felt that I've known anyone well enough to ask them if they would like to take part in it with me. I've always imagined that it might upset most men, I mean, them being there, and me wanting to play with myself, rather than fuck.' She paused, and then went on 'There have been occasions. You know, I've done it with you, where I've played with my pussy, sort of lazily, between sex with you, or before, or after. But what I'd love to do is have a whole, complete masturbatory session, from start to finish, with no need or reason to hurry, with you watching. May I do that? Will it upset you? If it would, then I wouldn't want to do it.'

'What a lovely idea, my darling,' I said. 'I can't think of anything I'd like to do more, right at this particular moment. I love to watch girls masturbating. It's a tremendous turn-on for me. And, as you say, it's not something you've ever done in front of me. Not seriously. Please feel free. Not only shall I not mind, I shall actually enjoy it. But there is one proviso.' 'What's that?' she asked, rather nervously. 'When you've finished,' – I said. 'And I do mean finished. Properly finished. Then I shall – with your permission, of course – I shall jump on you and, as you suggested when we left Tiffany's earlier on, fuck the living daylights out of you. I shall be so wound up, so horny, watching you wank, I shall be standing here, with my prick in my hand, waiting. Is that all right?' 'How lovely,' she said. 'I can't wait.'

We went into the bedroom, and undressed. When she got down to her undies, I was surprised to see that she was wearing a pair of unbelievably sexy, tiny, pure white silken knickers. The crotch of them was absolutely sopping wet. She saw where I was looking, and took them off, and gave them to me, smiling. 'Here you are, you old knicker fetishist,' she said. 'Sniff those while I masturbate. That should help get you ready for some serious fucking.' I grinned at her, taking the knickers and pressing the inside of the wet crotch to my nostrils. It gave off the unadulterated odour of fresh, wet cunt. Magical. 'Not half, my darling,' I said. 'What a lovely treat. One off the wrist, and then my own pair of damp-crotched knickers to sniff, while I watch you play with your wet little pussy. What more could a male fetishist: possibly want?'

She grinned back at me. 'I don't know the answer to that question,' she said. 'I've often wondered. What else are you into? Used tampons?' 'Jesus, no,' I said. 'I don't mind fucking you when you've got your period, if that's what you fancy, but I'm not into tampons, used or otherwise. What makes you think I might be?' 'I didn't think that,' she said. 'I only asked.' She lay on the bed, naked, her feet inches away from the foot of it. She splayed her legs. 'Come and sit on the floor here in front of me,' she said. 'It'll be like sitting in the front row at the theatre.' I grinned at her. 'But a lot more fun,' I said. She grinned back. 'Maybe,' she said.

She reached down and slowly rubbed the flat of her hand – her whole hand, as it were – over her exquisitely bald pussy. She lay her head back now, flat behind her, so that I couldn't any longer see her face. Not from where I was sitting. I could see her feet, her legs and ankles, the inside of her thighs, her hand, hiding, for the moment, both her bald pudenda and her cunt itself, and then, over and behind that, her flat stomach, rising up to her full, firm breasts, surmounted by erect nipples, and that was where my view ended. She began to rub her hand slowly back and forth, still flat, across the area between her legs. I couldn't see, from any angle, what was happening beneath her hand during this exercise, but I could hear a tiny sort of soft, squelching noise, which I took to be the noise produced by rubbing the flat of her hand slowly across the wet, by now slightly engorged, lips of her cunt.

She then took her hand away for a moment, and wriggled her hips – almost obscenely – presumably getting herself into a more comfortable position. She then reached down, still with just her right hand, but this time her middle finger was extended, and she began to rub it around on the outside of her vaginal lips, which were shining wetly from the lubrication that she must have been producing for some time. Probably since she began wanking me, I judged, by the quantity that was flowing out from between her pinkly wet pussy lips. It ran down the inside of her thighs, and I had to stop myself from reaching out and rubbing my fingers in it so that I might lick them and taste her sweet nectar.

And then I remembered the white silk knickers that I was still holding, but which I had forgotten about. I raised the crotch to my nostrils again, and breathed in deeply, inhaling the heavenly scent and feeling the dampness, and then – as I licked and sucked on the narrow strip of cotton-lined silk that had so recently been between her legs, guarding the lips of the very cunt that Annabel was now playing with – I tasted the forbidden flavour of her sex. My erection was so hard, it was hurting me. I wondered if, at this rate, I could last out Annabel's masturbatory session without indulging in a masturbatory trick or two of my own.

As I breathed and tasted the strong flavour and scent of her knicker-crotch, Annabel started to move her middle finger down inside her pussy, raising and lowering it, revealing it covered in the mucus of her lubrication, as she simply rubbed it in and out for a while. She then pulled it all the way out, and, bringing down her other hand, she used the fingers of both hands to spread her vaginal lips wide, thus affording entry now to two fingers of her right hand, which she inserted deeply, moaning slightly as she did so. She was obviously feeling with those two fingers for her clitoris, which she found almost immediately, and she began to stimulate it with rhythmic strokes, and she began also to move her hips to the rhythm, as her fingers gradually increased both their speed and the pressure with which she was using them. The sight of her fingers, delving wetly into her open cunt, and the expression of sheer, unadulterated lust on her face, with her eyes closed, her mouth open, saliva in the corners of her mouth, was one of the most erotically stimulating sights I had seen for a very long time.

That sight was now accompanied by the rising sounds of her

increasing excitement as she felt her orgasm approaching. The moans became almost groans, and here and there words were just about decipherable in between them. They didn't make any kind of grammatical sense, but I could hear words like 'fuck,' and 'come,' and even 'cunt.' They were squeezed out almost, in between heavy breathing and the faster and faster movement of her fingers, until she suddenly collapsed in a sweating, panting, moaning bundle of sexual happiness, her lewd expression gone, replaced by an almost dreamy smile, her eyes still closed, and her hand now still.

I had become so sexually excited myself whilst watching this totally salacious, blatantly physical exposé of female masturbation, that my erection felt as if it were about to burst. I was just wondering what best to do with it, when Annabel opened her eyes, and immediately saw my predicament. 'Oh, you poor darling,' she said. 'Here, let me attend to that for you.' So saying, she pushed me down onto my back on the bed, and clambered on top of me, spreading her thighs, and lowering herself onto me, her fingers spreading her dripping love-hole as she took me inside it. She was warm, wet, and tight, as she closed herself around me with those amazing muscles of hers, and began to fuck me. I didn't last any time at all, being on the verge of exploding from the moment she sucked me in, and within seconds I was joyously spurting jets of come up inside her welcoming pussy, welcoming the ensuing sexual relief. Annabel grinned down at me. 'That feels good, my darling,' she said. 'I think I'll have another sneaky little come with you now.' And so she did.

The following day was 4th July, 1976. The Independence Day Bicentennial. A public holiday. I reached out and switched on the local radio station, and the announcer was saying 'So get up and get out of there. It's the Bicentennial. Enjoy it, for you sure as hell won't be here for the next one.' It was a glorious July day, with strong sunshine, and with a good breeze blowing in off the East River, auguring well for the arrival of the sailing ships.

We made our way slowly downtown, making for the apartment block just off Battery Park where friends with an apartment with a balcony facing south, and on the thirtieth floor, overlooking the park, had invited us to their party, timed to commence at eleven a.m. The first of the ships were due around noon. The whole of New York – it seemed like the whole world – was in festive mood. Gone were the usual bad tempers, the pushing and shoving, the traffic snarl-ups, and the hooting cars with their shouting, fist-waving drivers, replaced by smiles and laughter, and happy greetings from complete strangers. It was as if New York had been transformed to a fairyland. We arrived, happy, excited, and thirsty, to meet most of the staff of *Tiptop*, plus a few friends of the owners of the apartment whom I didn't know. This was Annabel's first meeting with anyone from the office and they all greeted her with welcoming enthusiasm. Even Eileen, I particularly noticed, seemed to go out of her way to make Annabel feel at home as much as possible. Our hosts were serving champagne continuously, but there was every other kind of drink available for anyone who preferred something else. Always happy to drink champagne, Annabel and I relaxed and enjoyed ourselves, chattering to fellow guests, and admiring the spectacular view, looking south-east, out towards the Statue of Liberty. Absolutely on schedule, precisely at noon, the first sailing ship hove into sight in the far distance, a spectacular, seven-masted barque, flying the Swedish flag.

She was followed at regular intervals by a whole procession – fleet, I should say – of beautiful old sailing ships, including, of course, one from Britain, manned by cadets from Dartmouth Naval College. The great old sailing ships were danced attendance upon by a flotilla of ships, from the traditional New York fire brigade vessels with their hoses playing spectacularly port and starboard, to a real armada of privately-owned little boats and yachts. Every ship and boat's siren in the New World seemed to be blasting out its welcome, and we raised a consolidated, apartment-block cheer for each ship as she rounded the bottom of Battery Park and headed off up the Hudson River behind us, finally to drop anchor there in midriver, off Riverside Park. Every balcony in the building, like ours, was holding its Bicentennial lunch party.

Our hosts did us proud with a magnificent meal, the centrepiece of which was an enormous turkey, to me always a symbol of the nation's independence, but more usually eaten on Thanksgiving Day, the anniversary of the landing of the Pilgrim Fathers, after their voyage from Plymouth, in New England.

The sailing ships had all made port by about four o'clock. The one or two stragglers were reported to be on their way, but were some hours out of New York as yet. They had come from all over the world. From – amongst other places – Russia, Australia, Hong Kong, Scandinavia, Britain and South America, and had spent the preceding months visiting ports all around the world, prior to concluding Operation Sailing Ship 1976 in New York as part of the Bicentennial celebrations. By six, the party began to break up, and we took our leave, knowing that we would meet up with many of the same people again later that evening. The second party of the day was set up to view the fireworks that were to be let off from barges anchored in the Hudson River, opposite New York's West Side. Our party was in one of the beautiful old apartment blocks on Riverside Drive, overlooking Riverside Park and the Hudson River. We found a cab, eventually, and slowly wound our way back uptown from Battery Park to Park Avenue, and Fred's apartment. We showered, changed, dolled ourselves up to rather dressier standards than lunch had demanded, and sat down with a glass of champagne to collect our thoughts before taking off for the party, where we were due any time after eight. The fireworks were scheduled to commence at nine.

'It's been a lovely day, so far,' said Annabel. 'Everyone seems so friendly. Is it genuine? The friendliness?' 'I think so, sweetheart,' I said. 'As far as I'm able to tell, it is. I might be standing in for the big boss while he's away in London, but I don't think New Yorkers feel about that sort of thing the way we British do. Work is work, and play is play, and never the twain shall meet. If they like you, they let you know. I don't think many of them can be bothered to pretend. I could be wrong, but I don't think so. But one thing that I've been told is that, if you are an unattached woman in New York, the men are mostly either married or gay. The ones that are left that are single and not gay are allegedly chauvinist pigs. But I obviously haven't got that first hand. Ask Eileen this evening. She'll tell you. She's the one that I introduced as Fred's secretary.'

'I know the one,' said Annabel. 'She seemed very genuine. She says that she works as your secretary whilst Fred's away. Is she good?' 'Yes,' I said. 'Very good. I think she probably does more of Fred's job than Fred does. She's certainly a tremendous help to me.' I looked at my watch. 'I guess we could probably move off, if you're ready, sweetheart. Shall I ring down and ask for a cab? It's bound to take a little while this evening.' 'Of course, darling,' she said. 'I'm ready now. I'll just powder my nose, and I'll be right with you.' She disappeared in the direction of the bedroom. I rang downstairs for a cab.

The apartment, when we got there, was beautiful. It was my first experience of this kind of New York apartment block. Probably it had been built around the turn of the century, and its elegant proportions, plethora of rooms opening off a central corridor, long, floor-to-ceiling windows, and beautiful pine panelling reminded me of those apartment blocks in London, next to the Albert Hall, where some of our more famous conductors have lived over the years. Sir Malcolm Sargent, for one. The party was in full swing when we arrived, with one large room set aside for dancing, and another set up for a buffet supper, whilst the main, longest room facing out over the park towards the river held the drinks, and was the one, we were informed, from which to watch the fireworks when they

THE FOURTH OF JULY

commenced. Champagne was on offer, so Annabel and I decided to stay with it. Our host was a Professor of Humanities at New York University, and was an unlikely friend of Fred's, who had passed on this invitation. I had telephoned, a few days ago, to ask if it was acceptable for me to use it, and had been given a delightful welcome. It was pleasant now to meet someone who had previously been simply a voice on the telephone.

I introduced Annabel, and our host, Professor Richard Williams ('Please call me Dick') introduced his wife, Alana. She was a gynaecologist, with, she said, a thriving practice, which she ran from the apartment. They both seemed charming people, and were genuinely welcoming. They introduced us to those people that we didn't know, and we greeted again those we had seen that morning. Altogether, there must have been some fifty or so people at the party. We felt relaxed and at home from the moment that we arrived, and, having accepted a drink, took ourselves off to dance. The apartment was, fortunately, fully air-conditioned. If you've never seen a New York firework display, then – in my respectful opinion – you've simply never seen a firework display worthy of the name. This event was organized by the city, under its mayor, and it was like being transported to a totally spectacular pyrotechnic wonderland. Even the sophisticated crowd with whom I was watching, accustomed as they were to this kind of thing, were *oooh*ing and *aaah*ing as unbelievable display after unbelievable display rose up, burst into a million tiny explosions, and fell, sparkling all the way down, back to earth. There were set pieces, broadsides of rockets, skies full of shooting stars. There were effects that I had never seen before, and have never seen since. It was the most magical firework display of a lifetime. It built up to a crescendo, and ended in an explosion of such magnificence that it drew long, enthusiastic, unrehearsed applause from the entire assembled party.

And when the firework party was over, the real party began. The richest, most powerful nation in the world was celebrating its two hundredth birthday. As representatives – presumably of the nation whom America had beaten in a straight fight, two hundred years earlier, we were genuinely welcome. No one had axes to grind. Political, national, moral, or of any other kind. The mood was one of celebration, and it was extremely infectious. We drank some, and we boogied some, and then we drank some more, and then we boogied some more. Annabel and I eventually left at four o'clock in the morning. We found a cab within minutes, and were back home fifteen minutes later. We were high, and happy, and absolutely dead-beat. I think both of us fell instantly asleep the moments our heads touched the pillows. My last memory, as I fell asleep, was of thinking what a lucky chap I was. It was a lovely, really happy thought to fall asleep with.

The next morning wasn't quite so euphoric. I awoke at noon, wondering why someone was knocking the apartment block down, only to discover that the hammering was inside my head. I managed some seriously black coffee, and took some through to Annabel, who was beginning to make noises as if she was in the same sort of pain. A long, hot shower later, we agreed that brunch at our neighbourhood coffee shop was probably the best remedy. Hangovers always bring out the need, in me, for either a really good dry martini, or a really good Bloody Mary. In my younger years I had spent some time in advertising and public relations, prior to becoming a freelance writer, and in that capacity I had, for something over five years, promoted Beefeater Gin in the United Kingdom. So I could – and, from time to time, did – mix a good martini. That morning, I went for Bloody Marys. Terrific, even if I say so myself.

Beefeater was, in those days, probably the premium gin in the States, where people are (always have been, still are) very specific about the brand of whatever it is that they like to drink. To demonstrate what I'm talking about, I'll never forget giving my first cocktail party as a married man in New York. We lived in Sutton Place, in Manhattan, which is rather like living in

Grosvenor Square in London. Very rich. Very upmarket. And, naturally enough, I was stocked up with everything. But every thing. Whatever you wanted, I thought, I could supply. This is from a Brit, brought up on parties where people say 'I'd love a gin.' Or a Scotch. Or a whatever. In New York, wrong. Totally wrong. The first guy through the door, known to my wife and I as Superfly, when asked what he'd like to drink, said, 'Oh, hey man, I'd just love a Tanquerey and tonic. Thank you.'

Tanquerey and tonic? *What the fuck's that*? I thought. 'I'm terribly sorry,' I said, 'I haven't got any Tanquerey. Can I get you something else?' He had a good look at the available bottles, and then said 'Oh, sure. No problem. Beefeater and tonic will be fine.' Yes, you've got it. Tanquerey is a popular brand of gin in New York. I know now, but I didn't know then, that Americans ask for their drinks by brand name. As in 'I'll have a Cutty Sark on ice, with club soda.' Or, 'Make mine a Beefeater martini, Straight up. Hold the olive.' Or, 'Gimme a Seagram's on the rocks.'

But that lunchtime, Bloody Marys it was. A lot of ice. Smirnoff vodka, Lea & Perrins Worcester sauce, Libby's tomato juice, fresh lemon juice, salt, pepper, a dash of Tabasco, and a celery stalk to stir it with. Mix well, and drink. Cheers! A jugful of those, and we both began to feel better. We made it to the small, friendly neighbourhood restaurant, where we started off with another jug of Bloody Marys, while we made our selection form the menu. Annabel had what was rapidly becoming her favourite New York brunch dish – oeufs Florentine – whilst I had my favourite corned beef hash. We walked back to the apartment through the early afternoon sunshine, well fed, relaxed and at peace with the world.

The telephone was ringing as we entered the apartment, and to my surprise it was Fred. Looking at my watch, it was only ten in the morning, London time. 'Hey, Tony,' he said. 'How's it going?' 'It's going fine with me, Fred,' I said. 'But more to the point, how's it going with you?' 'It's good. All is resolved,' he said, to my genuine relief. 'Wally has backed down about how many hours I actually spend in the office. I've negotiated an excellent package for you. I'll give you all the details when I see you. I'll be back Wednesday of next week. I've told Eileen, so they'll all know in the office. So leap off down to wherever it is you're taking your girlfriend, and I'll be in New York when you get back. How's that?' 'That's terrific,' I said. 'Thank you.' 'Don't thank me,' said Fred. 'Thank Eileen. I don't know what she's been saying to Wally about you, but as far as he's concerned, the sun shines out of your you know where.' 'Can't be bad,' I said. 'See you. Cheers, Fred. And thanks again.' 'Cheers, Tone,' he said. 'Take care.'

Thank God for that, I thought. Wally needed Fred. As long as those two were getting on together, all was well with everyone else. But if Fred and Wally were at loggerheads, look out! Wally always seemed a reasonable sort of guy but, in my opinion, it was Fred who kept him reasonable. Wally trusted Fred. I don't believe that Wally ever really trusted anyone else. So if he thought – as he obviously had done recently – that Fred was letting him down in some way (even over something as mundane as the actual number of hours that Fred spent in the New York office) then heaven help the rest of us. Booze, drugs, sex, and rock n'roll didn't bother him. Loyalty did.

I left Annabel in bed the following morning, and went into the office, mainly, I must admit, to arrange the reservations for our forthcoming trip to Puerto Rico. I rang Charles Dainton to check the dates, and he called me back after having spoken to his wife Jo, to say that yes, the day after tomorrow would be great. Just let him know the flight times, and he'd meet us at San Juan airport. And yes, the temperature was in the high nineties, the same as New York. But there was the breeze off the Caribbean, he said, which made it seem cooler. And bring lots of sun oil, he said. I got Eileen to book the tickets on *Tiptop*'s account with a Madison Avenue travel agent, and went, as Fred had suggested, club class rather than tourist. The tickets were hand-delivered, about an hour later.

I checked through a pile of outstanding matters with Eileen, and spoke to Dave, the art director, and Angie, the deputy editor, to see if they had any problems. They didn't. I spoke as well with John Boyce, the advertisement director, and I also checked with Bill Carlson that there were no distribution problems. I called Pauline, who was away on a trip. I left a message on her answering machine. I also spoke to Lucy, to Dee Dee, and to June, at the brothel. She said the girls were missing me. I said that I was missing them. I don't actually know whether I was, or not. And finally I spoke to Jenny, who asked me if I had been able to do anything about my suggestion that she model for the magazine. I hadn't, but I didn't tell her that.

To be honest, I'd forgotten all about it. But I told her a lie, and said that yes, I had started to put something in motion, and that she would hear from me, or from Dave, shortly. Then I told her another lie, and said that I had to fly back to London for a meeting, and that I'd contact her as soon as I got back to New York. I did then actually dictate a note to Dave, giving him Jenny's telephone number and address, and asking him to set up a test shoot. Life with a fiancée, I was beginning to realize, had its complications. What on earth would life with a *wife* be like? But there was no point in worrying about things like that. Not right now. Annabel and I were off to the Caribbean to relax, and lie in the sun. What more could anyone ask? I rang Annabel to tell her that everything was fixed up, and suggested that she meet me at Michael's Pub for dinner. Michael's Pub is a bar and restaurant on East 55th Street, just around the corner from Third Avenue, probably most famous for the fact that Woody Allen plays clarinet there some evenings. That aside, it is a popular place, serving excellent food. Americans, for reasons that I don't understand, think that Michael's Pub is very English. Most English people think that it is very American. Whatever your view, it's a good place to eat and drink. I asked Eileen if she would care to join Annabel and me for an early dinner there. Despite looking rather surprised, I thought, she said that, sure, thank you, that would be great.

I had arranged to meet Annabel at Michael's Pub at seven, so Eileen and I stopped off at P.J. Clarke's for a drink or two after the office. Eileen was drinking Manhattans. I drank my usual scotch and water, no ice. P.J. Clarke's is at its most crowded at the end of the day, the beginning of the evening. It is full of attorneys, advertising people, publishing people, wheelers and dealers, movers and shakers, either throwing a few down before they catch their trains home to their wives and families in the more expensive suburbs, or perhaps buying their mistresses a quick drink or two before doing the same. If they've got an excuse to spend the evening in Manhattan with their mistresses, they probably won't start off at P.J. Clarke's.

Whatever your reason for being there, it is a fascinating bar to drink in when it is really busy. Any English pub regular would be amazed at the speed with which you get served. If you want, say, ten different drinks for ten different people, just reel them off. Once is enough. You'll get them all, moments later, and absolutely correctly. All you need to say the next time is 'The same again.' The other tradition in New York bars that has always appealed to me, as a serious drinker, is the one where, if you are a regular customer – this simply means if you go to the bar often enough for one of the barmen to recognize you – then every fifth round – give or take a round – is on the house. I find that extremely civilized.

At about six-forty-five, Eileen and I finished our drinks and slowly walked the block and a half to Michael's Pub, where the early evening crowd was as thick as the one we had left behind us. I bought Eileen and myself a drink, and left her to it whilst I went to have a word with the restaurant's *maitre d'*. He could offer me a table for the three of us at eight, he said, which seemed about right, and I happily accepted. I slipped him a five dollar bill, which would ensure that he didn't give my table to anyone else.

Annabel arrived promptly at seven. She was carrying bags from Bloomingdale's, Saks Fifth Avenue and Macy's, so we all knew what she had spent the day doing. That particular year, Bloomingdale's bags didn't say Bloomingdale's, they simply said Big Brown Bag, but everyone knew where you'd been shopping. She was full of how much cheaper clothes were in New York than they were in London. *Tell me about it*, I thought. It has always been thus. We Brits get ripped off at home by everyone, for everything. We pay about a third as much again as do our European counterparts (now our EU comrades) for our motorcars. Clothes in London tend to cost in pounds what New Yorkers pay in dollars. As do, for another example, prescription spectacles. I've saved myself a fortune, over the years, simply by buying my glasses in the States. Florida, New York State, or New England, it makes no difference. And the quality and standard of service is so much better than anything offered at home.

When I got back to the girls, they were chattering together as if they had known each other all their lives. I got the impression that they genuinely liked each others' company. Eileen was complaining about the lack of attractive, available men in New York. 'Is it really as bad as they say?' asked Annabel. 'I guess it is,' said Eileen. 'Take the office, for example. Apart from Tony here, and with Fred away, the men are either gay, or married. I'm not sure which is worse, for a single girl. I mean, I don't, like, have any problem with the gays. They're amusing enough. They're actually quite a lot of fun. But as far as, you know, sex is concerned, I mean, well, forget it. Obviously.'

'As for the married men, they never seem to think of anything else. I reckon I could get laid a dozen times a day. I don't know if women stop putting out once they get married, but it certainly seems like it. That's if you believe what the married men tell you. It's "How would you like to suck my cock, Eileen?" and "Boy, I'd sure like to get into your panties, sweetheart," all day long, from first thing after they arrive in the morning to the last thing before they go home at night. I couldn't believe it this evening, just as I was leaving that John

Boyce – he's our advertisement director,' she said, looking at Annabel, 'he came into my office, and said "Why don't you I take me home and fuck me, baby?" Just like that. I mean, forget any goddamn subtlety. Not that I'd fuck him if he was the last man in the world,' she said. 'But, you know? I mean, how about "Can I buy you a drink, honey?" Something. *Anything*. But no. Just "Why don't you take me home and fuck me, baby?"' 'What did you say in reply?' asked Annabel. Eileen laughed. 'I said "why don't you go home and fuck *yourself*, baby? You'll probably think you're a better lay than I would."' We all laughed. 'You have to laugh, really, don't you?' said Eileen. 'Otherwise you'd cry, wouldn't you?' Annabel and I agreed.

Woody Allen certainly wasn't playing at Michael's Pub that particular evening, but they had a very listenable to little jazz trio competing with the conversation, the laughter, and the clink of glasses. They were playing classic stuff for piano, bass and drums. Earl Hines, Benny Goodman, Earl Miller, Count Basie, that sort of music. Most English jazz fans would have left home simply to be able to listen to it. Here it was *gratis*, and I don't think anyone was really listening. Except me.

I excused myself from the girls for a moment, and went over to the pianist. I waited until he'd finished what he was playing. It was an arrangement I hadn't heard before of Wes Montgomery's 'Finger Pickin',' I applauded. 'Thank you,' said the pianist. 'Thank *you*,' I said. 'That was something else. But tell me,' I asked. 'Do you play requests?' 'Sure,' he said. 'Provided that we know them.' 'How about "Give Me the Simple Life"' I asked. 'Oh, yeah,' he said. 'Man, you got it.' 'Thanks,' I said. 'My pleasure,' he said. I think he meant it. 'OK, fellas?' he asked his colleagues. They nodded, and he tapped his foot for the beat. They played it beautifully. Ella Fitzgerald would have been proud of them. I raised my glass, across the room, as they finished, and the pianist grinned, and nodded. If I could play the piano, you could have my share of girlie magazines, I thought. Any day. But then, I wonder if playing the piano in Michael's Pub in New York is the epitome of what that particular pianist wanted from life? I guess not.

I've no idea how much he would earn by plying there. One assumes a fair wage. Anyone doing anything creative, be it writing, painting, drawing, playing an instrument, taking photographs, whatever, does it basically for money. But once they are able to earn a decent living at whatever it is, then they want it to be read, looked at, listened to, by appreciative people, in good surroundings. Writers want their work to be printed in successful newspapers and magazines, or they want to write books that are published, and that sell. Writing, by itself, if it's not published, is totally meaningless.

The pianist, presumably, would prefer to play – with his colleagues – to a crowd in a concert hall, or on television or radio, where people went, or switched on, because they wanted to hear his music, rather than simply providing background music to the sound of people's conversation in a noisy New York bar. I was happy editing one of the most successful men's magazines in the world. For me, being at the top, or near the top, of one's profession, is what life is all about. There are, I know, many people who would disagree with me. *But enough of that*, I thought, turning back to pay attention to the two beautiful girls who were with me. At that moment the maitre d' approached. 'Mr Andrews?' he said, I nodded. 'Your table is ready now, sir.' 'I'll be right there,' I said. 'Thank you.' We finished our drinks, and I ushered the girls across to the restaurant area. We had a relaxed and pleasant meal, the three of us together. Eileen kept Annabel amused with her stories of her ongoing battle with life as a bachelor girl in New York. Her sense of humour and her instinct for survival were obviously her most valuable weapons, but it is patently a tough city to survive in as a single girl, working as a secretary.

America doesn't have (or didn't have, in those days) the social support systems, with which we British have become so cocooned. Back in the 1970s, if an American drew unemployment benefit for six months, then it ceased, and he or she had to work for six months before qualifying to draw it again. With the high rents demanded in Manhattan, and the high cost of living, the system simply didn't allow for anyone being out of work. Ever. Salaries were certainly higher than in London, but competition for jobs was undoubtedly greater, and it wasn't at all unusual for a highly skilled person to be out of work for a couple of years. Advertising is perhaps the prime example of that particular situation. If a big advertising agency loses a major account, they can lay off a total of as many as fifty or sixty people, if you add together the creative people – art directors and copywriters – the account handlers (planners, they're called today) and the back-up administrative and secretarial personnel. Only a small percentage of those people would find immediate employment, while the balance – most of them in no way responsible for the losing of the account – would be thrown on the unemployment refuse heap. Magazine publishing is a similar business. Should a magazine fail, for whatever reason, a large number of people are inevitably thrown out of work. And magazines *do* fail. If circulation drops, or, put more basically perhaps, if sales fall, then advertising revenue automatically falls too. You can't charge advertisers for readers who aren't there. If advertising income falls, then sooner or later the publishing company will almost certainly have to cut the number of pages published each week or month. As the magazine gets thinner, and loses the appeal of a fat, happy, glossy, successful publication, it will almost certainly lose more readers. A genuinely vicious circle, almost inevitably leading to its failure. And, of course, times change. Habits change.

Television has been responsible for the disappearance of a myriad newspapers and magazines, all around the world. Television programmes draw more viewers than newspapers or magazines draw readers, with the result that advertisers spend their money where it will do them the most good. On television. There is only so much advertising money around. So newspapers and magazines lose out. These days, people also spend much of the time that they used to spend reading – whether they were reading newspapers, magazines, or books – watching television. Which compounds the problems for publishers. Hence the move by many international print publishing companies into television.

Eileen, Annabel, and I spent some time discussing the problems inherent in magazine publishing, whilst enjoying the delights of Michael's Pub's food and wine, and then, at around nine-thirty, Eileen announced that it was probably time for her to head homeward. I paid the bill, and found a cab for Eileen, before Annabel and I took one back up to Fred's apartment. I decided not to go into the office the following day, but to relax, and do the small things that one does the day before going on holiday. Buy film for my camera, sun oil for both of us. Find a book or two to read. That kind of thing.

In the end, we got up late, had some breakfast, and then went back to bed and fucked lazily. Luxuriously. There's something about sex during the day, at a time when normally you would be working, that makes it infinitely more pleasurable than sex at any other time. Annabel's body was made for fucking, and I made the most of it that day. I had locked the bedroom door against being disturbed by Fred's cleaner, and we heard her try the door just once, before she took herself off. She would be accustomed, I guessed, with Fred, to him still being abed during daylight hours. We eventually showered and got dressed at about eight that evening, and went out to eat sexually replete, hand in hand, looking for a new restaurant in which to indulge our appetites.

We found one not far away, a couple of blocks north on Madison Avenue, that looked promising. It was one of those small, friendly, neighbourhood Italian restaurants, run by an Italian couple. It had the obligatory red and white checked tablecloths, and there was an ample supply of Chianti flasks racked up behind the small bar. We were greeted with a warm welcome, and given a secluded table towards the back of the room, suitably removed from the other couples – mostly obviously married, some with children – who were there before us. We took the patron's advice, and ordered the dishes of the day. We ate some beautiful home-made soup, followed by equally delicious home-made pasta, served with a really fresh mixed salad. I recognized neither, but made a mental note to return to the restaurant as soon as we got back from Puerto Rico. We slept well and awoke early, and when we were ready to leave I got the doorman to find us a Checker to take us to Kennedy. Checkers are the big, old fashioned cabs you sometimes see in New York. They are marginally nearer to the London idea of a cab than the rest of the city's taxis (which are just ordinary saloon cars, painted yellow) and are called Checkers because they have a black and white checked stripe around their middle. They're not made any more, for some reason.

The Pan Am flight down to Puerto Rico was pleasant and entirely uneventful, and Charles was there, true to his word, waiting for us as we came out of Customs and Immigration. The sunshine, even after New York in July, was hot and strong, and we were glad to find that Charles' Pontiac was air-conditioned. We drove seemingly out of town, and along the coast a little way, keeping the Caribbean sea on our left, and we soon came to a completely modern, circular apartment block twelve storeys in height, built literally on the perfect, golden-sanded beach, where the waves were breaking gently onto the shore some hundred yards away. 'You're not far from the beach, then?' I said, as we humped our bags out of the boot of the car. Charles laughed, but I think he'd heard it before. To Annabel and me it was pure magic.

Charles's apartment was on the sixth floor, and whilst it was air-conditioned, the air conditioning wasn't switched on, since there was a beautiful, fresh sea breeze blowing in through the open windows. Jo turned out to be a tall, lithe, tanned New York blonde, with a ready smile and a nice sense of humour. 'Welcome,' she said, giving a warm, firm handshake. 'Charles tells me you publish dirty magazines.' 'Something like that,' I said, grinning back at her. 'I hope you've brought some with you,' she said. 'I haven't yet got a work permit here, so I've not too much to do, except lie in the sun, and complain. A few dirty magazines would cheer me up considerably.' 'I haven't actually brought any with me,' I told her. 'But I'll get some put in the post for you.' I made a mental note to take out a subscription in Charles name. 'Presumably they're legal here, the same as in the States?' I asked. 'Oh, sure,' she replied. 'We have exactly the same laws. But not quite the same manners. You'll see what I mean later.'

'Charles and I assumed – after you've had a drink, of course – that the first thing that you will want to do is to leap out onto the beach and into the sea. At least, that's what everyone else who comes here wants to do. Does that appeal to you both?' We both said that, yes, that appealed very much, thank you. 'Good,' she said. 'I've put beach towels in your room. Are you all right for sun oil?' We nodded. 'Good,' she said again. 'Then I'll pour you a drink, and I'll leave you to it. We thought we'd take you into old San Juan for supper this evening. It's the prettiest part of the city, by far, and the nicest restaurants are there. The seafood is really excellent, as you can probably imagine.' She looked at her watch. 'It's almost three now. Please feel free to do whatever you want to do. And if there's anything you need, just shout. If we don't see you before, shall we meet on the balcony at six for a drink before supper?' That would be good, we said.

One thing I do differently in the tropics, or at least when I am in the sunshine, is that I tend not to drink my habitual scotch and water, no ice, but rather go for the local hooch. I can't explain why. I just do. That means I drink ouzo in Greece. Tequila in Mexico. Arak in the Lebanon. (Not that anyone goes to the Lebanon any more, but there was a time in my life when I used to go there regularly. Before their war, of course. It was a delightful place then). And, of course, rum in the Caribbean.

Puerto Rico is where Baccardi comes from. Amongst many

other rums. They mix killer cocktails – using all of them – for tourists at all of the major hotels in San Juan. My advice is to stick to a single rum, with whatever your favourite mixer is. I give this advice, having drawn a round of applause from the gathered diners in the rooftop restaurant at the Hilton Hotel in San Juan, simply because – having indulged in far too many of the aforementioned killer rum cocktails – I managed to stand on my head. Everyone else thought I was too drunk to do it. Only I knew that the only time I actually *can* stand on my head is when I am drunk. So, a couple of Baccardi and cokes later, Annabel and I wandered down across the soft, golden sand of Puerto Rico, and stood, hand in hand, in the warm Caribbean sea. Annabel looked good enough to eat in a minuscule bikini which hardly covered her firm breasts or contained her taut, full bottom.

I squeezed her hand. 'It beats Brighton, doesn't it?' I said. 'If only because there aren't any pebbles.' She laughed. 'There's that, of course,' she said. 'And then, the temperature must be, what? Ninety-something?' 'About that, I guess,' I said. 'And then there's this beautiful, golden sand. Just like warm icing sugar. And those are palm trees over there, aren't they?' she asked. I had to agree that they were. 'And the sea is a sort of turquoise colour, isn't it?' she asked. 'Not grey, like the Channel at Brighton?' 'Yes,' I said. 'It is.' 'I don't suppose they have rock here, though,' said Annabel. 'Do you?' 'Probably not,' I said. 'It wouldn't seem right, somehow, would it?' 'Not really, I suppose,' she said. 'Puerto Rico Rock. It hasn't got the same sort of ring as Brighton Rock. Doesn't quite flow off the tongue properly.'

'But then, they've got things here that they don't have in Brighton, so I'm told,' I said. 'What sort of things?' asked Annabel. 'Well,' I said. 'I'm told that, if the male Puerto Rican, lying on the beach in his swimming trunks, sees a pretty girl passing by, probably in her bikini, and he wants to pay her a compliment, let her know how pretty he thinks she is, he doesn't raise his cap, and say hello, like one might at Brighton.

THE FOURTH OF JULY

In any case those awful baseball caps don't lend themselves to being raised, somehow. No. So, instead, he hauls out his cock and starts jacking off in front of her.'

'You're kidding,' Annabel said. 'No, I'm not,' I told her. 'I think that's what Jo was referring to when she said they don't have American manners here. Do you remember?' Annabel looked around, with interest, but there wasn't a person in sight, not for miles, apart from a few kids playing at the water's edge. 'I don't believe you,' she said. 'You're pulling my leg.' 'I'm not,' I said. 'Really I'm not. You ask Jo when we get back.' 'I will,' she said. We plunged into the sea, and forgot about Puerto Rican wankers for quite some time. Annabel raised the subject again over our pre-supper drinks later that evening, out on the balcony. 'Oh, so you've heard about that,' said Jo. 'Yes, I'm sorry to say. It *is* true.' 'Have you had it happen to you?' Annabel asked Jo. 'What on earth do you do?' Jo laughed. 'Well, at first,' she said, 'I pretended not to notice. But all you get if you ignore them is a lot of jeering, and rude comments So what I do now is I stop and look at them, and then I put my fingers like this,' she said, holding out her hand, with her thumb and forefinger about an inch apart. 'They get the message, I think. But it doesn't stop them doing it. Apparently they think it's very macho. They're all so fucking blown up with what they think is Spanish macho, they're appalling. Absolutely appalling.'

The conversation moved on, and after a decent interval, Charles drove us into old San Juan. We had a quick look at the old Spanish fortress, which looks beautiful, floodlit as it is at night, with its old cannons, and then we walked through narrow, cobbled streets, alive with lights and music and people, to the restaurant. Over our excellent seafood, Charles asked us if we would care to go sailing at the weekend. He didn't own a boat, he told us, but on occasions he hired a small, Puerto Rican fishing boat, together with its captain, which sounded delightful, and we said yes, please, we'd love to. That gave us a couple of days, to get something of a tan going, in order to protect ourselves, before venturing out to sea.

The evening passed pleasantly. It transpired that neither Charles nor Jo were particularly enamoured of Puerto Rico. They had made a few good friends, but, generally speaking, they didn't take to either the island or its inhabitants. They had been there nearly two years now, and Charles' agency's head office in New York had promised him a posting to Jamaica, to which, they said, they much looked forward. I told them of my friend John Lane, and it transpired that he and Charles knew each other from New York, some years ago. At the end of our first day in San Juan, we went to bed tired but happy, feeling a long, long way away from any kind of problems. If only we had known.

We spent the next couple of days on the beach, and in the sea, carefully gaining a tan which, using plenty of good, protective sun oil, arrived rapidly and satisfactorily, without any sunburn. Come the Saturday, we all piled into Charles's Pontiac, laden with picnic hampers, drink coolers, and the whole paraphernalia of a day at sea in a boat, and took off for the north coast. An hour and a half later, we arrived at a small fishing village, where our captain and his boat were waiting for us. We set off in about half an hour, with everyone (bar the captain, who stolidly retained his trousers, shirt, jacket, shoes and socks) stripped down to the very basics. The boat was not fast, but was comfortable, and we sailed along the beautiful, exotic coast of Puerto Rico, eventually anchoring in a small, deserted bay, where everyone was left to do whatever it was that they wanted to do. Swimming, sunbathing, snorkelling – Charles had two sets of the equipment – drinking, talking. We all did some of everything, and after a delicious lunch, put together the previous evening by the two girls, we sailed back feeling relaxed and happy, with that wonderful feeling that a day at sea in the sun always seems able to produce.

The rest of the week passed quickly, if extremely pleasantly, and before we knew it, Annabel and I were bidding our grateful goodbyes to Charles and Jo, and catching our flight back to New York.

I sat on the plane with Annabel, feeling bronzed, fit, and well, and looking forward to what the immediate future was about to bring. In order of events, it looked as if, first of all, I would see Annabel off from New York the following day, with her returning back home to await my arrival to sort out our future together in America. Then I would have my conversation with Fred, to hear the details of the package that he said he had sorted out with Wally for me. And then – presumably quite soon – it would be back home for me, and marriage, before returning to start a new life in New York. If only I had known it wasn't actually going to turn out anything like that at all. But that's quite another story.